THIS IS HOW WE END THINGS

A NOVEL

R. J. JACOBS

sourcebooks
landmark

Published by Sourcebooks Landmark, an imprint of Sourcebooks
P.O. Box 4410, Naperville, Illinois 60567-4410
(630) 961-3900
sourcebooks.com

Cataloging-in-Publication Data is on file with the Library of Congress.

Printed and bound in the United States of America.
VP 10 9 8 7 6 5 4 3 2 1

This book is dedicated to the memory
of Father Joe Beattie, OSFS, for his
commitment to teaching and coaching,
and for his tremendous patience.
May the road go on forever.

Prologue

XX XX

FROM PSYCHOLOGICAL REPORT

INTERVIEW MATERIAL

AUDIO RECORDING

October 20, 2013

Evaluator: Simon Martin, PhD

...

"This is confidential, right?"

"It's our seventh meeting, and you ask that every time. And yes."

"Meaning nothing leaves this room?"

"Again, basically. There're some exceptions. Legal issues. If you report child or elder abuse, even in the past, I have to

make a call. Or if you say you're planning to hurt yourself or someone else, I have to report that."

"Planning to?"

"Right."

"But things that happened in the past, that've been investigated already..."

"...They aren't required to be reported, no. And won't be. On that, you have my word. Protecting a patient's privacy is a critical part of what I do."

"..." *[The subject pauses, approximately fifteen seconds pass]*

"It sounds like there's a story you want to tell, but you're reluctant to start."

"I mean, I've never told anyone."

"That's what trust is for."
[A ten-second pause]

"I think there's something very wrong with me."

"Well, maybe there is, and maybe not. Why don't you tell me a little about what makes you think so, and we can figure it out together?"

"...You swear on your life it won't get out?"

"Aside from the exceptions, yes, I swear."

[The subject audibly exhales] "In eleventh grade, I murdered the man who killed my parents."

"I...okay, I'm listening."

"I knew I would from the moment I read his name on the police report and started being careful, even then, to avoid any internet research or contact with him that might raise suspicions about me. See, you're fidgeting. I can tell you're..."

"I was just surprised is all."

"You're sure you want to hear this?"

"Please, go on."

"Will you put that pen down?"

[A clicking sound]

"I killed a man named Douglas Mitchner. He hit my parents' car, head-on, at nearly eighty miles per hour. The police report I got said he was a type 1 diabetic who lost control of his vehicle after going into insulin shock, falling forward into the steering wheel as his foot pressed the accelerator. I knew he didn't mean to hurt anyone, but for some reason, that made me want him dead even more. Family money on my father's side sent me to boarding school instead of state's custody, but he took my adoptive parents away—the only family I ever knew."

"You'd mentioned you were adopted."

"At birth."

"Continue, please."

"After their service, going in my parents' room seemed disrespectful? Somehow? But I circled their bed. The corners of the white comforter tucked neatly beneath the pillows. It was the kind of bedroom that had lace doilies. On my father's bedside table, the lamp was still switched on. I turned it off and could feel the heat from the bulb that had been lit for two days. On my mom's nightstand was a picture of me in a silver modern frame that matched nothing else in the house. I think it had been a gift. The image kind of captured the hopes she had for me, and the way they'd cared for me, the best way they knew how. They took me in at my most vulnerable. They'd loved me."

"And you loved them."

"No, I don't think I did, I don't think I could. I respected them. I was loyal to them. If my mother knew about my dark side, she never let on. She was cheerful, always. But my dad knew very early; he could see my...emptiness but was warm and loving anyway, fully aware he could never be loved in return. I admired him for that.

"I retrieved my things, took a shower, then began plotting the most satisfying way to murder Douglas Mitchner, wondering how long I would have to wait to avoid drawing attention to myself."

"I see."

"I decided four months was safe, but in hindsight, I really should have waited longer."

"Longer?"

"Definitely. Boarding school was actually easier than my suburban Catholic high school, so I had some time on my hands. In October, I bribed a homeless man to buy a revolver from a pawnshop with cash I tucked away after the funeral. He passed it to me in the alleyway with the nonchalance of someone who would've given a teenager an atomic bomb. I tested its weight in my palm, noticing the number thirty-eight etched into the silver metal, then slipped the gun beneath the seat of my car before buying ammunition at a rural gun range, also using cash. In the second week of November, I caught a taxi to a neighborhood where I assumed drugs were sold. I mimicked a movie scene and asked to buy 'rock' cocaine from some guys in an alleyway. The dealer made a comment about my long hair, but when I flashed the emptiness, the vacancy in my eyes, and smiled, he relented. 'Some kind of vampire,' he said, about me. I stored the crack cocaine in a Tylenol bottle on a shelf above my roommate's bed, in case it was somehow discovered. Not a nice thing to do, but like I said, something's wrong with me. You keep looking at that pen. Please don't take notes."

[A ten-second pause]

"I'm listening, go ahead."

"I bought a button-down shirt, a pair of pants, and a pair of nondescript running shoes at a thrift store and kept them separate from all of my other things. I forced myself to cry during a counseling appointment and made a point to appear unrushed at the end, lingering to make some extra small talk. I stole two sets of latex gloves from the student health center on the way out the door, then put on the thrift store clothes. Then I left my phone under my pillow and slipped out the back door. It was just after seven p.m. The drive took two hours, and when I got to my hometown, I parked in the shadows of an oak tree behind a church, then took a taxi to a shopping center near Douglas's home, paid the driver in cash, and walked the rest of the way. It was a quiet night except for the crickets. I cut through a side yard where a wind chime clinked around. He had a bowl of something resting on his big bulbous stomach, pale turquoise light from a television flashing over his dumb features. Far away, a dog barked. I remember that. I knocked on the sliding glass door at the rear of the house. An outdoor light switched on."

"You must have been scared? You were a kid."

"No, listen. When he stepped outside, I shoved the butt of the revolver under his chin. And he blubbered, something or other about a gold and sapphire ring. 'You'll need the keys,' I said, 'Open the garage and start the car.'

"He did as he was told, and we were on our way. It smelled sour in the car. His gray shorts he wore were stained dark from where he'd wet himself. I directed him, 'Take your next right.' He was whining, 'Where are...?'

"I motioned with the gun's barrel, like I'd done all this a hundred times before. On a side street, I pulled several of the crack cocaine rocks from my pocket and held them to Douglas's lips. 'I need you to swallow this. But don't chew.' He was scared out of his mind, but did he it, wincing at the bitterness while his Adam's apple bobbed. He was crying and mumbling to himself, and his shirt was getting dark in places from his sweat. I needed it to cycle through his bloodstream."

"The rock cocaine?"

"Yeah. I scattered the rest of it across the floorboards. As I was doing it, he got brave or scared, I guess. He swung his elbow at me, trying to fling himself out of the car. Caught me right here [points to their left eye]. Yeah. It was bad; he stunned me, and I almost lost my grip on the gun and barely managed to get outside before him. He screamed once, like a sound that wasn't really a word; I think crack dust had coated his mouth. In the distance, I heard a porch door creak open and slap shut. Someone called out, 'Hello?'

"I shoved the gun under his chin and forced him back into the driver's seat.

"I kept opening and closing my eye because my vision was turning blurry. He'd done some real damage to it.

"He started hyperventilating. His wheezing made me sick.

"I walked around the front of his car and fired six shots into him through the windshield.

[A pause]

"You're okay? You wanted to hear this, remember?

"I ran off into the night, like any normal jogger. I heard the first siren as I slipped the gun into a food waste bin behind a pizza parlor. I ran all the way back to my car, then two and a half hours later, I was sitting in my dorm library, reading Rolling Stone magazine. I'd showered, and my hair was wet. Two kids I'd met earlier that semester burst through the door.

I could smell alcohol on their breath from across the room. One asked, 'Geez, you're still up? What happened to your eye?' They bragged about someone firing a potato shooter from a rooftop and told me everyone had ended up in a neighborhood swimming pool. Regular kid stuff. 'You could have come,' they said. And had I given any more thought to coming home with one of them over winter break? Someone's folks had a place.

"I said, 'You boarding school kids are too wild for me.'"

"They had no idea?"

"Not until five days later, when I was in handcuffs. The cop who arrested me wasted no time telling me I'd need a psychological evaluation."

"And you mentioned none of this at that time? About you thinking something was wrong...inside?" *[A thumping sound, likely the interviewer touching his chest]*

[A pause]

"No. I started thinking about how I should lie."

"That was five years ago?"

"Yeah, I wasn't tried as an adult, so my sentence wasn't very long."

"So now you're doing ongoing counseling and assessment as part of your parole. And you're finally putting words to this feeling..."

"It's a lack of feeling, more of an absence than a presence. When you're like me, you have to hide what you are."

[A long pause]

"Do you want to see the emptiness? I'll show you, if you want. It hides in my eyes."

"..."

[laughs] "Both of them, even the fucked up one. Maybe especially that one. Do you want to see?"

[A pause] **"Okay."**

[Mumbling, indeterminable sounds, possibly a chair creaking]

"I'm..."

[Laughs] "See? I knew you'd be scared. Everyone is."

CHAPTER 1

SCARLETT

Robert and Scarlett watch through the thick glass of arched windows while vehicles lumber down University Avenue. It's late Thursday afternoon, and the lobby of Hull Hall, home of Dorrance University's Psychology Department, is freezing, even for March. Most years, the coldest days have passed by spring break, but this year winter was late to arrive and stayed like a party guest who couldn't read the room. The building's architecture is impressive by any standards, even if the vaulted Gothic ceilings have always seemed vaguely haunted to Scarlett. She bounces on her heels in a thin thrift store sweater, teeth chattering as she checks the time on her phone. "Any chance she's waiting at the back entrance?"

Robert raises an eyebrow. "Surely she wouldn't stand at a locked door for this long? And I can handle her orientation thing if you're pressed for time."

"I'm a single parent in a PhD program, pressed for time is my normal state," Scarlett says, her smile determined and warm. "This'll go faster with two of us. Especially since you have all your ducks in a row, like always."

Robert chortles. "I appreciate the vote of confidence, but I'm not sure I have ducks, and they're not in a row. This semester, it's like I have squirrels and they're at a rave."

"In that case, you've fooled everyone, including me." Scarlett shrugs. As usual, Robert has her smiling—even when the situation might otherwise be tense. She's heard the term *work spouse* before, but had no reference point for it. But Robert probably is that to her, she thinks, even if it looks mostly like a close friendship. Which is perfect. Three years after an emotionally wrought divorce, a close male friend is what's comfortable.

Two years have passed since Robert led Scarlett's own orientation, and since that time, the two have worked together on every project that's come their way, including the most recent one—about which only the grad students and department chair, Joe Lyons, know the details.

Scarlett checks the time again. The department may not have the same budget as Engineering, but considering their team has become nationally prominent, the heater should at least work. "It'll be an adjustment getting used to another team member, but I guess it's past time, after winter graduation. I know Joe needs six on the team. You, me, Britt, Chris, Elizabeth, and now…Veronica, if she ever shows up. I hope she's open to writing grants."

Robert cocks his head slightly.

"What?"

"Joe hasn't told you? Veronica doesn't have a research background. Joe offered her a place in the PhD program, but she just finished her JD."

"She's a *lawyer*?"

"Not admitted to the bar anywhere yet, as far as I know, but yes, respecializing in psychology research methods."

Scarlett traces the toe of her shoe along a tile as she takes the information in. "Why would the fearless Joe Lyons want someone with a legal background on our team?"

"Between you and me?"

"Of course." Scarlett elbows him.

"My sense was that she pushed him, hard, lobbied to join, and eventually sold him on it."

Scarlett considers this. The team receives innumerable applications, most of which are never read. "Yeah?"

"You know Joe, he has to think something is his idea." Robert shrugs. "But I think this person Veronica convinced him we would benefit from oversight."

Scarlett swallows. "He's worried?" Risk was Joe's reputation.

A sly smile emerges on Robert's lips. "See? That's just it. We're all too close to the research now. Even you, supposedly the team's moral compass."

Layer by layer, the details of the experiment had been revealed to her: a study on dishonesty that necessitated deceiving the subjects. It was the daring kind of experiment that modern institutional review boards never green-lighted anymore because of its potential for causing psychological harm. But it was also precisely the kind of study that made Joe Lyons prominent in the field.

No one took risks in research like he did.

Not for forty years.

Joe Lyons leads an exclusive group of graduate students with one mission: expand the field of psychology with cutting-edge research. The team functioned best with six members and had been down one for three months. Now Veronica, handpicked by Joe, was about to arrive for her orientation. Had Scarlett put blind faith in the legendary Lyons? He's a rock star in their insular world, his publications playing out like *events*, like an anticipated *world premieres*.

A publication beside his name opened a lot of doors.

A recommendation letter from him paved a professional road.

Codesigning an experiment with Joe Lyons guaranteed tenure at most Research 1 schools and positioned your name to be referenced in psychology classes for generations.

Psychology, Scarlett knows, is a young science. A student can still go to a conference and listen to a lecture by someone in their textbook.

But Robert's comment echoes in her mind. The moral compass, was that really her role? And if so, where were the moral compasses of the other team members? She hadn't thought of the team's deception as more than harmless mischief, but had she lost her directionality? Was there more danger in the experiment than she dared to face? Scarlett idealized the team early on: the close–knit planning sessions, endless drip coffees, and stacks of papers were exactly as she'd pictured them when she'd applied. University life in general suited her, strolling manicured paths between storied lecture halls and world–class laboratories, while guitar notes from students drifted in the wind, felt invigorating enough to justify the worrisome debt she'd taken on, the bills she struggled to pay, and the unvarying meals of noodles she and her daughter consumed.

But now she had seen the collegiate curtain pulled back. She watched Joe's maniacal habits cost him a marriage and navigated suspicions around campus because of the department's secrecy. And now Joe was bringing on someone with a legal background? For oversight?

She knew Joe Lyons valued loyalty above all, demanding no information leaks, no gossip.

Nor talk of the affair that everyone—as of two weeks earlier—knew for a fact he's been having.

Robert suggests, "Let's check that back door?"

Their footfalls echo as they descend the half flight of stairs to the building's rear entrance, where the ancient overhead lights make hexagonal shadows on the walls. Through the windows, she sees red brick covered with literal ivy.

When the new first–year candidate, Veronica, appears in the glass rectangle in the door, Scarlett and Robert exchange a glance.

"I didn't say a word," she says.

"You wouldn't because you're too nice, but you're teaching her multiple regression, not me."

"Aww, she's just turned around."

Behind her, bits of ice dot the walkway. All the landscaping is either prickly evergreen or deceased. Robert flashes his impish smile before pushing the door open. "Veronica?" he asks.

A blast of frigid air fills the stairwell. Veronica nods. She has severely cut jet-black hair, a bright-orange puffy jacket, and enormous earmuffs. "Your door was locked," she says, her voice crackling with contentiousness as she shifts her weight back and forth between the sensible flats she's wearing.

"Our fault for not being clearer," Scarlett says as she guides

Veronica in. "This weather must be quite a welcome from New Orleans! Let's get you upstairs, I promise it's not always this cold here."

"Oh–kay," Veronica agrees irritably.

Over Veronica's shoulder, Scarlett catches Robert's eye. Her gut tells her this meeting is not about to go well, but his smile is contagious. "I'm sure you're eager to hear about the experiment," he says.

———

In the hallway, students rush with prebreak haste. A bright blanket of rooftop snow shines through three more arched windows on the student lounge's far end as they enter. A round wooden table covered in condensation rings sits in the center, while the near wall is lined with mailboxes all stuffed with multicolored sheets of paper. Each is affixed with a name tag: Robert, Scarlett, Britt, Chris, Elizabeth, Veronica. The room smells like coffee and also like copier ink.

Veronica bends to admire the mailbox tag bearing her name, then smiles proudly. The three of them settle around the table and politely catch up about her move. It turns out that geography is a ubiquitous topic in grad school, everyone either having recently moved from somewhere or preparing to move to somewhere else—people following partners or relocating for internships or for a million other reasons. Having only ever lived in North Carolina, Scarlett notices the subject always comes up immediately. "Robert tells me you just finished law school. What was it like?"

Veronica's gaze shifts back and forth in a way that makes Scarlett aware Veronica's making the same mental adjustments she had a moment earlier—before this morning, they had only "met" through email and a conference call.

And how well can you get to know someone like that?

"It was interesting," Veronica answers, measuredly. "The law has always fascinated me."

"Oh," Scarlett says, unsure how to respond because…who actually talks like that? "Was there a particular area of the law that you focused on?"

"JD-PhDs tend to become quite specialized in one area. Mine is managing liability."

Something about Veronica's voice makes Scarlett feel like the building is on fire.

"Sounds useful," Robert chimes in, fiddling with his laptop.

"For sure," Scarlett agrees. "I'm definitely interested to hear your thoughts as we get you oriented."

Veronica wrinkles her nose. "I'll be discussing most of those observations only with Dr. Lyons."

"Oh," Scarlett says.

What on earth?

Robert, she notices, has resumed grinning. They both know Joe Lyons can't run the department without them, so whatever "observations" Veronica anticipates keeping between her and Joe won't stay hidden for long.

Robert taps the tabletop. "I suppose we should get to why we're here. Obviously, your TA assignment won't start till next semester, but there's no reason you can't start helping with the experiment now, and doing your…assessing or whatever? I queued up a video of the procedure so you can get a sense of how the script is delivered. Sound okay?"

Veronica folds her hands in her lap and nods.

Robert navigates to a clip he'd readied, then lowers the lights so the screen is more visible. Pictured is a medium–sized room with one–way glass along one wall and a circle of chairs in the center. One at a time, people enter and sit, occasionally issuing a small nod or wave.

"This is the team," Robert says. "You recognize Scarlett, obviously. The real subject will be the last one in the room and isn't aware the others know each other. A week before they participate, they each complete what they think is a screening for mental health concerns, as if they're verifying they're not too anxious or depressed to complete the study."

"Except it's not actually a screening measure," Scarlett clarifies. "Not most of it, at least. It's already part of the experiment to establish a baseline for how honest they are."

"It's a little devious," Robert admits, "but on their release form, they give us access to their application materials to the university."

"Hmm," Veronica says, then raises her hand as if in class. "I don't like it. If the screening tool is just to see how honest they are, how do you actually make sure the subjects are mentally healthy?"

A quick glance passes between Scarlett and Robert. "The first few questions *are* for self–reported distress. But we haven't run into any problems so far," Robert says, and Scarlett, for the first time, glimpses Joe Lyons's logic in inviting Veronica to join the team. She hadn't considered that the experiment might be causing anything more than immediate discomfort, although she had begun to notice how casually words like *deception* and *agitated* were now casually tossed around—words that might have caused everyone's ears to perk up in undergraduate school but now hardly elicited a shrug. Still, who did this person think she was?

"Every element of the experience has been considered," Scarlett says, as gently as she can.

Veronica brushes her fingertips through her curtain–like bangs.

"Thirty minutes before the experiment begins, half the subjects get a phone call from someone who says they're an administrative assistant to the department head," Robert says.

"Usually it's Elizabeth, but sometimes I do it," Scarlett says.

"They're told they're missing a prerequisite. Everyone's nightmare, right? That they've somehow overlooked a course they need to graduate? They're told they're being put on automatic academic probation because of the error, and that they'll be disenrolled if they don't get an A in their current psychology class, which is why they've signed up for the experiment: they're getting extra credit. Because of the timing of the call, they don't have time to consult the catalog or talk with an advisor."

Robert continues: "The subjects are asked to silence and store their cell phones during the experiment, during which the 'assistant' calls back to say there's been an error and the academic record is actually fine." He motions toward the laptop screen. "Here, I'm about to follow the subject in, close the door, and read the directions. The participants are told they're taking part in a test of groupthink."

On the screen, the lights dim in the experiment room, and Robert's voice can be heard describing the series of images that the participants will see. He tells them, "Afterward, you'll be asked a few questions about what you can recall from the images and asked to solve some problems based on the information you received."

Veronica wrinkles her nose as if she smells something acrid.

Robert fast–forwards the clip, saying, "Now they're shown a series of images of everyday objects. Afterward, they'll be asked if they can recall which ones they've been shown, but that part's baloney; everyone always gets twenty out of twenty."

On the screen, the room's lights come back up. The students all pass their clipboards to the person on their right. "This is where they're told that only the three highest scorers will actually get the extra credit. They're asked to score their neighbor's test to ensure 'the highest level of accuracy.'" Robert makes air quotes around the phrase. "That's giving us the data we're actually collecting. It turns out that so far, subjects who experience the stress of the phone call are four times as likely to lie to make themselves look smarter. In fact, they'll harm their fellow student to accomplish that. On average, they mark two more wrong on their neighbor's paper than if they didn't get a call making them think they were in academic trouble."

Veronica's expression is unreadable. "Wow," she says.

The laptop closes with a clap sound as Robert looks up. "Interesting, right? Of course, Joe wants to take it a step further, but an institutional review board proposal is still in the works."

"What…does he *hope* to do?" Veronica asks.

Scarlett shakes her head subtly, hoping Robert will notice. They've only covered the most recent study, and Veronica seems eager to punch a hole in their research. Who knew what she'd say about the previous semester's study in which students were told their partner had a serious medical diagnosis? Or the condition from the summer semester, where participants were shown violent videos, then asked to administer what they thought were disciplinary sanctions?

Robert answers calmly, "He wants to add a condition that pretends to take away the student's financial aid as a punishment for too many 'wrong' choices, then see if losing it makes it more likely they'll 'punish' the others in the group. The subject will think they're choosing whether or not to take away the others' extra credit."

"Robert thinks they would," Scarlett says. "But I don't."

"Scarlett's an optimist. If you stress someone out, they're more likely to lie and act in their own best interest. If you take away something they care about, they'll turn vindictive." Robert stands. "Liars aren't born, they're made. And people want to hurt others the way they've been hurt."

Veronica's brow darkens. "Made, not born? You really think that's always the case?"

"*Always* is hard to say. Something like three percent of the population are sociopaths, right? Most have bad upbringings, but not all. Not by any stretch." He thinks about this for a second, then smiles. "Come on, let's go meet the rest of the team."

SCARLETT

Robert leads the way. "The next condition should be about fifteen minutes. You called the subject in this one, right?"

Scarlett nods. "Just before we met Veronica."

Veronica smiles humorlessly.

Scarlett considers her as they make their way down the now-empty hallway. Isn't it odd that a PhD candidate would be so... uninitiated? Still, Joe Lyons's process for selecting candidates has always been mysterious. When Scarlett had been admitted two years earlier, it was a pleasant surprise. Joe told her at the time that, given her qualifications, he had no choice but to take her on—such an odd way of making her an offer. Robert had run the orientation then too, and loyalty developed between them effortlessly. Maybe a connection will develop again with Veronica, Scarlett considers. Maybe Veronica actually has a brilliant legal mind and her insights will come in handy, although it seems doubtful when she thinks of how she shut down Veronica's question earlier.

"How much have you read about dishonesty?" she asks Veronica.

"Enough. Dr. Lyons mostly wants me to just observe and audit for a while."

"Audit?" Robert asks, "Was that the word he used?"

"It was," Veronica says. "When will the others be here?"

"In a hurry?" Robert asks.

They pass a stray student sitting cross-legged, typing on a device in their lap. The rhythm of college life is so palpable, Scarlett estimates she'd be able to *sense* the date without looking at a calendar. At the end of the hall, they ascend a stairwell to the third floor, which is completely empty.

Robert clears his throat. "A little background, then. Lying usually peaks in adolescence, but most adults *self*-report lying in about a fifth of their conversations. College students lie to their mothers about half the time, and to their *own therapists* more than that. So the fact that we could nudge the circumstances to make it extremely likely? It doesn't surprise me."

Robert can't help but be professorial, Scarlett thinks, his briefing beginning to take the tone of one of his class lectures. She lingers slightly, her gaze falls momentarily on the snow again. Dishonesty is a part of everyday life, she knows—show up late to a meeting, and there's a better outcome if you make up a traffic jam—but there's something unsettling about *creating* the circumstances that guarantee it.

"Here we are," Robert says. He unlocks a door and then turns on a light, which flickers briefly before the three step inside.

The room is the one shown in the video clip: windowless, aside from an enormous mirror on the far wall, which gives it the feel of a basement despite being on the third floor. Four heavy–looking chairs are arranged in a circle in the room's center, while one sits alone in the corner.

"This is where it starts," Robert says. "The subjects have all signed up for a study on group decision–making in their intro psych class. We didn't hire confederates because…"

"Confederates?" Veronica interrupts.

"Actors," Scarlett clarifies the jargon. "We want to control the environment as much we can."

"And don't want word to get out about what we're doing," Robert finishes. "Small community. You may have noticed on the drive in."

Veronica walks over and touches the chair in the corner. It resembles the others, but is far heavier and designed to stay in place.

"It's set aside on purpose," Robert says. "To make sure the subjects feel more like outsiders."

"Oh." Veronica unzips her jacket and folds it over her fore-arm. Dark patches of sweat have formed under each of her arms. She motions toward the mirror. "What's behind there?"

"That's for observing the interactions that take place during the discussion, making notes on their movements and behavior," Robert says patiently.

There's a knock on the door. Veronica jumps a little, and all three of their heads turn.

A young man steps in, his hair is combed with model preci-sion. He flashes a smile at Scarlett, then nods at Robert. "Guys," he says.

Robert gestures like a party host making introductions. "Veronica, this is Chris. He's finishing up his first year. Chris, this is Veronica, the new candidate. She's going to watch the first half of the experiment run."

Chris issues a playful nod as he folds down the half–popped collar of his polo shirt. "What's up, Veronica? I jumped in on the last part of your Zoom interview."

"I remember," she says.

Scarlett clears her throat. "Chris manages the cameras and data transcription."

"Guess I'm the first one here," he says, flicking his chin to knock the hair from his eyes before dropping into one of the chairs.

Scarlett begins to say, "Probably any..." when the door then opens wider.

Two women enter. The first has black hair and eyeliner and wears dark jeans and a denim jacket. She makes no eye contact with anyone except Chris, whose shoulder she touches before sitting down.

"Britt, this is Veronica, she…"

Britt interrupts by holding up her palm. "I read your vitae, I remember. You're new, you're going to watch us do this, I got it. I need to get into character, so please don't talk to me." She leans forward and removes her septum piercing before rolling down her sleeve to cover her tattoos.

Chris snorts and shakes his head.

"Nice to meet you," Veronica offers stiffly.

Britt does not respond.

"Britt's expertise is analysis and data integration," Robert volunteers.

"And this is Elizabeth," Robert says, motioning toward the woman who entered just behind Britt. Elizabeth is tall with blond hair that falls nearly to her waist. She tucks it behind her ear and extends her hand to Veronica. "Hi," she says as they shake. "Good to meet you, and welcome. Hi, everyone."

Chris and Britt seem to pay no attention, but Scarlett circles behind her and squeezes Elizabeth's shoulder, wondering how obvious the coolness of the others toward Elizabeth is. Only two weeks had passed since suspicions about her affair with Joe had been made obvious when the rest of the group spotted Elizabeth climbing out of Joe's Saab one morning.

"Well, look who had a sleepover," Chris had said.

Britt had frowned.

"Young teach-er, the sub-ject, of schoolgirl fan-ta-sy," Chris had begun singing as Scarlett's stomach tightened. Rumors were one thing, but they were getting blatantly careless.

"I guess that's what it takes to get a key to Joe's files," Britt had sneered. "Must be convenient for her research. Nice little advantage."

Robert hadn't commented that morning, Scarlett had noticed. He'd silently pushed open the door to let everyone in.

In her tight brown pants with her hair blown, she looks like Farrah Faucet, Scarlett thinks. She catches a hint of Elizabeth's perfume a faint spice like coriander. "Elizabeth has been here two years and helped design the study," she tells Veronica.

"Is that so?" Veronica asks, arms folded.

Elizabeth shrugs as she hurriedly sits. "Sorry I'm late, everyone."

"Are you?" Britt asks. "Sorry?"

"What on earth could have made you late?" Chris asks, bitingly.

"Guys, let's all play nice," Robert says, moving toward the door. "I'll go meet the subject in the lobby. Just a reminder, we're running the worried condition."

"Copy that," Chris says, rolling his shoulders.

"Let's go watch from behind the glass," Scarlett suggests to Veronica, leading her back into the hallway and then into the small observation room, where three chairs sit in a row.

Veronica chooses the chair furthest from the door, and then Scarlett closes them in and sits beside Veronica. The room is movie–theater dark. Gradually, their eyes adjust to the light coming through the glass from the lab room. Elizabeth's perfume still lingers in Scarlett's nose, but from Veronica, she detects no scent at all. Scarlett can hear Veronica's coat rumbling as she fiddles with it beside her. "I know this is a lot to take in all at once," she offers. "But it's great you'll be able to watch in real time. You'll be up to speed on everything in no time, I'm sure." The others relax as Robert disappears into the hall. "The dialogue is completely scripted to keep the data clean. The first time we ran this, it was like we were putting on a high school play, everyone rehearsing their lines, so nervous."

Veronica stares into the experiment room.

Such seriousness, Scarlett thinks, before Joe's words come back to her: "We're making *history*." Slightly hyperbolic, maybe, but she's noticed the way people look at Joe at conferences and can even feel the gazes of faculty on *her* as she walks through campus.

"The experiment might seem cruel," Joe told her once, "But in the age of disinformation, understanding what makes someone be dishonest might shape society."

Scarlett taps her scuffed Converse sneakers. Who knew what might happen next? She glances at Veronica and decides to extend an olive branch. "I remember it being a lot the first day too, so just to go back through everyone's names, I'm Scarlett, which is easy to remember because I have red hair." She tugs on the ends of her curls. "And Robert." She nods.

"He led my interview," Veronica says.

Right, Scarlett thinks. *Everyone remembers Robert.* "Exactly, he's the one who looks like Clark Kent with that dark hair and those glasses." Scarlett points at the woman who looks like Ally Sheedy in *The Breakfast Club* if she'd been goth. "Then, there's Britt. You have to be assertive with her. And Chris, who may seem like a smart aleck, but he can be really helpful and down to earth once you get to know him. He respecialized too, actually; his background is in sports psych. Rumor is he beat the tennis coach during tryouts. And…" She points again. "That's Elizabeth with the long blond hair, looking at her phone. Don't worry, there won't be a quiz afterward."

Scarlett follows Veronica's gaze toward Elizabeth, who slumps forward, typing something quickly before dropping her phone into her purse and zipping it closed. Is Elizabeth even more preoccupied than she's been in the last few weeks, or is she imagining it? She seems so rattled—shifting in her chair, tugging at the sweater—that for the first time, Scarlett wonders if she'll be able to complete her part of the script.

Had she been texting Joe? Even now?

Chris smirks as he leans toward Elizabeth, his voice echoing slightly through the speakers, like the flight captain talking over a loudspeaker. "Study date makes for a late night?"

"Let's get this over with," Elizabeth tells him, studying the screen on the far wall with her eyes.

"Everyone knows," Britt says in a monotone voice.

"But your secret is safe with us," Chris adds.

Elizabeth's head turns, her cheeks visibly reddening. "Robert will be back with the kid any minute," she mutters, pulling her hair into a ponytail.

"What are they talking about?" Veronica whispers, watching hawkishly.

"I'm not sure," Scarlett lies, brushing some imaginary lint from her jeans. "Probably nothing."

Veronica stares into the double reflection of her own glasses on the observation window. "Can…they hear our voices?"

Scarlett considers joking, before thinking better of it. "No, it's soundproof. The room is rigged with a mic, and the sound only comes through a little speaker there." Scarlett points at the ceiling.

The lab room's door opens again, and now Veronica makes a small shushing sound as if reminding Scarlett to keep quiet.

She really is on edge, Scarlett thinks, Veronica's seriousness practically contagious. Through the glass, they watch a lanky young man in a fraternity T–shirt that says *Woodser* enter the room.

Britt and Chris do not look at him. Elizabeth gives him a small wave.

No one even glances at the glass as Scarlett checks the tablet in her lap. "That's Tom," she whispers.

Robert motions toward the heavy chair in the corner, and Tom drops into it. He looks at the others and, for a heartbreaking second, attempts to scoot his chair forward toward the obviously closed circle, straining as he leans forward before Britt shoots him a frosty glance that stops him in his tracks.

Scarlett glances at the tablet. "He's a twenty–year–old Caucasian male. We haven't had an enormous sample size, but the demographic balance has been close to the population, at least for North Carolina. It's skewed young, of course."

Tom's leg bounces anxiously, she notices, though he hadn't sounded particularly thrown off in her short phone call to him earlier. He'd taken the "news" about being on probation with such stoicism, Scarlett had been tempted to repeat herself. Then, he'd simply hung up. His puffed–up posture reminds her of her younger brother's friends from the high school football team, their tough façades proportionate to their discomfort.

Robert moves to the front of the room and reads: "You're

here because you've signed up for an experiment on group decision–making. The experiment begins with a short cognitive warm–up, then a presentation, followed by a short assessment. The group will be asked to make several determinations about the presented material. The purpose of this experiment is to see how the decision–making process of this group compares to the decision–making process of other groups. When I say, 'Start,' you'll be presented with a series of slides. Completing the assessment afterward should take approximately five minutes. Afterward, you'll be asked a few questions about what you can recall from the images and asked to solve some problems based on the information you received."

The first set of images flashes on the screen: a hammer, a wheelbarrow, a violin.

After twenty images, a slide pops up announcing the second part of the experiment.

"Remember," Robert says, "place a check beside the line corresponding with the image only if you're seeing it for a second time."

Robert gets a particular twinkle in his eye in moments like this, Scarlett thinks. It's good that he actually knows what he's talking about, she considers. He dims the lights; then the series of images shown in the video clip from earlier flashes on the screen. The projector makes a slight buzz that the mics pick up and is audible even in the observation room.

Scarlett has seen them all dozens of times by now. "See how Tom is in the corner? Being alienated from the group further increases the chances of him lying later," she says.

After a few minutes, Robert tells the group to set down their pencils.

But Tom hesitates. He looks around squirrelly, as if he hoped no one would notice he stole a few extra seconds taking notes. It takes Robert stepping closer to him for him to actually pause his work. "For the purpose of record keeping, please score the measure you've just completed. Do not write your name or any other identifying information on the page."

Scarlett whispers, "The handwriting makes it obvious which one was completed by the subject, but actually, he's the only one with a black pen. The others have blue."

Tom shifts restlessly in his chair. The grad students pass their assessments to the right, but Tom resumes marking intently on his paper. He seems so tortured; she feels for him. The experiment isn't supposed to be this hard on people. *Poor guy*, she thinks, *he must be really worried about his grades.* She reaches for the phone to place the reassuring phone call to him when Tom's hand shoots up.

The others ignore him.

Veronica whispers, "He looks pretty upset."

She's right, Scarlett thinks just as Tom stands.

"This is complete bullshit," he yells. "Isn't it?"

Every head in the room turns.

"I should at least get to finish the test. I…deserve that, don't I?"

"What's…?" Veronica begins to ask.

"This hasn't happened before," Scarlett answers.

"*Don't I?*" Tom yells, then throws the paper he's holding across the room, the sheets drifting to the floor.

Robert holds up his hands. "Why don't we all just…?"

"*Fuck you*," Tom says, pointing.

Veronica's eyes go wide.

Robert raises his palm and speaks in a slow, calm voice. "If you'll just sit back down, I'll explain what's…"

"I'll *not* fucking sit back down! There's something wrong with this chair, it's way heavier than it should be. But you already know that, don't you?" He paces toward the screen, poking at it with his finger. "This presentation makes no sense. It's too simple."

Elizabeth's and Robert's expressions turn nervous.

"You're fucking with me." Tom points at the glass. "Someone's behind there too. Who is it?" He stalks toward the window, raking his hands through his hair. "Yet another *woman* who wants me to back down, be quiet, not be heard?"

"*What*?" Elizabeth asks.

Britt sits forward. "What did you say?"

"You all think you're so smart and I'm the joke here, right? Because I'm not some good–looking, rich guy?" He glances ever so quickly at Chris. "Well, congratulations. I'm probably not even getting credit for this. My advisor screwed up, so apparently I'm get-ting kicked out of school! I really just came down here to tell you all what I think about this *stupid* department and your experiments."

"Nobody's getting kicked out of school," Robert says.

"The lady said, 'probation,' and I'm already *on probation*, so I know what that means. What am I supposed to do now, *huh*?"

Scarlett picks up her phone, the screen illuminating the dark as she dials. "You need to get up here," she says as Joe Lyons answers. "Something's wrong."

"On my way," his voice says, the thump of his footsteps audi-ble through the phone before he hangs up.

Veronica stands and backs away from the glass. "What hap-pens now?"

"Joe's coming. Just sit tight, he'll stop it."

Elizabeth stands and steps toward Tom. "Tom? It's Tom, right? You're obviously upset, and maybe you're right to be. Let me try to explain what the experiment is about."

"And *you*. *You* know it's all fake. You TA my class and signed me up. I only came here because of you, and you just wanted me to look *stupid*."

Elizabeth continues, "I think we should all go back downstairs, and you should get the explanation you deserve. I'm happy to be the one who…"

"No, you're in on it! Stay away from me, Elizabeth *Ann*."

She stops. "How…do you know my middle name?"

Scarlett wonders the same thing, her neck turning hot, the way it does when she panics. The turn of events is dizzying. A few minutes ago, it was clear that what was real was actually fake. Now, what's fake has become real in a way no one anticipated. "Come on, Joe," she mutters under her breath.

Two seconds pass that feel like ten minutes. The door opens, and Joe Lyons walks in.

"*How*?" Elizabeth repeats.

"You happy now?" Britt asks Tom.

Tom turns. The question seems to make something snap inside him, like a glow stick that's just popped.

Joe Lyons opens his mouth just as Tom lunges, arms extended toward Britt.

Which is when Chris shoots from his chair, grabs Tom by the shoulder, turns him, and with a swift punch, knocks him out cold.

His body falls with a thud that shakes the wall.

"Oh my gosh," Scarlett says.

"Christ," Veronica echoes.

Joe rushes toward Elizabeth, his eyes wide with concern.

In the experiment room, they exchange glances as Chris rubs his hand. "And people said grad school would be dull," he says.

Robert crouches down to inspect Tom, whose back gently rises and falls. "Can somebody call the police?"

CHAPTER 2

LARSON

Detective Alana Larson crunches through frozen pine needles while scraping ice from the windshield of her twenty–year–old Tacoma, when she hears her work phone's curt chirp. Her work phone and personal phone have different ringtones—a protocol she adopted as a cadet to immediately distinguish the two. "When you have to drop everything to save someone's life because Keith Urban starts blaring," she told her mother during the first year on the force, "you start considering a basic chime." That was four years earlier, on her first job in Charlotte. She'd anticipated fewer "drop everything" moments in her new position as a detective in Shepard, North Carolina, even if everyone told her they actually happened from time to time.

But in the time she'd lived there, none had.

Six months in, there had been plenty of minor crimes to investigate—and plenty of hats to wear—but not a single emergency. Which was exactly why she'd accepted the job. After working as an investigator in Charlotte, a smaller district sounded like a lot less stress than beat work in the city.

She sets the scraper onto the truck's floorboard and reaches across the passenger seat for the phone. The call is from a campus number, she realizes, her breath a white mist in the cold.

"This is Larson."

The woman on the line sounds tentative. "…I work in the Psychology Department at Dorrance. There's…been a fight here, someone was punched upstairs. Professor Lyons asked me to call for help. I…had your number after a break–in at my apartment last month."

The voice is familiar, but Larson can't place it; minor property crime has been her bread and butter so far in the job. "You'll want to call campus police for that," she says, pausing as she remembers it's Thursday morning. "Ask for Officer Patrick King, he'll be there in no time. If someone's injured, dial 111 for medical first. They'll notify law enforcement if you explain the situation."

She's always liked Pat King. She remembers a video that went viral online a few years earlier: King was directing traffic at a local high school's graduation when he noticed one of the seniors struggling with a necktie. King stopped the boy, knotted the tie around his own neck, then passed it to him to wear—all without missing a beat as he continued directing cars. He'd had no idea someone filmed the encounter, but that twenty–second clip captured him perfectly: community–minded, confident, kind.

The woman thanks Larson before ending the call.

A fight at the *Psychology Department*? Slides from a lecture in her first–year class at NC State seven years earlier flash through her mind. Larson stifles a smirk as she retrieves her ice scraper, the beginnings of a *Far Side*–esque cartoon forming in her mind:

was there some mischievous use of a bell and some meat powder, maybe?

The ice chips into white shavings as she pushes the scraper across the glass. It's an odd time of day for a fight, Larson thinks, even in the twenty–four–hour world of a university.

She'll make sure to follow up with Officer King.

The woman on the phone had sounded shaken.

KING

Officer Patrick King has worked on campus for twenty years but hasn't been inside Hull Hall for a decade. By and large, his work has been in the parking garages on the far ends of campus, where vehicle break–ins are a weekly occurrence, and in the dorms, where students sometimes got carried away with booze or other contraband they'd snuck inside. A fight, which is what the dispatcher told him he was responding to, happened three or four times annually on campus, max. And *every* time had involved alcohol.

King can't recall a single fight before 8:00 p.m.

When he pulls up in his cruiser, he sees that the EMTs have indeed arrived first; an ambulance from the medical center idles at an angle in the loading area, wisps of vapor rising from its tailpipe. Sunlight reflecting off the snow–covered landscaping makes the building seem otherwise idyllic, like a photo in an online campus tour.

Like a place where bad things could never happen.

The snow blanket mutes the morning sounds, and the cruiser door issues a gentle thump as King pushes it closed.

A fortyish man with shaggy brown hair and glasses stands in Hull's doorway, a glint of recognition in his eyes as he extends his hand. "Officer King? I'm Joe Lyons, department chair. The EMTs have just gone up to the second floor. I think the kid is still out cold."

Lyons wears khakis and a fleece over his blue button–down, as if he's conforming to some sort of professor dress code, King thinks. He follows Lyons up the stairwell, trying to mask the heaviness of his breathing as the reedy professor bounds upward two steps at a time. "What happened?" King manages to ask.

"I walked in after everything started, but apparently they were in the middle of the experiment, and the subject..."

"The subject?"

A quick glance over Lyons's shoulder. "Sorry, the kid who was participating. Apparently he got upset, started yelling, and attacked one of the grad students."

In the third floor hall, Robert, Scarlett, Chris, Elizabeth, and Britt stand in a circle around a doorway. A dark–shirted EMT with close–cropped blond hair emerges from the room they face. "He's okay, just coming to now," the man says evenly to King. "Bell's rung though." He looks at the students. "Which one of you is the heavyweight champ?"

Chris gestures with his hand.

The man laughs, then reiterates to King. "Kid's gonna be fine, so there's nothing really for us to work on. Unless you want us to give him a ride to the medical center."

"Give me a minute with him," King says, before turning to the group in the hall. "I want to talk to him first, but I want to hear from each of you shortly, so don't go anywhere."

They all nod in agreement.

King enters the lab room to find a chair knocked over and another shoved aside. He'd been a bouncer years ago after his stint in the army, and the pattern of overturned furniture looks familiar. He hears a groan and sees a young man rubbing the side of his jaw. The ball cap he'd evidently been wearing lies beside him on the floor, King notices, and his socks are mismatched. He keeps his distance so as to not appear imposing, but squares his shoulders.

The young man winces as he stands, his gaze conveying pure confusion.

"What's your name, son?"

"Tom," his voice creaks.

King glances around the room as if asking for an explanation. "Things get a little out of hand here?"

Tom closes his eyes, apparently falling into a state of deep contemplation. His jaw works back and forth before he says, "I lost it…lost my temper." King's deciding how to respond when Tom adds, "Her smile always was fake."

"Whose smile?"

Tom motions with his chin toward the hall, where a woman leans against the wall, blond hair falling over her shoulders in waves. When she senses the pressure of them looking, she turns and walks away.

King nods. "You'd met her before today?"

"That's Elizabeth, the TA for my Tuesday–Thursday psych class."

"You wanted to impress her or something?"

"Until I found out I was getting kicked out of school." Tom

winces as he rests his back against the wall. "I lied about how school is going when I signed up for this; I was already on academic probation. I messed up, didn't I?"

"I won't say you didn't, but we're gonna get you some help, maybe see about that bruise on your jaw. Come on." King extends his hand, helping Tom to his feet.

"St–still…" Tom stammers as they start toward the door.

"What's that?" When King looks into his eyes, they're cloudy and confused.

"I…thought she was special. But Elizabeth is just like every other girl, isn't she?" Tom asks through gritted teeth. "And now she owes me an apology."

KING

After King feels satisfied Tom is calm enough to release, he authorizes his transportation to the university medical center for evaluation. "Any time I've taken someone to the hospital in the back of a patrol car, it's felt like a mistake. Sends the wrong message to everyone," he says, joining Chris and Lyons at the same circular table where Robert and Scarlett had started Veronica's orientation earlier that morning.

Chris, King notices, has an open cut on the knuckle of his middle finger that looks like the jagged streak of a red marker. He chews gum while Lyons sips nervously from a bottle of water.

"Walk me through what happened before you punched the kid?" King asks.

"Dude gave off a weird vibe the second he walked in the room, to Elizabeth especially. I'm not sure why Robert even brought him up. Before he lunged he was saying something about how she'd tricked him; I guess she'd signed him up. He said something…oh, he said *her middle name*. Creepy. She was shaking."

King makes a note on the tablet in front of him.

"Then he went for my friend, simple as that," Chris continues, his expression hardening as he raised his right hand. "Now, if we're done here, I need to go get a tetanus shot. Oh, and if you want to know? I'd gladly knock his ass out again. Not sorry."

SCARLETT

In the midafternoon, Scarlett's phone rings. Robert's picture appears on the screen, and she answers, tucking her red curls behind her ear. "Well, that was quite a morning," she says. "You were still there when I left. What'd I miss?"

"They carted him over to the medical center to get checked out, even though he seemed fine, physically. After that, just a few short interviews with the cop, King. He realized pretty quickly everyone was saying the same thing."

Robert sounds…something. His speech is slower that its normally caffeinated pace. "Are you still rattled?" she asks.

There's a pause in which she pictures Robert pinching the bridge of his nose. "I guess so. I'm supposed to be a leader in the department, but I didn't feel like one today. I should have shut down the session and called for help right when the kid started to get upset."

"Everything happened really fast," Scarlett says reassuringly.

"Still, I shouldn't have let it go on. I was the one who brought him up. The others didn't notice the look in his eyes—it was the worried condition, so they weren't supposed to even look at him. I think he managed to freak out Elizabeth; she was crying when she went home."

Who wouldn't be freaked out by someone yelling like that? Scarlett thinks. "She has a lot on her already. And that guy made my skin crawl; he was saying something about *women?*"

"Something like that. I missed how *angry* he was," Robert says, sighing.

Scarlett changes the phone to her other ear. Through the sliding glass doors adjacent to her balcony, she can see how much the snow and ice that had accumulated the night before have melted. Patches of gray and green have emerged on the ground. "Don't be too hard on yourself, we're all overworked and on edge. Do you think we succeeded in scaring Veronica off? Think she'll be able to watch another trial soon?"

"That's partly why I'm calling. Joe wants to have a meeting with everyone there tonight to talk about what happened and decide what needs to change going forward. Seven p.m. in the lounge."

Scarlett glances over at her daughter, Iris, who has arranged a set of markers in a neat rainbow arc across the apartment's tattered carpet. "That sounds ominous. I wouldn't be able to make it normally, but Iris's dad is here for her spring break, and I'm sure he wouldn't mind hanging out with her for an hour or so. I'll check with him to make sure that works, text you in a second."

Scarlett ends the call and finds Mark's number in her phone, then types: "Sorry, I know you've just gotten here and are settling in at your hotel, but is there any way you could come over tonight for a few hours? Our chair called a meeting about an emergency this morning. It starts at seven."

Dots wave on Scarlett's screen within seconds, indicating that Mark is typing before his words appear: Not a problem. As if I'd say no to more time with Iris 😊. See you at six thirty.

You're the best. Scarlett types back, a smile creeping across her lips. Mark actually *is* the best in so many ways—so comfortable to co–parent with, and so easy to be with generally. She conjures an image of his calm, steady presence and wonders, once again, *Why did we get divorced?* They had their problems, sure, but could they have been worked through more fully? Could she have found a way to close the distance that had opened between them, gotten him to open up more? And had *she* been as open as she could've been?

Doesn't *every* couple have problems?

Even if married life wasn't perfect, it was less worrisome, certainly, Scarlett thinks as she spies the water bill affixed with a magnet to the refrigerator. She rocks on the stool on which she's perched and observes Iris lying supine on the carpet, ankles crossed, coloring with her markers. There's a certain joy in knowing you're about to make someone's day. "Iris, honey, I'm going to go back to school for a bit, but your dad is going to come over in a little while."

"Dad!"

And, like that, her daughter is on her feet, jumping, then dancing, and then tearing into her room to find the picture she drew earlier for Mark.

Scarlett picks her phone back up to text Robert, All good here. See you soon.

I don't think the meeting will last long Robert texts back.

SCARLETT

At ten till seven, the group begins to congregate in the lounge. The sun had set hours earlier, and their faces are reflected on the arch–framed windows. Joe Lyons paces back and forth along the length of the far end of the room, nervously tapping his fingers on the countertop as the heat pipes make a coughing sound overhead.

Robert, who arrived first, watches Lyons over the bridge of his glasses. "Joe, if you keep pacing like that, people will think we're dismantling the whole college."

Lyons snorts aggressively before pulling out a chair and sitting. "You're right, that's probably not helping. Thanks." He looks up and nods as Britt and then Scarlett enter the room. Veronica comes in a few seconds later, and Joe stands and extends his hand. "Good to finally meet you in person, and sorry this's been your introduction to where we are procedurally. We'll talk through what happened this morning and get a plan together." Joe sounds uneasy, even apologetic.

Veronica shakes his hand formally. "I'll be taking notes during the meeting for us to review later," she says before crossing her arms as she sits.

Britt's eyebrow rises. "What's up with your minion, Joe?" she asks, as if it were just the two of them in the room.

"Let's all be professionals here," Joe says. "In a way, Veronica couldn't have come at a better time. Her advice is going to keep us out of situations like today's."

Chris enters before Joe can say more, and Britt removes her jacket from the chair beside her so he can sit down. Elizabeth comes in last and takes the final chair, closest to the door, which

Lyons closes behind her. She scans the room searchingly, as if trying to recall something.

"Tell us what's going on, Joe," Britt says directly. "I feel like the principal's visiting our homeroom."

He walks to the windows, then turns to face the group. "I'll get right to the point. We have to stop the experiment."

Groans erupt. Gazes fall onto Robert, the loyal lieutenant. "Not my idea, for the record," he says.

Joe shoots Robert a look saying *thanks a lot*, then clears his throat. "What happened this morning revealed procedural holes that need to be addressed before we go any further."

"Holes?" Chris asks, incredulous.

"And which procedure do you mean?" Britt asks. "The whole thing...?"

Lyons raises his palms, his expression turning stern. "This isn't actually as bad as it sounds, but it does mean shifting our priorities. I want to go over our *actual* screening and figure out what could have been done to identify Tom as a risk. He obviously has something going on we missed."

"Obvious this morning, but maybe not two weeks ago when Elizabeth signed him up. A lot could have happened in that time," Britt says.

"Which is exactly what we need to look at. I want our screening, experimental procedure, and follow–up to be airtight before we run another condition, and that means canceling everything that's scheduled for now."

Another round of groans.

"Trust me when I say this is our best option. If we do this right, the experiment will be able to continue."

"Meaning it might actually *not* continue?" Scarlett asks.

"We have a lot of data already, so *work* doesn't have to stop. Someone could run an analysis on where we are with this experiment, call it a feasibility study."

Britt barks out a cruel laugh. "I'm sorry, did you say a feasibility study? This is my part of my PhD work, Joe. Besides, don't we already have a pilot study going on that no one's talked about?"

Joe closes his eyes and quickly raises his hands. "Not officially. Hold on."

"Hold *on*?"

"This will probably be okay," Robert quickly interjects. "We just have to tighten up."

"*Probably*?" Chris asks with a laugh. "This is getting more uncertain by the second."

Scarlett raises her hand as if the group were in middle school, then lowers it as she realizes how it looks. "Joe, can you estimate a time frame? If we're talking about a significant delay, some of us'll have to communicate with the graduate school and the other members of our committees, and some of the journals we've already queried."

"I'd guess a month to be safe."

"That puts us nearly into summer," Chris says, a sharp edge to his voice.

Robert speaks up. "Joe, with all due respect, you're slamming the brakes here on all of us, putting our professional lives in a weird place. You don't have to worry about as much—you're tenured…"

"With a nice little forensic business on the side to generate income," Britt says.

"That's…been closed for several years," he replies, quickly scanning everyone's face in the room.

Robert leans forward. "Maybe we could analyze the procedures without fully stopping. I've already sent out grant applications contingent on us collecting this data in the next month."

Chris chimes in, "Which maybe you should have thought about before bringing that kid into the room."

"And *maybe*, Chris, with any *luck*, you won't get sued for assaulting him this morning," Joe fires back.

Chris shrugs. "My attorney would bury that guy. Not to sound like a dick."

"You always sound like a dick," Elizabeth says.

Heads turn.

"And there are other people besides you in this department, in case you haven't noticed," she finishes.

Chris's jaw works the gum in his mouth.

Veronica clears her throat loudly. "I'm afraid to say that Dr. Lyons is right. It would be wantonly irresponsible to continue."

"Oh my God," someone mutters.

"We're stopping," Joe says, an edge in his voice now. "Because that's what's right—for the university, the department, and frankly, for us. I'll tell you something else that no one's said yet: this morning, the police found a knife in that kid's backpack. Let that sink in for a second. It was inside in the lab room."

Silence settles over the room.

"This is for more than just appearances, and I'd appreciate the team's support." Joe's eyes dart around the table feverishly, like he's second-guessing himself and becoming more resolute at the same time.

"It's a hard pill to swallow, but it's the right move," Robert says.

"I'm with Joe," Elizabeth adds quietly.

The others look at her. The tilt of her chin suggests she's used to that.

"*Of* course you are," Chris says.

"We can talk about your love life some other time," Britt says, but the barb is too personal, too mean to truly land.

"I said, I'm *with Joe*," Elizabeth annunciates, more defiantly the second time, making eye contact around the table as the double meaning hangs in the air. Scarlett feels her eyebrows shoot up. "Look, that kid is obviously the one at fault for what happened, and he'd clearly googled me or whatever, which I'm trying not to freak out about. But right now? Tightening this up is what *we* can do."

Joe rubs the side of his neck. "She's right. Some version of that story is going to get back to administration. And when it does, we'd better be prepared to show some data to show that Tom got into that room despite rigorous barriers, and that he would have fooled anyone. If not, we'll get shut down for good. Including everything we have planned going forward."

"I concur," Robert says.

"Reluctantly, I do too," Scarlett adds.

Veronica clicks the pen she's holding closed.

"I guess we're done here," Chris says.

Joe stands. "I'll send out an email by tomorrow morning with a plan and a timeline for getting back on track. In the meantime, there's still plenty to do with data we've already collected."

The room fills with the friction sounds of a chair sliding over laminate flooring.

"I'll look forward to following up with you later," Veronica says to Joe, then stands and leaves. Joe, Robert, and Scarlett file into the hallway.

"Text you later," Chris says to Britt as he zips his jacket and follows the others.

Britt remains seated, evidently contemplative. "You don't have to agree with everything Joe says, you know," she says to Elizabeth. "He's not going to look out for you if push comes to shove."

Elizabeth eyes her as she wraps a red scarf around her neck, her blond hair spilling over it onto her black wool jacket. She forces a smile as she slings her bag over her shoulder.

"You know, you could file a complaint against him and eat his lunch."

"Britt, if I need your advice, I'll ask for it."

"You know why other women don't like you?"

Elizabeth stops and her smile disappears. For a second, it looks as if she may cry before her expression hardens. "Britt, what I *meant* to say was, if I need your *jealous*, self–involved advice, I'll ask for it, okay?"

Britt shakes her head as Elizabeth disappears.

"It's like you're trying to get hurt," she says, just before the door closes.

CHAPTER 3

VERONICA

She didn't even recognize me.

Veronica lights a gingerbread–scented candle, then runs water over the blackened match. When it sizzles, she throws it away. Better safe than sorry. She feels like stomping her feet and does, then brings her fist down, hard, on the Formica counter-top, sending sparks of pain up her arm. The candle flame makes her new living room glow orange yellow, the stacked cardboard boxes casting shadows on the walls.

How could she not *remember?* The thought plays over and over in Veronica's mind, the repetition torturous.

The idea seems impossible, yet there was no hint of recognition—no widened eyes or stammer when she spoke. In fact, Elizabeth hadn't spoken to her *at all*. Not a word. Just that same above–it–all nod that had inflamed Veronica's last nerves as an undergrad seven years earlier.

Veronica's hair is different now, true. As are her glasses—she found a stylist before internship interviews in her second year of law school. But she'd *enhanced* her appearance more than changed it, she thinks. *It's not like I'm unrecognizable.* Except to someone as utterly, malignantly selfish as Elizabeth Colton, Veronica thinks, rage simmering in her chest. Instinctively, her fingertips brush the straight line of her dark bangs.

You'd think a person would recognize someone who got them kicked out of their sorority. It was Elizabeth's sophomore year at Tulane—Veronica had been a senior, chairing the committee that enforced the alcohol rules at campus social events. Elizabeth had it all then: she was brilliant and beautiful and wanted everyone to know she was *going places*. Oh, she'd thought she could do whatever she wanted then too. She'd given Veronica a nickname—Officer Safety. She'd called her that drunkenly one night, and everyone had laughed and laughed while Veronica's cheeks had burned, turning crimson.

Twenty-year-old Elizabeth had thrived on attention—male attention specifically—like it was the oxygen she breathed, and had half of the male student body wrapped around her manicured finger. And when her thirty-year-old musician boyfriend was stopped bringing two grocery bags full of booze into the house by campus security, questions were asked.

Whispers began.

It was a minor incident, true, but rumors caused damage. Sanctions could be levied against the entire chapter.

Somebody had to answer.

Reputations were at stake.

A rule was a rule, after all. No alcohol or foreign substances in the house. No nonstudent visitors after 8:00 p.m.

Rules meant order. They kept everyone safe.

And they *also* were a handy way of shooing away inconvenient people.

So a complaint was filed by a senior member of the sorority—who just maybe was Veronica—which brought Elizabeth in front of the chapter council, who then politely asked her to resign her membership.

Oh, Elizabeth had cried. She'd looked right at Veronica as she had.

And Veronica, for better or worse, couldn't hide her satisfaction.

Because *who was taunting who, now?*

So one would think, Veronica muses, that Elizabeth Colton would at least remember who she was.

She remembered, and in fact had jumped with glee when she realized who it was she'd be working beside on Joe Lyons's research team. Here she came again, Officer Safety, years later, at a completely different university, ready to impose some structure.

Veronica picks up a box cutter that is resting on the countertop and slices through a line of packaging tape, the tool's weight pleasant in her palm.

It was going to be fun watching Elizabeth realize who was right beside her.

ELIZABETH

Elizabeth sits rigidly in Joe Lyons's bed, the meeting, if you can call it that, having concluded an hour earlier. There have been ashen circles beneath her eyes for weeks—long before this morning's event with Tom, or that fiasco they'd just left in the student lounge, where Joe yanked everyone's research to a halt.

No, she *anticipates* something—she's sure she does—and it feels like it threatens to swallow her whole, like the pull before a giant wave crashes.

She's been looking over her shoulder, her intuition scream-ing. At night, she's woken up twisting in the sheets like she meant for her whole body to wring them out. Has the hiss in the wind really only been audible to her? She's snapped at every-one, including Joe. She's felt tension mounting for months and thought it had come to a head when her eyes met the other grad students' from Joe's car two weeks earlier.

Now, she can hardly look at him as he pads toward her with a cup of tea. It's a comfortable house he lives in, with warm gray wood floors and a fireplace, better than she expected him to find after his divorce last year. The back windows look out on a wooded area that reminds her of the view from trailers she stayed in growing up.

Men looked at her—they always had—but Joe had been so familiar, charming her by recalling delicate details of her past that she'd dared to share with him. His fearlessness—in and out of the lab—had cast a convincing spell that everything would somehow turn out okay. But now her doubts close in like subtle symptoms of a disease she was terrified to consider.

When Joe kisses her shoulder, she jumps.

"You're tense," he coos. His tone is so different from an hour earlier that she wonders if his anxiety during the meeting was theater.

"How can I not be with everything going on?"

"Every department goes through something like this. You'll get three papers out of that data. Your committee will be patient about any..."

"Fuck my committee," she snaps. "Until *today*, I did all the work we'd agreed to."

He takes a step back, rubbing at his chin. There's a haze of fear in his eyes as if she's scared him for the first time, as if, just now, her anger makes him understand that their affair has been a risk all along.

Elizabeth senses an opening. There's never time to actually talk about things, and there will never be, so she goes right at it. "Everyone knows about us, Joe. You heard how they talked to me at the meeting."

"That's just Britt. I'll meet with her."

"It's not just Britt, Joe! And it's not the snide comments; I can handle those, believe it or not. Scarlett actually felt *sorry* for me earlier; she thinks I'm stupid for being with you, I can tell. And Britt and Chris take the liberty of calling us out. They saw how I sided with you."

Joe rubs his chin as if she landed a glancing blow there. "I don't want to be stealthy about us either, but that...discretion won't last forever."

She avoids his hand when he reaches for her, and instead stands, her arms wrapped tightly around her ribs, just under her breasts. "No? I need to look after myself, if you won't. I need to start making better choices."

Joe looks at her sorrowfully, his eyes round and dewy. He has such a heart. *If only*, she thinks... If only he weren't so busy, and idealistic, and also reckless.

Is there actually a path forward for them?

"I've put myself in positions like this with guys my entire life," she says. "I'm not doing it again. Maybe it's because I didn't know my dad, or that I have no self-esteem. You tell me, you're the professor. But I'm *not* getting kicked out of here or shamed around campus because you're embarrassed that I'm your girlfriend."

Joe follows her to the window. The floor creaks the way old houses do at the end of winter, surfaces hard and brittle. "What can I do? What would help? What's mine is yours already. You have a key to my house and office, I trust you."

Trust. He had trusted her with access, and she explored his assessments, measures, old reports.

Even the one he'd told no one else about.

The one that even Joe didn't like discussing.

She'd read it from start to finish and understood completely why it needed to be kept under lock and key.

"I don't give anyone else that kind of access to look things up whenever they want," Joe says. "Not even Robert."

"And it drives them crazy."

"I can't control that."

"But you can. It would make sense…if we were married." She turns, facing him. Her face is half lit by the moonlight streaming through the window as she moves her hands to her hips. "Step by step, right? You could let the graduate school know about us, then sign off for me to have a different committee chair. People switch committee members all the time; it won't be a big deal, just find someone from another department. Education, maybe. We could be a public couple, no more hiding."

"I…"

"Then we could get engaged."

The word hangs in the air. It seems momentous but also inevitable the second she says it. "I could move in here. Tell me you don't want that too," she adds more softly.

Joe presses his knuckles against his eyes as he takes a step back. "This is a lot all at once."

"Is it? We've been doing this for about fifteen months. We're the worst-kept secret in North Carolina, if you're concerned about that. I don't want to live alone anymore. No one has to know about when we started…"

He turns and walks toward the kitchen. It was true that no one knew when they'd started their affair because Joe wasn't divorced at the time. He wasn't even separated. As far as anyone on campus knew, he was a happily married workaholic. But their team worked together closely, and long hours together aggregated into shared meals, inside jokes, trips. After a seminar in Dallas, he'd invited Elizabeth up to his suite after the others left the bar. "There'd be no going back," she'd said that night, playfully, both of them tipsy.

"Then let's go forward," he'd said, light from the chandelier aglow in his eyes.

Now, she'd wondered if he regretted having said it, or resented her for her part in blowing up his personal life.

"Is the conversation over?" she calls after him.

"What you're talking about would be self-destruction. You know that."

Elizabeth explodes like a bomb detonating. "What do you think this *is*, Joe? What do you think *I am*, your plaything? Is this just what you do? You have affairs, get to know someone, make them fall in love, and mess up their lives? I know this isn't your first time."

She'd heard no whispers of Joe's dalliances—everyone so painstakingly *loyal*, after all—but she could sense them nonetheless, the way her ears rang after concerts long after the music stopped.

He turns and looks at her, but for the first time, she can't read his expression. The ambiguity is disorienting, startling.

"I'm just not ready," he says.

Elizabeth purses her lips before saying, "Well, *I'm* ready." She knocks the dish towel off his shoulder as she storms toward the front door. "Maybe I ought to talk to the dean myself."

"Wait," Joe calls.

She throws the door open so hard, it slams against the opposite wall. More snow has fallen since she's been inside. Her white car blends with it, a circle of bluish light cast over everything by the lamppost in Joe's front yard.

She steps into the icy air, her shoes sliding some as she makes her way down the walk. Joe calls out her name, but she ignores it—a test, she knows, to see if he'll follow or make more of an effort to move their relationship forward in the coming days.

She opens her car door and slips into the driver's seat, dizzied by how quickly the tenor of the evening had changed. She's probably let things go too far already, but what was said was *needed*, even if she had no intention of actually talking with the dean. She breathes into her hands as the heater comes to life, the engine of her beat-up Lexus chugging despite the cold. She fights a longing desire to run back inside and make things right with Joe.

No.

As she shifts the car into reverse, she can see he's still at the door, completely still in his pajama pants and white T-shirt, the angle hiding his face. When she and Joe met, he was going through the classic midlife crisis at forty-seven, and she told herself she didn't care what anyone thought—the practical and reputational risks were mainly his, after all—but the sideways glances and digs had begun to make her heart feel raw. Now it feels like wearing a bright red A on the center of her chest.

What was that blank expression in his eyes a few minutes earlier?

She shivers as she backs out of Joe's driveway.

It was the second time in a single day a man's gaze had sent a chill up her spine.

ELIZABETH

The chill lingers as Elizabeth unlocks the first floor entrance to Hull Hall that all of the grad students use. The exit sign above the door colors the snow around her pink as she pushes her way into the dark stairwell. She shoulders her backpack and shakes off the cold—North Carolina winters being less forgiving than those in Louisiana, where she'd spent time as a child after her mother's third marriage. Her boots echo percussively—*clip-clop, clip-clop*—in the closed space as she notices the seam of yellow light beneath the second-story door.

It's an irony, she thinks, how deeply she hates being alone; she's alienated everyone in her life, methodically, recreating her lonesomeness again and again. *Even Joe's had enough*, she thinks, even if their affair holds him hostage. She can sense he's looking for an exit.

Clip–clop, clip–clop.

She feels a flash of her childlike fear of the dark, a distant feeling that she'll be safe only after pushing into the lit hallway. But there's something *else* she senses, isn't there? *Still there?* Anxiety makes her glance over her shoulder. Too many troublesome events have been packed into one day, she thinks. That kid, Tom, had *said her middle name*. Had he been following her? She hums to herself to feel less vulnerable.

Pop goes the metal door handle as she shoves her way onto the second floor. Elizabeth catches tiny glimpses of her reflection in the office windows she passes, the red scarf and her black coat zipped to the top. Unsurprisingly, some of the lights are on, the other grad students already refining the procedure.

The floor is linoleum tile squares, some slightly darker than others, having been replaced at various times, and Elizabeth's footsteps squeak a little with each step from what remains of the snow on her boots. A lime–colored flyer for a concert dangles from a piece of masking tape on the wall. She rushes past the first office, where Robert works, not wanting to hear any questions about the stats she now has time to run for him.

Maybe Robert's seniority gives him an unofficial leadership role in the department. Or maybe it's his smarty–pants, 1950s–collegiate persona, with his horn–rimmed glasses and neatly parted hair. Not that he had been on the ball earlier that morning; his unflappable persona had sure crumbled in the heat of the moment. True, Tom had been an extreme case. Based on how freaked out some of the students seemed during previous trials, going through the experiment was more stressful than anyone—including Joe—had predicted.

But the students don't expect class credit for nothing, do they? They shouldn't. *Spoiled brats at this preppy college*, Elizabeth thinks. She'd worked to help put herself through Tulane, then gutted out the social isolation after that *incident* at her sorority. Now, an advanced degree is her way out. No more factory town with its collage of crushed beer cans and bleak gas stations for her.

No, she would not go back.

What's the line from the Milgram obedience study? *It is imperative that we continue with the experiment.* Elizabeth wonders: *would she shock another participant if it meant getting ahead*?

Honestly?

Maybe so.

She continues on, glancing at the office that Scarlett inhabits. If Scarlett were any less virtuous seeming, Elizabeth might guess she and Robert were sleeping together. But truly, she senses nothing but wholesomeness between them. Her gut says that best buddies is all they are.

To each his own, she thinks, even though they'd make up the kind of couple she'd always wanted to be in—straightforward, collaborative, caring. Maybe there was still that possibility with Joe; maybe it wasn't too late for them, she considers, shoving her cynicism aside.

Figures also that Scarlett, clearly everyone's favorite, somehow ended up with the office that has the best view of the courtyard. Her door is closed, but a soft light escapes where it meets the floor, and the faint symphonic sounds of the campus radio station are audible. Typical liberal academic listening to NPR.

Since she's started working for Joe, nonuniversity news seems foreign and like a distraction.

She rounds the corner and slams chest–first into someone, a startled yelp escaping from her throat.

When she looks up, Chris glares at her, brushing his brown hair from his forehead—God forbid it's ever mussed. He grins at her, tauntingly. "Eyes up, Elizabeth." His grass–green collared shirt makes him look every bit the trust–fund kid he is. The mood in the department was fraught periodically, but when had it become so ferocious? Was it the knowledge about her and Joe? Or the insane hours they'd all been working?

"Just trying to get by here," she says, switching her backpack to her other shoulder.

"You're the one scurrying around. But maybe you can help me. Have you seen our beloved Professor Lyons this evening? I'm trying to get feedback on a questionnaire I made up last year that might work for screening, but he won't answer his phone. And since you're obviously so agreeable to his ideas, I thought maybe you…" Chris looks her up and down, his eyes seeming to flicker. Men do this to Elizabeth. The fact that she's used to it makes it no less gross. "…might have some knowledge of his whereabouts."

Chris's ease in composing himself is unnerving. She cuts a wide berth around him, ducking as if he might reach for her.

"Don't flatter yourself," he says. "Dual relationships aren't a turn–on for me."

"Fuck off, Chris."

"Good job setting the department back six months by backing the stoppage."

Elizabeth extends her middle finger as she strides down the

hall. Chris has always mildly creeped her out but is probably harmless. There's no time to think about him anyway; what she needs to do is glue herself to a chair and crank out the lit review she'd promised Robert after the meeting. She uses the bathroom, then hears footsteps outside the door as she washes her hands. The hand soap smells like Lemonhead candy.

Another door opens and closes. Then, a heavier one, like the door leading to the stairwell, slams and she jumps. "Easy," she tells herself, ripping two brown paper towels from the dispenser.

She moves back into the hall, noting the ancient elevator groaning at the end of the hall. It was hardly ever used. Strange Chris would have taken it instead of the stairs.

The office beside Elizabeth's is Britt's. Britt's door is closed, but her music—if you could call it that—thumps away inside. It sounds like Nine Inch Nails being played inside a blender, except faster. How can anyone concentrate with that racket hammering away? Whatever little speakers she's using must be maxed out because the bass can be felt through the tile in the hall. Which means that in Elizabeth's office the music will be a *presence*.

She pictures Britt's snarl and steels herself. If Elizabeth is the most disliked in the department, Britt is the most feared. Early on, Joe had coached Britt on keeping her appearance "neutral" for the sake of consistency in the experimental conditions—this was a woman who once wore a safety pin through her nose to a departmental meeting—and relayed afterward that Britt hadn't taken the advice well. "Stormed out" had been his words.

She clears her throat and knocks on the door.

No answer.

It's no wonder. The music vibrates Elizabeth's shoes.

Elizabeth knocks again, harder, and the volume drops. "Go away" comes from inside.

"Britt, I need…"

The door flings open, Britt staring up at her, a look of plain disgust on her face. Her jet–black hair is spiked with some sort of glossy gel that catches the hallway light. When Elizabeth hesitates, Britt bugs her eyes out, conveying her impatience. "What?"

"I'm just asking you, politely, to turn that down. I'm going to be next door and have a ton to get done tonight."

Britt stares, squinting her eyes as if noting something ponderous about Elizabeth for the first time. Her head leans slightly left, signaling she's deep in thought. "No," she barks, before closing the door.

Or tries to.

Elizabeth sticks her boot into the doorjamb and lets the rubber tip catch the door's edge. She steps inside the office, her shadow falling forward as Britt's eyes flash in surprise. Elizabeth's voice takes on a honeyed tone; it's the voice she uses when she holds back tears no one will ever see. "I tried asking nicely. You *don't* have to be a bitch about the volume. I have a right to work in quiet. Lower it, and we'll be *all* good. 'Kay?"

"Are you threatening me?" Britt sits up.

"Take it however you want," Elizabeth says.

Britt's eyes flick toward her purse.

"Seriously? You're going to tase anyone tonight, weirdo? Just turn the music down," she says, then slams the door herself.

How quickly things can devolve, she thinks; it's a wonder any of them collaborate. *Villains never think of themselves as villains, do they?* she thinks, tears stinging her eyes. *Herself included.*

Her key ring is jangly in her fingers as she opens the office door. A few deep breaths later, she powers up her laptop and finally gets to work. *The sooner she's published and defends, the sooner she can start looking for faculty positions—anywhere but here,* she thinks fleetingly, suddenly missing the openness of Louisiana's rolling green fields, the plains outside Alexandria, where she felt like she could breathe.

After an hour, the screen begins to blur. She notices a mistake, then, circling back, another. It's a simple one, a decimal out of place, but her attention has clearly waned. She fixes both errors and looks out at the empty alleyway, yellowed by streetlight as a cold wind hammers her window.

Caffeine is her only hope.

The ancient Coke machine on the first floor only accepts change and dollar bills. Joe keeps a little petty cash in his desk drawer, she knows—their love of Diet Coke a commonality. She slips her white puffy jacket back on, and she shakes it loose as she makes her way into the deserted hallway.

BRITT

Britt feels the tremor of the door closing in the office beside hers.

Elizabeth must be leaving, she thinks.

She turns down her music and hears the soft echo of Elizabeth talking to someone in the hall, the old building's acoustics making it seem nearly haunted, especially at night.

She peeks out. Nothing visible, then the whoosh of a dark uniform passing.

A janitor, Britt thinks. Makes sense at this time of night.

Then, Elizabeth's office door opens and closes again. If Britt didn't have so much to do, she might ask what was going on.

A minute passes, a cursor blinking steadily on Britt's screen.

Then, Elizabeth's door opens and closes a third time, her footsteps clicking fast down the hall.

Wherever she's going now, she's in a hurry.

Soon, Britt thinks, Elizabeth's choices are going to catch up to her.

ELIZABETH

The building feels airless. Her footsteps squeaked earlier but echo now. Elizabeth hears her own breathing as she strides down the hall, her hands trembling as she tries Joe's number.

He doesn't answer—of course—it's late.

But what she just saw can't be a coincidence.

And there's only one way to find out if what she suspects is the case. And aside from Joe, she's the only one who can look.

The brass doorknob of Joe's door is cool on her palm as she turns it and pushes inside. Enough light spills in from the hallway so that she can see her way to his desk. She can see the file cabinet is already open.

The door closes before she can turn around, her thigh knocking bruisingly into Joe's desk as she stumbles backward.

"Britt? Chris? I swear to God, I…"

A hand reaches over Elizabeth's mouth, stifling her scream. She flings her fists but connects glancingly, her jacket's fabric a fury of slick friction. She opens her mouth wide enough to bite into a finger, but a white–hot streak lashes into her side.

The pain is so sharp, she gasps.

Her hand finds her abdomen, sticky and warm. *Opened up.* She mumbles half words, panting.

This is shock, she thinks.

This.

Is shock.

She opens her mouth to scream just as her mouth is covered again. The warmth spreads across her chest.

Then, pain rips through her neck.

It's too late, she thinks.

It's all over.

CHAPTER 4

LARSON

Detective Alana Larson listens to forty-year-old country as she drives—what her mother would have called *real* country. The airy melody offers to take her places she doesn't want to go—back to the pool halls she wandered as a kid, and to dusty alleys outside the honky-tonks, listening to her mom belting out covers, trying to make it as a country singer.

It wasn't the worst childhood, even if her father was long gone—Alana knew that even at the time—but the travel was uncommon—late nights in cities like Nashville, Raleigh. She became familiar with odd glances from barkeeps who fed Alana peanuts and Dr. Peppers as the gigs installed a world-weary distance in her mom's eyes. More than once, her mom exhaustedly buzzed the tires of their Buick Riviera on roadside rumble strips in the pale near dawn.

The tours also precipitated a visit from a school resource officer when Alana was nine—her first time talking with a cop, who told her she'd check to make sure Alana didn't miss one more school day.

And that it was always better to tell the truth, even if that was hard to do.

Larson's eyes sting at the memory, but she turns the volume up anyway—the song one that's made for driving—her familiarity with it like a religion she'd long ago stopped believing.

The roads are clear on the Friday morning before spring break, students having departed to sunny destinations like Destin, Panama City Beach, Daytona. From the top of the hill, she can see Dorrance's stony peaks—of one of the country's most prestigious universities, the sort of idyllic place Larson never thought of as an option when she was a kid. It's adjacent to a downtown that's equally charming, where historic markers dot walkways. Brick is ubiquitous and well scrubbed, and fountains anchor a central courtyard.

Shepard isn't all that way, of course; there's an untamed periphery where ivy won't grow in any university town, twisting roads where ponderous students don't venture. Or are afraid to. There are shadowy houses in disrepair, where novels are written by candlelight and weeds hide paths into deeper woods, where chaos is spoken of like an art form, and creatives go to be left alone.

But even those places don't report much crime, which is fine by her.

She flexes her dry hands on the Tacoma's steering wheel as snow sprinkles onto her windshield. Her work phone chirps, the blue hue of the dashboard lights reflect on the screen.

"This is Larson," she answers and immediately hears a blur of speech—tearful, frantic. In the last six months, Larson's never heard the septuagenarian dispatcher talk so quickly. She's saying something about a disturbance on campus. "No, no," Larson tells her amid a flutter of relief. "I got a call about the fight yesterday. I told them to call Patrick King, I'm sure he handled it."

The dispatcher's voice breaks. "Alana, someone's been murdered."

Larson's pulse accelerates, then begins to pound as she turns the wheel and then splashes down an alleyway toward campus. The dispatcher's words are a rushing stream, Larson getting the gist in bursts. "Stabbed or cut was what they said. A female… maybe in her late twenties. She was screaming…blood. They said *so* much blood, they…"

"Slow down. I'm almost there."

Crime statistics in Shepard are tame. Most are substance related: DUIs, underage possession, open–container charges. Bike theft is relatively common. She'd worked on her share of sexual assault cases, each one making her stomach turn, and investigated a dozen fistfights between neighbors.

Once, she'd arrested a grad student for collecting explosives. Never in Shepard had she investigated a murder.

She turns on Third Street, then shoots down Main, five blocks from campus. "Verify the name of the building for me?"

"Hull Hall."

"That's…?"

"It houses the Psychology Department."

LARSON

Five minutes later, Detective Larson stands outside Professor Joe Lyons's office in Hull Hall. She'd had to duck beneath yellow police tape and show her badge at the building's front entrance, then again at the top of the stairway that opened to the second floor. Pat King—somewhere in his late fifties, graying—stands beside the door she was looking for. He's put on weight since Larson had last seen him—pandemic weight, maybe, or just the aggregate stress of keeping everything together on a college campus. He's been in his position since long before Larson joined the city force and had been consistently helpful to her, even affable. It probably took a bit of affability, she'd thought before, to navigate the shenanigans of eighteen–to–twenty–two–year–olds.

The office door is open, and King stands just outside in the hall. He greets her with a solemn nod. "I wish I could say, 'Good morning.' The office manager found her. She's apparently the first one in every morning, and she noticed blood coming from under the door." His voice has the weariness of a man nearing retirement who has already begun dreaming of spending his days elsewhere. He points to a semicircular blackish pool in the hallway. So dark it hardly looks like blood at all, more like someone spilled acrylic paint from the university studios.

Mars black.

She takes a small step back, bullet points from her academy training flooding her mind.

King says, "Goes without saying I was shocked to take the call. There's not been a murder in the eighteen years I've been here. We secured the building around eight a.m., within about fifteen minutes of first notification. It's lucky spring break's started, otherwise locking this down would have been a mess."

He's right. Who knows how many students would have been up and down this hallway already on a normal Friday morning.

"Do we have an ID on the body?"

"The assistant who called ran without taking a long look, but she thinks this is Elizabeth Colton, a second–year PhD candidate in psychology."

Larson forces her gaze onto the woman's face, her lightless eyes. There's no getting used to that. Her fist instinctively covers her mouth as she examines Elizabeth's arm hanging languidly from the desk chair. She gauges the color of the blood and the degree of bruising around the entrance wounds and makes mental notes, then gauges the smell, which she knows will worsen exponentially by the hour, and understands the real horrors of decomposition haven't yet begun. This woman was killed in the last twelve hours.

King follows her gaze around the room. "Do you think it's possible she stayed in that chair and didn't slide down?" His voice trembles like he's trying to keep it steady.

"Possibly, but she could have been placed here after she was killed." Larson tries not to come off as pedantic, even as King's naivete reminds her that in some ways that she's on her own.

"How good are the security cameras for the building?"

"There's one over the rear entrance, which the office manager seems to think she likely used to enter the building, and one in the first floor entranceway, but that door had been locked since six p.m."

"Good, that way there's a limited number of…" Her head turns as she senses movement in the hallway. "I thought the whole building was blocked off," she says, already hurrying past King, then looking down the hall just in time to see a figure rounding the corner.

"Hey," she calls, rushing after the figure.

She knows the medical examiner personally, and this person is not her—which means someone has trespassed onto a crime scene, contaminating it. "Excuse me," she yells, breaking into a trot. "You need to stop where you are."

At the corner is a woman—slight, with dark spiked hair, black puffy jacket—glancing at Larson as she turns a key in an office doorknob and then disappears inside, slamming the door closed behind her.

"Stay there," Larson barks back at King.

Larson's hand finds the handle of her gun as she breaks into a run, her heart racing and thoughts spiraling. Whoever this person is, they're either very brave or very desperate, having come in the building's back entrance, ducked under police tape at least twice, and managed to slip by the campus cop who's supposedly securing the building.

Larson pounds on the wooden door with the base of her fist, then steps slightly back. The placard says "Britt Martinez". "Shepard PD, you'll open this door immediately and move into the hallway."

She clears her throat to yell again when the door lazily falls open. The young woman spins in her desk chair, and Larson's eyes are met by a gaze of impatient disgust. "Can I help you?" Britt asks her.

"Hands over your head now, and move into the hall."

"I don't have time for any police games right now," Britt says, nudging the door with the tip of her boot.

Larson feels her eyes widen and the base of her neck begins to warm. She's grown nearly immune to disrespect, but this is beyond. She shoves the door open further. "You're going to leave this area now, or you'll be placed under arrest. Am I being clear? This is a crime scene."

"Well, *I* didn't commit any crimes, and I have a lot of work to do."

Larson senses *something* in her tone—a kind of dispassion—that reminds Larson of a cousin who was able to recall specific statistics and numbers that seemed irrelevant to most others. Universities are a refuge for people who are different, Larson reminds herself, before releasing a small sigh and the handle of her pistol. "One of your colleagues has been killed," she says, slightly out of breath from the trot down the hall. "I need you to leave this area."

Still no reaction.

Suspects commonly return to crime scenes, but this woman either isn't comprehending the situation or doesn't care. "A graduate student in this department has been killed," Larson says.

Now Britt sits up straight. "Was it Chris Collins?"

Larson blinks, caught off guard. "No."

Britt's chest heaves with relief, and her neutral expression returns.

King appears, speaking into a radio attached to his shoulder. A second later, another uniformed campus cop huffs at the top of the stairs. Larson stops herself from asking how someone could slip by him so easily and instead says, "Please escort this person outside and take down all her contact information. She's not to be up here." She then says to Britt, "I'll be talking with you later."

The officer points toward the back stairwell as Britt picks up her pack with a sigh and closes her office door.

The totality of the encounter troubles Larson, but two details stand out: Britt assumed that Chris Collins, whoever that is, was who'd been killed.

And when she learned the victim was someone else, she didn't bother asking who.

She returns to where King has taken position. "We're going to need a little more vigilance on securing the building, especially until the ME gets here."

"Agreed. Sorry she got through."

"You responded to that call about the fight yesterday?"

King nods. "Something like that. Even before, the Psychology Department has had a cloud over it. Maybe it's just my perception, but the secrecy around some of the research makes everyone suspicious. Last I heard, undergrads were giving them access to their personal information. I can't think of a good reason for that, it's nothing I'd do."

"I've had my own issues with psychologists," Larson mutters quickly. "Has anyone else been notified about Ms. Colton yet?"

King shakes his head. "She apparently has very little in the way of family. The office assistant mentioned the department chair, Dr. Lyons, could identify the body. She indicated…"

"What?"

"That Ms. Colton and Lyons were involved." King raises his eyebrow. "I'll get you his number."

Larson looks again at the scene where Elizabeth lies, morning sunlight now streaming in through the window. Nothing juxtaposes neutrally with death, she thinks, her hand returning to her mouth as the sight of the blood again makes her stomach turn.

There's no telling what's happening in that office—the rest

of the building hasn't been cleared for evidence or swept for additional threats.

"Send me Lyons's address along with his number. I want to go over there myself and see how he takes the news."

JOE

Lyons is brushing his teeth when his phone rings. He strides back into his bedroom, cupping his hand beneath his chin. The incoming number is from the university—it's too early to schedule meetings about what happened with yesterday's experiment—so he sends the call to voicemail, spits, and rinses away the pale blue paste from his sink.

Another call comes within seconds. Same number. Maybe the provost calling—known to be insistent—in which case, he'll need a cup of coffee first.

He's not yet to his kitchen when his phone rings a third time.

The hair on the back of his neck stands up.

The instant he hears the office manager's voice, his fingers begin to tremble. "Something's happened, Joe. I...don't know how to say this. Are you sitting down?"

His stomach sinks as he braces himself against a doorframe.

At the same moment, there's a loud knock at the door, and Joe's head jerks toward the sound. "Hold...hang on." Lyons makes out a dark-blue uniform through the frosted glass beside the front door, his mind connecting the call and the cop who's come to his house. "I'm going to have to call you back," he says.

His hands are clammy as he opens the door, squinting at the harsh daylight. A police officer—female, early thirties, sandy–blond hair pulled tightly back—stands there. Her somber expression tells Joe this is about more than Chris clocking that student the day before.

"I'm Detective Larson," she says in a low voice, showing her badge.

His mouth trembles involuntarily. "Is Kate okay?" he pleads, hardly able to utter his daughter's name, the world a buzz of confusion as he considers the worst catastrophe first.

"I'm here because of an attack on campus," Larson says.

His mouth dries. "Attack?"

"May I come in?"

They go into the living room and sit on the sofa he bought just after his divorce, which still feels firm and new. He and Elizabeth sat in the same spot the night before.

"I'm sorry to have to be the one to tell you this, but a woman has been killed. The attack was last night in a department office—in your office, actually—and she didn't survive. We believe the woman was Elizabeth Colton. I know hearing this must be very hard."

It's like Larson is speaking another language. Time slows down. *I may be going into shock,* Joe realizes—disbelief insulating him from deep pain soon to flood in. His gaze wanders up the hallway from the living room, searching for the corner of his bed, visible if he cranes his neck, where Elizabeth had spent nights with him—often enough that he'd begun thinking of the left side as hers.

"Are you okay, Professor?"

He blinks a few times in succession. "That's…this is impossible; why would she be in my office?" Even as he asks, he knows the question is peculiar.

But what is there to say when the world falls off its axis?

"The investigation is underway now. We're gathering evidence and will need your help. In the meantime, we've had some difficulty contacting her family. The office manager seemed to think the two of you were close. I know it could be very hard, but will you be able to identify her body?"

Joe's phone rings yet again. He looks down and realizes he's still clutching it in his palm, then answers, aware the calls will keep coming if he doesn't. "I'm with the police now," he says, then hangs up. His eyes refocus on Larson, aware that she is gauging his reactions, shock refocusing his attention to odd details: the shine of her badge, scuffed white streaks on her boot, a bird's indifferent call outside. "I'm sorry, you want me to identify her?"

Larson nods. "Several people mentioned you had an intimate relationship with Ms. Colton."

Several people.

Elizabeth is right.

Was right.

Sweat forms under Joe's arms and cools his forehead.

"Would you say that's true?" Larson asks. "That the two of you were very close?"

His gaze wanders.

How foolish he has been.

How incredibly *foolish,* Lyons thinks.

He shifts restlessly, feeling such a powerful urge to lie.

SCARLETT

Scarlett checks the time on her Timex as she sits beside her six–year–old daughter, Iris, who picks at a small rip in their couch. "Just leave that, honey," she says. The view from their living room is of mature trees in a common area nestled between other apartment buildings. It's in an older part of town, and the scene looks stately in the mist. Their apartment itself isn't much—dated, nicked countertops and patchy drywall—but it's close to campus and situated in one of the best school districts in the state. Most of the neighbors are also grad students, which means infrequent loud partying, no bass thumping through walls or drunken late–night conversations on the porches.

Iris cranes her neck to look out the front window.

"Not yet, baby," Scarlett tells her as she cleans their breakfast dishes. "Your dad said eight thirty, and it's still quarter past."

Iris, dressed in jeans and a pink hoodie, traces a clockwise circle over her wrist where a watch would sit. Their furniture is secondhand but tidy, aside from an occasional tear. Guests have told Scarlett they can't believe she and Iris actually live in the place. "It's like it's staged," her sisters once said. Growing up in a house with seven siblings, everything was always a mess. Her parents were classic southern churchgoers—a pastor and his wife—and the family moved every time her father took on a new parish. The family had no shortage of love, but no amount of warmth could furnish a home.

Still, the place and everything in it is all theirs. It's an unexpected silver lining to her divorce—one she hadn't anticipated—she can keep things just the way she likes them.

"If there's a knock on the door, it may be Robert. He's supposed to pick me up right around the same time," she calls to Iris as she retreats to the bedroom.

Iris considers this with a sly smile. "Is Robert your boyfriend?"

Six–year–olds aren't known for subtlety, but her unexpected directness makes Scarlett laugh. "We're friends who work together, that's all. Robert's nice about giving us rides to school since it's on his way."

"He told me he lives by the arboretum. That's the other direction."

Scarlett pats Iris's pillow before crossing through the hall. *You're not wrong*, she thinks, impressed with how cleverly her daughter picked up on that detail. "I guess that's true, but it's nice to get a lift when it's so cold outside, don't you think? The buses can be drafty."

"Robert's funny. He teases me, but I like it."

I like it too, Scarlett thinks, smiling to herself. Robert's rigidity around Iris always elicited a smile from her for some reason. Maybe it was watching someone so capable struggle awkwardly with an interaction so simple. Or maybe it was that despite Robert's stiffness in those situations, his efforts gave her a glimpse of some inner warmth.

She pulls a sweater from her closet.

Is Robert interested in her? *One of the mysteries of the universe*, her youngest sister might tease. If so, Scarlett thinks, an interesting scenario could unfold any minute. He and her ex, Mark, may arrive at the same time. Mark was never the jealous type, but might he be suspicious? Iris evidently is. Even if Mark was that perceptive, *she's* only ever sensed flickers of romantic tension with Robert amid the marathon of data collection, analysis, and writing. If Robert wants something more than collegiality with her, he's paced his approach glacially.

As she finishes getting ready, the hair dryer cries out shrilly when she turns it on. She hears a knock on the door just as she turns it off. "Honey, hang on, let…"

She hears the lock click, then the door squeak as it swings open. Robert stands in the cold, so oddly formal around Iris, hands folded at his waist. "You can come in, silly!" she tells him.

"Well, thank you very much," he says, lamplight reflecting warmly on his glasses as he cautiously steps inside and closes the door. "Kids terrify me," he'd confessed to Scarlett, once.

Scarlett tells him she'll be just another minute as she fiddles with an earring.

"I'm not going to school today," she overhears Iris inform him.

"I see. You've gone on strike?"

Iris giggles.

"Promoted then? Skipping a grade? Sent directly into the workforce?"

"It's spring break! My dad is visiting."

"That sounds like much more fun."

"I thought you were him when I heard you knock," Iris says.

Scarlett again emerges from the bedroom and meets Robert's eyes as she continues to stand awkwardly by the door.

A perfunctory knock lands on the door before it flings open, then Iris bounds past Robert. "Dad!"

Mark steps inside wearing a charcoal sweater and a brown barn jacket, his dark hair slightly blown about by the windy morning. Mark scoops Iris into his arms, his eyes pinching with pleasure as he absorbs his daughter's hug. He extends his hand as he steps forward, Iris still clinging to him as if attached with Velcro. "Good morning, nice to meet you. Mark Simmons."

His tone is clear and even mirthful, without a hint of jealously, Scarlett thinks, pushing away her tinge of disappointment.

Robert's expression is quizzical as he extends his hand. "I'm Robert. Sorry I hadn't expected to meet you, but hi. I function as a chauffeur for Scarlett and sometimes your little one when the timing works out."

"That's nice of you," Mark says, rubbing noses with Iris, who has lit up.

There's something vaguely incongruent about watching these two men interact, Scarlett thinks, stepping forward with her arms folded over her chest. Characters from two separate worlds, like Indiana Jones walking onto a *Star Wars* set. "Mark, you're welcome to stick around here if you want a place to hang out for a while; there's an extra key…"

Mark waves off the offer. "The two of us have a little adventure planned. Breakfast, then shopping, then maybe see about the indoor pool at the hotel. All of that sound okay?" Iris nods as Mark smiles contagiously.

Scarlett picks up her book bag, her head cocked with a reluctant smile. "Not too much sugar at breakfast, okay? And no to the pool if it's cold. I don't want a frozen Iris showing back up."

"You have my word," Mark says. He shakes Robert's hand again before they all head down the stairs, four in a row. The handrail's flecked paint reminds Scarlett of how modest her circumstances are compared to life before the divorce, and she feels a desire for Mark to be impressed by how well she's done on her own. Part of her wants to announce that she's off to do research at one of the finest psychology programs in the country, which she still isn't sure how she was lucky enough to be accepted into.

She climbs into Robert's decade–old Honda Civic and spies the gray–blue shiny canvas of Robert's book bag in the back. Across the parking pad, Mark secures Iris in his new–looking BMW X5—a small whiff of smoke wafting from a tailpipe.

"He looks familiar. Where's he from?" Robert asks, buckling his seat belt and starting the engine.

Scarlett laughs, partly from relief at how smoothly the exchange had gone.

"What?" Robert chuckles.

"The familiarity thing. That's what everyone says, they always have. People think Mark's famous or on TV. I can't tell you how many times we were stopped and asked if he was the actor in *Spider–Man 2*, or on the local news anchor in Kansas City in the nineties, or something like that. He just has one of those faces people think they recognize."

She sometimes worked at the front desk of a clinic he visited as a pharmaceutical rep, and he asked her out twice before she'd said yes. He'd offered to cook for her on their second date— invited her to his apartment for a dinner he prepared. She'd marveled years later at her own naiveté in accepting an invitation from a virtual stranger, but the evening had turned out magnificently. He'd made stir–fry, or something like it, which they'd eaten on Fiestaware in his kitchen. He had mason jars for drinking glasses and no experience using the dishwasher since he lived alone.

His fumbling charmed her, and a month later she was fibbing to her parents about where she spent her evenings.

Two months after that, they were engaged.

Robert nudges the windshield wipers to clear away bits of sleet. "He seems...nice."

"Five years of marriage and never a cross word," Scarlett says.

They watch the BMW's taillights cycle through as Mark shifts into gear, then glides over the small hump of the parking area onto the foggy street. "So why the divorce? Please tell me if it's none of my business."

Scarlett sighs and looks at him with the quizzical smile she uses when figuring out what to say. "It *is* none of your business, but I'll tell you anyway. The relationship has officially been over for two years, but it probably ended at least a year before that. The short answer is that we grew apart. His career in medical sales took off, which meant more time traveling. Iris and I were alone, and I was completely overwhelmed. I started wanting to go back to school, and I think he wanted to be married to a stay–at–home mom who wanted more kids."

And now I wonder if he's seeing anyone, if he'll remarry, Scarlett thinks. *If Iris will have a new family someday while I pursue my career.*

Robert's phone rings as they rumble down the quiet road toward campus. He silences it. "That's the front office. I can handle whatever they need in a few. Mark still travels just as much?"

"More. I wonder sometimes whether I should have tried harder to make it work. You see how happy she is around him. He's such a good dad, but honestly? He got royally screwed when we split up. He acted like he was going to put up a big fight for custody but then settled really fast, which was best for her, and for me. I felt like I was taking advantage of him, but…"

Scarlett's phone begins to ring too, and when she sees the department is calling, she looks at Robert. "They just called you a second ago. Something's wrong." She presses her screen and says hello.

Instantly, her eyes widen and she stares straight ahead.

Robert glances back and forth between her and the road as she acknowledges what's being said.

"What was that?" he asks as Scarlett hangs up.

Her eyes drift to the telephone poles they pass, one after another, so bare–seeming in winter.

"Talk to me," Robert insists. "What's going on?"

Scarlett draws a breath, stunned. "That was one of the assistants in the front office. She said the police are interviewing everyone. I can't believe what I'm about to say. Elizabeth is dead. Her body was found in the department. I was *there* last night." She looks at him, the air thick now as the tires rumble. "Weren't you there too?"

Robert grips the wheel. He hesitates before answering, "All six of us were."

VERONICA

Shortly after 9 a.m., Veronica picks lint from her red plaid sweater as she approaches Hull Hall and is confronted with cruisers blocking both sides of the street. *Great.* Waiting at a locked door in the cold yesterday and now *this.* She lowers the window of her sedan as a uniformed officer approaches, palm raised.

"What's going on here? I work in this building. I have a meeting with Doctor Lyons in fifteen minutes." She aggressively taps the face of her Mickey Mouse watch.

"Uh, not today you don't. There's been an incident. I'm sorry to tell you this, but someone has been killed."

"*What?* Who?" she asks.

"I'm afraid I can't release that information now, ma'am, but no one is allowed in or out of the building at this time."

Did he say *killed*? The reality of what she's being told settles over her as another vehicle approaches from behind. Veronica begins to sweat as she looks past the officer, then gauges the width of the street. "I have to turn around, but it's going to be a U-turn," she tells him, her voice shrill and unsettled, before raising her window to begin the maneuver.

Just as she does, her phone rings, the caller ID flashing a Shepard PD number.

Her heart skips a beat. Her assumption, right until that instant, had been that whatever happened didn't involve anyone she knew.

But what she also didn't know was that within twenty-four hours, someone else in the group would be dead.

CHAPTER 5

LARSON

Larson can feel the temperature dropping as she waits for Joe Lyons to get dressed. She calls the morgue to verify that Elizabeth's body has been moved. "Just now," the voice says. "I'd give them another half hour before heading over for ID."

"That timing should work out pretty well on this end," she says, then hangs up and calls King. "I picked up a cruiser from the station and am at the professor's house. I'm taking him to ID the body."

"Roger that. Things moved fast here after you left," he tells her. He sounds slightly less rattled than before, as if he's making an effort to shift into a professional mode. Still, she can detect a tremor in his voice. "The medical examiner obviously is going to run blood work, but indications are that the body wasn't moved after the struggle and that the cause of death was loss of blood from the stab wounds. She thinks the victim died somewhere between eleven p.m. and two a.m." He pauses. "Even in a town like this, the media could work themselves into a frenzy pretty easily. I'm afraid they'll start wanting to know if this is the start of something, like Ted Bundy or the Gainesville murders in the nineties."

"Let's hope to God not," Larson says. Far too early to make comparisons like those.

"With no precedent, it's hard not to speculate," King says.

She gets his anxiety. In King's entire career, he'd never responded to a murder scene on campus *in a departmental building.* The guy is doing his best to hold steady. "I'll keep you up to speed on anything happening on this end. After this, I need to talk to the kid who got the police called yesterday."

"I'm already on it, just sent you his name and address. Tom Campbell. He rattled everyone pretty good, caused a disturbance during their experiment. And, well, he brought a backpack into the room. Alana, there was a knife inside. It was small, the folding kind for camping, but it could have done a lot of damage."

He brought a knife to the floor where someone was stabbed to death hours later, she thinks. "Noted," she says.

"It's in the report and it wasn't returned to him. He checked himself out of the ER around five p.m., so the timing makes it possible that he was here, but between you and me, I don't think he… Oh, hell, to be honest, I don't know what to think about him. He seems more like an impulsive kid than a cold-blooded murderer. Even though…" Larson can practically hear King wince. "He *did* admit, in a way, to having some kind of fixation on the victim. *Damn it.* I hate every part of this."

Larson thanks King before hanging up. She never met Elizabeth Colton, but the image of her body left a raw weightiness in her chest.

Larson stomps her boots on the driveway from the chill in

the air as Lyons moves into view in the front windows of his house. A few seconds later, he emerges wearing a black hiking jacket, jeans, and gray New Balance running shoes, like he's about to run some usual weekend errands.

"This way, Professor," she says, opening the rear door of the police cruiser for him and then starting off. He stares numbly out the window, seemingly in a trance, like he's trying to decide whether he's in the middle of a bad dream. The police radio crackles and Larson silences the volume, appraising Lyons in the rearview mirror. She's not sure what to make of his and Elizabeth's relationship, but her intuition tells her he isn't at the top of her list of suspects. Even if Lyons did want Elizabeth dead, why would he take her to his own office—then leave her there? That makes no sense.

When they arrive at the morgue, she knocks once on the glass door before glancing up at a security camera, then hears a buzz and click as the door unlocks. She leads Lyons into the hallway, which feels barely warmer than outside, their footsteps squeaking in the dim, windowless space. She can see their breath as Lyons shuffles forward, rubbing his temples like he's too overwhelmed to think. He hasn't said a word since they left his house.

Larson nods to the medical examiner, who opens a door at the end of the hall and leaves as they enter the room where faintly green light reflects dully off the stainless steel doors. The place has a sickly sterile smell, like a hospital but more pungent, as if it were a place where nothing at all is meant to live. The last chamber door is open, and Elizabeth's body lies exposed on the metal surface. Some of the blood has been cleaned from the wound on her neck, but the gash on her arm still looks jagged and sticky. The coagulated blood is purplish black.

Larson follows a step behind Lyons, who halts five feet from the body.

"It's her," he says curtly. "Can I go now?"

Larson walks him back outside, where jet contrails criss-cross an expansive sky. Lyons scans the parking lot, directionless. When Larson begins to guide him, she realizes he's sobbing, his shoulders rhythmically heaving. She escorts Lyons back into the police car and begins driving him home.

The streets are completely empty now, and a train whistles in the distance as they bump along. She glances up at the wispy clouds. It had been a cold winter; the temperature was low for this time of year, but not unprecedented.

"Joe," Larson begins softly, hoping a familiar tone may mitigate his shock. Lyons jumps nevertheless, eyes darting about. He's middle–aged, but suddenly looks like a little boy. *Careful*, Larson thinks. "I know this is hard, but can you think of anyone who was angry with Elizabeth?"

"Angry?" He sounds confused, like emotions tangled his thoughts. "Not angry *like that*, like murder for God's sake, no, *no one*. She may not have been the most popular person in the department, but I can't imagine anyone would want…*that*. Want her *dead*…"

"What makes you say she was wasn't popular?"

His mouth opens, then closes again.

"Was it because of your affair?" Larson asks this matter–of–factly and realizes as she asks that she hasn't judged Elizabeth and Lyons's relationship at all. Her mom always had more than her share of romantic messiness, and she never thought of her as a bad person.

"Am I being questioned right now?" Lyons wipes at his dewy eyes.

Larson can smell the sweat on him. He's either petrified, or so skillful an actor that he can control his endocrine system. "I'm gathering information, Professor. Let me back up. I understand that you're the department chair. What do you do in that role?"

"Research, mainly, at this point. Grant writing to secure funding. I contribute to papers, overseeing day-to-day procedures, that sort of thing. I usually teach two classes a semester, one if I can talk someone else into taking one for me."

"Sounds very busy."

He rubs his eye with his knuckle. "It's the same at all top research universities. I was part of a forensic assessment practice on the side until a few years ago, but I shut that down. No time. I got a sizable grant and wanted to focus on running experiments full time."

"Forensic assessment?" Larson bristles but forces her emotions aside. "As in, criminal cases?"

"Civil cases, mostly, evaluations for hiring and things like that. Companies want to avoid the liability of hiring the wrong person."

She eyes him.

"I don't see what that has to do with finding out what happened to Elizabeth," he says.

"Like I said, I'm just gathering information." Larson's gaze shifts back to the road.

"That practice's been closed for three years. But to your earlier question about our relationship, *probably,*" he says. "Word got out, then the others saw us together a few weeks ago. It was awkward. It's rubbed some people the wrong way," Lyons says, sounding so sorrowful he's forgotten his concern about being questioned.

"Elizabeth's death was within a few hours of midnight last night. Who else might have been in the building?"

"I'm sorry, can you pull over?" Lyons meets Larson's eyes in the mirror, and she can see his face is pale.

She turns the wheel, and the tires crunch on the gravel by the side of the road. For an instant, Larson looks at the woods and wonders if Lyons might try to run. It would be a dumb move—he'd be cuffed and charged within half an hour—but she'd seen dumber escape attempts, people giving freedom their best shot but going nowhere.

He's barely outside the car when she hears the sound of him throwing up. From across the hood, she sees him crouched over, elbows resting on his knees, the back of his jacket heaving. Larson cuts the engine and steps outside to keep away from the smell of what's left of Lyons's breakfast that morning. The wind blowing in through his open door has whipped down off the ridge above where they are and is freezing cold. After a minute he stands upright, and with a wobbly nod, gets back inside the car and shuts the door.

Larson restarts the engine, reenters the road, and the hum of the tires on the asphalt returns.

"Sorry," he says.

"Take your time," Larson says. "You were telling me about who else could have been in or out of the building in the last twenty-four hours."

Lyons wipes the back of his sleeve across his lips. "Up until this week, I would have had no idea where to begin. We've been running the experiment."

"I keep hearing about this experiment," Larson says, leading him.

"It's on why misinformation happens, how people mislead, and how others react to being conned. Timely, right?" Lyons's voice sounds marginally solid, and even confident, for the first time today. "Experiments like ours seem simple, but the implications are profound. In the fifties, psychologists looked at obedience to measure how and why soldiers follow orders. In the sixties, they studied kids' self–esteem after desegregation. Investigating social science is what my team does, and we probably all have our own personal reasons for being so drawn to it."

Like a cop who wants to create order after a chaotic childhood, Larson thinks.

Lyons's voice cracks. "But regarding the investigation? We've had over sixty participants come in, mostly undergraduates, but a few people from the community too."

"There was an incident yesterday…"

"…that I'm still turning over in my mind," he finishes. "Some percentage of the subjects got…upset during procedure. We had a few minor verbal exchanges, but nothing like what happened yesterday morning."

She eyes him skeptically and makes a mental note to check with Pat King for records on that call. "I'm assuming you have records on everyone who participated?"

"Absolutely," Lyons says. "Very well organized."

"That may be helpful." Larson silences her phone as it buzzes in her pocket. She assumes King has texted her Tom Campbell's contact information by now, and wonders if he took off for break after leaving the hospital. Dorms close during university breaks, but King made it sound like he lived off campus. Even still, if Tom had a job or grew up far from where he attended college, he might still be around. She'd been in both of those situations as a student— working a part-time job through school, having moved as far as possible from where she grew up with no intention of returning.

She approaches Lyons's driveway and the cruiser bucks as it takes the incline. The trip to the morgue took less than an hour, but it feels like they've been gone for much longer. Maybe the cold has quelled the day's pace, or the new emptiness of the college town has seemed to slow time.

Lyons rests his hand on the door handle. "We stopped the experiment for the time being. After the incident yesterday, I realized we weren't screening well enough and that going through one of the stress conditions was harder on subjects than I realized."

The seat creaks as Larson looks over her shoulder. "Question, then: Why run an experiment like that in the first place, if you knew if would cause distress?"

Lyons pinches his eyes shut, and for a second, Larson thinks he may be sick again. "Because we're swinging for the fences here. The most valuable insights into human behavior have always come from ethically questionable studies. The Stanford Prison Experiment. Most people think it couldn't be done today, and they're right, but that data gave us a cornerstone of the field. We learned, immeasurably…except when that kid yesterday…" He rakes his sleeve across his lips. "Look, I've just brought on someone with a legal background to help keep everyone safe. I was taking steps. I didn't want to be responsible for inspiring some tragedy."

Lyons seems to choke on the word as it leave his mouth, the realization appearing to wash over him. Larson doesn't have to say it: a tragedy is exactly what his work might have inspired.

"None of the team wanted to stop, but Elizabeth took my side in the meeting last night. Some of the others were angry with her about it."

Larson immediately pictures the blank expression in Britt's eyes earlier that morning.

Like he's reading her mind, Lyons continues, "There are five other grad students who now have access to that building, and they all come and go at all hours. You should have no trouble finding them: Robert, Scarlett, Britt, and Chris. Veronica is the newest member, the one with the legal background. She just started yesterday morning but also has full access. She's probably the least likely to have anything to do with this. Robert is the most senior; he's been here the longest and helped me bring the others on board. I'd talk to him first." Larson detects an angry edge in Lyons's voice, as if seeing Elizabeth's body had cleared his mind, focused him on finding her killer.

There's *something* he's not saying, she thinks. "You sound a little suspicious of them," she says.

The cruiser door creaks as he pushes it open. "I trained my team to deceive people, detective. You can't think you're the exception to anyone's rule."

LARSON

A white news van is parked in front of the police station, a reporter with straight dark hair pacing beside it, her long beige coat buttoned up beneath her chin.

"Oh boy," Larson says under her breath, finding her way to the side entrance, where she swipes in. Once in her office, Larson's door partially blocks out sounds in the backdrop to her daily life: an old-fashioned phone ringing on the front desk, the electronic gurgle of the fax, another cop raising his voice at someone from the local television station. She drops into her desk chair, willfully ignoring the emails waiting in a queue on her computer monitor as she thinks about what Lyons said: none of the others cared for Elizabeth, and those bad feelings crescendoed as she took Lyons's side the night before.

But poor professional relationships are hardly murder motives. Could what happened to Elizabeth be the result of some disagreement that went south? Quite possibly. But Larson's instinct tells her otherwise. She pictures her body positioned in the chair, the dark blood pooled beneath her, and the deep slices into Elizabeth's arm and neck, and suspects that King is right. Someone with a history of violence, who didn't hesitate to create pain, had killed Elizabeth Colton.

She picks up her phone and calls King.

"Some good news that possibly makes our lives easier," he begins unsteadily. If his voice conveyed weariness before, it sounded exhausted now. "Timestamps from the security system show the building's doors did lock last night at seven p.m., as scheduled. The front door opening would have set off an alarm, and it didn't open back up again until this morning at seven a.m., just before the office manager came in."

Larson listens carefully, picturing Hull Hall in her mind. "Okay, that leaves the back door."

"Right. The back door would be the only other way in, aside from breaking a window, and the CS team found no signs of forced entry."

"So we're looking at the back door between the hours of say, seven p.m. and two a.m. Unlikely our killer would have hung around too long afterward. Tell me there's a camera monitoring the back door?"

King sighs. "That's where things get weird. There's a camera, but it's disabled."

Larson sits forward. "Intentionally, I'm assuming? Last night?"

"It's tricky. There's no way to know whether or not it was broken intentionally, because, ready for this? It happened about a month ago. No one noticed there was no video feed because there was no reason to check the footage before now. We couldn't figure out why it wasn't working until we kept backing up the date. On February eleventh, it stopped."

"So there's no way to know who went in and out of the back door around the time of the murder?"

"Well, the door does lock, and the only access is with key cards. To unlock the door, you have to swipe in. And between seven p.m. and seven a.m., there were only seven swipes: The five other grad students and Elizabeth Colton."

"You said seven."

"The other was the cleaning crew member who accessed the building around nine thirty. I have a call in to check the IDs of whoever was on that team and where they all went afterward."

Larson pictures members of the janitorial service at the college that she had ever interacted with. Hardworking quiet types, often first–generation Americans. Probably the most indispensable service providers on campus and often the least considered. Everyone had seemed content to do their work, then leave. Hard to imagine why any of them would have been bothered enough by Elizabeth Colton to plot her murder, but she supposed it was worth checking out. "Sure," she says. "But I don't think we should spend much time there. I'm going to stay focused on the people who have any kind of motive: Elizabeth's boss and lover, Lyons; the kid who attacked her yesterday; and her colleagues who apparently didn't like her."

"The office manager said as far as she knows, they're all still in town, so you won't have to work too hard tracking anyone down. And the kid who caused the fight was instructed to not leave campus. You spent the morning with Joe Lyons; what's your sense of him?"

"He's beside himself," Larson sighs. "Upset. He seemed genuinely shocked when I told him, and was sick after identifying the body. Not a guy with a taste for blood."

"So, what are you thinking so far?"

Larson pinches the bridge of her nose between her thumb and forefinger. Perhaps the morning's intensity had worn her a bit too. "A few possibilities. It's possible Lyons was the intended target, and whoever killed Elizabeth meant to confront him but was surprised. There's some chance it started as a robbery, but it's an academic's office, so what's there to steal? Maybe if it was one of the hard sciences, there might be some valuable tech or information, but who's that acutely interested in social psychology? Which leaves us at the beginning: she was killed by one of the participants in this experiment, which apparently pissed some people off, Joe Lyons, or one of the other grad students who didn't like her."

"Their contacts are in your inbox."

Larson's gaze flicks back to the screen she'd been ignoring. "Thanks. The kid from yesterday, named…"

"Tom Campbell," King finished. "He's been skating on the edge of expulsion for three semesters, apparently."

Larson makes a mental note to call him first.

She ends her call with King, sets down the receiver, finds Tom Campbell's number, and dials it. On the second ring, he answers. Larson introduces herself and says she needs to speak with him immediately.

There's a ding in the call's background. A microwave, maybe. "How about tomorrow?" Tom asks.

Larson feels her eyebrows rise. "I'm sorry, Tom, but this can't wait."

"I've prepared a meal and I'm about to eat," he explains with obstinate calm.

You little shit, she thinks. Larson checks Tom's address, then maps the route. They all send her through downtown. She checks the time and sighs. "One hour. That's two thirty on the dot," she says, deepening her voice to sound more stern. "Are we clear on that?"

No answer. Then a slurping sound.

"Mr. Campbell?"

"I'm clear," Tom says and then hangs up.

Larson stands and pulls her coat from her chair. She can use the extra few minutes to take a statement from Robert. Maybe Lyons just wanted the attention off of him, but he seemed eager for the two of them to talk.

BRITT

Britt's Doc Martens clomp down the freshly swept walkway into Chris's condo building. The emerald–green boxwoods lining the entranceway are as magazine worthy as the rest of the landscaping, even this late in winter. The elevator has a gleaming stainless steel interior, and pop music plays as she rides to his floor. The doors open with a subtle tone.

When a neighbor, an older man in a beige coat, emerges from the condo beside Chris's, Britt drops back onto the landing and waits until he is gone. She's already had more than her share of interactions for one day. Chris is the only one she wants to see. She looks over her shoulder, plucks Chris's mail from the box, then retrieves his spare key from the place behind the light fixture where she knows he hides it and lets herself in.

The interior resembles a modern furniture catalog. Britt wouldn't be surprised if it was the nicest condo in the city. Maybe even the state. It's a far cry from the utilitarian furnishings in her own place across town, but she looks over the living room approvingly—the designer rugs and clean lines of the Danish pieces Chris prefers are arranged perfectly on the oak floors. Chris has always had money but became beguilingly wealthy after coming into an inheritance.

She knows she'd be jealous if it were anyone else.

Spiteful, even.

Chris emerges from the bathroom shirtless with a fluffy white towel around his waist. The results of his workouts and meticulous diet are apparent. He shakes his head as Britt hands him the mail, then sets it beside him on the marble countertop.

"Did you check your phone yet?" she asks.

"I just got up," he says, locking the door behind her. "But you should really start knocking before you come in. If I thought someone broke in, it wouldn't be pretty."

"At nine a.m.?"

"*Or* I might not be alone here, ever think of that?" he asks, jeeringly, before softening to add, "Just knock next time, okay?"

Britt frowns but nods on her way to the refrigerator, where she retrieves a bottle of water. Chris's housekeeper has arranged them in neat rows, just the way he likes. On the lower shelf are the prepared meals he's ordered and the protein supplements he takes each day. The bottle cap twists off with a crackle, the water clean and pleasantly cold as it slides down her throat.

"Ready in fifteen," Chris's voice echoes as he starts down the hall.

"Hey, come back."

He returns, his expression flashing irritation. "What? Help yourself to whatever, but I need to get…"

"Elizabeth Colton is dead."

Chris stops, his expression melts into a shocked smile that's pure disbelief. "What did you say?"

"You'd have noticed the calls from the department if you ever checked your messages."

He ignores her scolding and sinks onto his couch, running his hands through his wet hair. "She *died*? I just saw her. Last night."

Britt takes another long gulp of the water. "You never liked her. It's okay not to be sad."

"What...happened?" Chris asks, ignoring her previous comment.

"No clue. I went in this morning, but a cop kicked me out. She was ready to cuff me. Take your time getting ready. We probably won't be able to get onto the floor for a while. I bet Joe cancels everything for the next few days."

Chris's eyes pinch shut as his head sways back and forth. "Wait, wait, what actually *happened* to Elizabeth? She died in the *department*?" Chris grabs for his phone.

Britt's facial expression doesn't change; she won't let it. But for the first time, raw emotions form a lump in her throat. She looks away from Chris as tears begin to sting her eyes. "That's what I'm saying. The police kicked me out of the office."

He opens his phone. "I have a ton of messages. What the literal *fuck*?" His gaze flicks up at Britt before he lowers it and begins to read, watching Britt out of the corner of his eye.

She lowers her voice and whispers, "How long were you in the office last night?"

Chris looks up, and they hold each other's gaze for a long time.

SCARLETT

Robert and Scarlett are seated in a booth at a diner near campus, their reflections like ghosts in the window. Dollar bills with quirky, Sharpie-penned messages adorn wood paneling, and the place smells comfortingly of fried food. Neon reflects off various surfaces. Robert rearranges a paper napkin in his lap while a jukebox in the corner plays an upbeat song about dreams coming true.

"I don't get *why*. Why would someone *kill Elizabeth*?" Scarlett whispers the words, but there's no one within earshot in the diner.

"It's unreal." Robert shakes his head. "I don't know what to think right now. We teach students about the stages of grief; I think I'm having them all at once."

"Fear should be one. Because right now, I'm terrified."

Robert's phone rings, and after a brief exchange, he says the name of the diner, then hangs up. "That was the detective working on Elizabeth's case. She wants to talk and is on her way here."

Scarlett nods, her eyes watery as she picks at fries in a red plastic basket. "I wonder how Joe's doing. I know theirs wasn't a public relationship, but he has to be devastated."

Robert nods silently as Scarlett takes hold of another fry, then drops it back onto the plate. "You don't think it's possible that Joe…" She pauses, her eyes communicating the question.

"No. I can't imagine him doing anything violent. And as far as I'm concerned, what was between him and Elizabeth was their business. It was a distraction, sure, but they were both adults, and I can't imagine Elizabeth felt taken advantage of. Joe isn't like that."

"I guess I agree," Scarlett says, reluctantly. She straightens her back in the booth as if she's seated in a pew. "I didn't like it and I try not to judge, but…"

"But what?"

"She was *murdered*, Robert. It's different than dying of an illness or an accident. And since it was in *his* office, I can't help but wonder if their relationship had something to do with it." Scarlett pulls her phone from her purse. "I need to check in on Iris," she says, tapping the screen, then nodding as the phone dings, registering his response. "He said they're at his hotel, eating room service and watching a movie. I suppose that's as good a place as any to stay safe." She pauses, and Daryl Hall's voice fills the silence. "At least she's with her dad right now and not near all this. To be a kid again."

Robert makes a slight cheers gesture with his Coke. "Here's to that."

A set of headlights swings into the lot, then darkens. A woman in a dark uniform tromps toward the front door through the snow, her arms wrapped around her chest.

"Just distract her, and I'll make a run for it," Robert says. "I'll send you a postcard from Mexico."

"Don't," Scarlett scolds, aware that Robert's odd humor is maybe his best defense against pain.

A flurry of snowflakes follows Larson inside, and Scarlett smiles sadly as Larson approaches the table. She and Robert stand to greet her. The cold has clung to Larson's jacket, Scarlett notices, the room temperature seeming to drop. Larson shakes both of their hands and slides into the booth beside Scarlett. "Thanks for meeting with me. I'm sure you've heard Elizabeth Colton has been killed. As I told you on the phone, I'm investigating her murder."

Scarlett swallows at the word *murder*. "It's confirmed now? That's how she died?"

Larson pauses a beat, like she's assessing Scarlett's sincerity. "That's what the evidence suggests currently, yes."

"How can we help?" Robert asks. His posture and the way he's folded his hands make him look like an Eagle Scout, Scarlett thinks.

A waitress stops by and asks if Larson would like to order. "Water, thank you," she says, opening her tablet. "Right now we're focused on the time between seven p.m. and two a.m. I spoke with Joe Lyons this morning; he said you know everyone who has building access."

"I work directly under Joe and issue all the key cards, so yes."

Larson checks the time, then taps the screen. "He said you're also very familiar with the…experiment? The student who attacked Elizabeth, did you sense he knew her?"

Robert shakes his head as Scarlett leans forward. "I was watching that incident from behind the glass. That boy just seemed kind of uneasy. He was actually reaching for Britt when Chris punched him."

"Those two are close," Robert says.

Larson's fingertip hovers over the tablet screen. "Britt Martinez and Chris Collins are a couple?"

Robert and Scarlett exchange a glance. "They've never come out and said that, no. And I may as well just say this because I'm sure you'll hear about it soon enough—they were both upset with Elizabeth, but I *highly* doubt they…" Robert pauses midsentence as the waitress reappears and sets a glass of water in front of Larson.

Larson takes a sip. "Noted. But you should know, I keep hearing that."

"What?"

"Everyone involved seems to highly doubt anyone else would have been so violent. What makes you say they were upset with Elizabeth?"

"Elizabeth supported Joe about stopping the experiment, for one."

"And for two?" Larson asks.

Scarlett twists the napkin in her lap, a moment of silence passing as the jukebox changes songs. Soon, Prince's falsetto echoes off the hard surfaces—there isn't a particular sign he's more compatible with.

"Look, I'm not trying to throw Elizabeth under the bus right now," Robert says.

"I'm aware of her and Joe Lyons's affair," Larson says flatly.

"Fair," Robert says evenly. "Let's just say no one was particularly excited about how much access Elizabeth had to Joe's things. His office, his data, his previous literature reviews."

"Cause for resentment maybe?" Larson asks.

Robert's head shrugs sideways.

"I think she had real feelings for Joe," Scarlett says quietly. "We suspected they were more than colleagues, but it kind of came out about two weeks ago when we saw them together in his car."

Robert rubs the back of his neck.

"Telling her what was going on can only help." Scarlett says to him, as he looks over his shoulder, uncomfortably. "Joe wants that, I'm sure."

Robert's head swivels back around. "You're right. It just feels wrong. Elizabeth's work had been slipping for a while. She was late to the experiment a few times and was slow to run analyses she said she'd do. Scarlett was picking up her slack."

"I didn't really mind," Scarlett says. "She was having a hard time sorting everything out with Joe, I guess."

"But the other two, Chris and Britt, were less understanding?"

"Maybe," Scarlett answers.

"Yes," Robert adds simultaneously.

Larson makes a note on her tablet. "Back to building access for a second. There've been a lot of people in and out in the last few months, I understand. Something like sixty participants, Lyons said. He's got a record of everyone, but why are there so many?"

Robert and Scarlett again catch each other's eyes. Robert begins, "Without giving you a thesis, we need a certain sample size to tell if there's an effect and enough diversity to compare groups. If the sample's too small, it makes comparisons impossible. When the subjects deceive us during the experiment, we want to be able to say the circumstances elicited it regardless of the person's background."

"The experiment makes them frustrated enough to lie?"

"It's one of the hypotheses."

"I don't mean to be naive here, but if Joe knew participants were going to get so upset, how did the experiment get a green light?"

"Joe didn't exactly come out and tell the university everything he expected," Robert says.

Larson eyes them both before making another note.

"He wanted the participants to get upset?"

Another sideways shrug.

"Okay. Officer King is retrieving data from the swipe cards, but I'll just ask if either of you were in the building last night."

"We both were," Robert says. "I was there from about six–fifteen until eight, maybe? I didn't see anyone but Scarlett." He nods across the table.

Scarlett shifts awkwardly. "Same. My daughter was with me. I said hello to Robert, then shut my door and did a little work."

Larson frowns. "You brought your daughter with you to the office last night?"

"Just for a minute, I had to run in. I forgot something after our meeting." Scarlett stumbles on the last word, her long–suppressed stutter making an appearance. "I...I heard Chris and Elizabeth having an exchange in the hallway. Sorry, I'm just remembering that now."

Larson's finger hovers above her tablet. "Did you hear what either were saying?"

"Not the words, just their voices."

A surge of something close to embarrassment makes Scarlett's cheeks flush, the sense of being a snitch. Then she remembers that Elizabeth is dead. Tears press in her eyes. "It wasn't a long conversation. But it was definitely Chris she was talking to; he has a distinctive laugh. In fact..." She pauses. "I saw Chris leave. My office looks out over East Lawn. I heard a door close and looked up. I saw the collar of his jacket turned up to cover his neck. He was walking in a hurry. I remember thinking at the time that it was because he was cold."

"You're sure it was Chris."

"I saw him from behind, but I'm pretty sure."

She makes eye contact again with Robert, whose lips are pinched tight.

Larson checks the time again before producing two cards bearing her contact information and sliding them across the table, one sticking slightly in the condensation from her water glass. She slips her jacket back on as she stands. "Please be in touch if you remember anything else from last night. As information comes in, I'll likely be in contact to fill in some more details."

Robert and Scarlett watch Larson head back to her cruiser. The lights blink on, then vanish into the snow.

Robert had seemed so collected during the interview, so steady. Now he fumbles for a twenty–dollar bill from his wallet and sets it on the table. "I guess you should take me home," she says and then pauses.

She touches his arm.

"You're shaking," she says.

LARSON

Larson's phone chirps, then King's voice is in her ear. "I just emailed you the full record on Tom Campbell."

"I'm on the way to talk with him now," she says.

King pauses like he's considering the best way to say what he's thinking. "Rough neighborhood. You want to wait to have someone go with you? Hard to picture a student at the college living there, to be honest."

"I'll be fine, thanks. I'll call if I need any backup." She doesn't want to tell King that one, she maintains the state record for pistol accuracy among cadets in the state, and two: she never asks for help. To the point of stubbornness, she recognizes.

But King's clearly well intended, so she adds, "Thanks for the offer and for sending the file. I'll swing by after I talk to him."

"I'll have a pot of coffee on when you get here," he says before they hang up. She can almost smell it—police station coffee— despite its reputation for grating the backs of throats, it has a special place in her heart; never in her life has she paid four dollars for it.

The cruiser rocks as Larson enters the parking lot to the

apartment complex King mentioned on the phone, which is as bleak as she remembered. Twice last month Larson had investigated burglaries here—at the intersection of poverty and crime in Shepard. Nearly all of the vehicles have broken windows or various parts affixed with duct tape. Most of the residents are either the working poor or can't afford to live anywhere else.

King was right, these are the wrong side of the tracks—exactly like where she lived with her mom growing up. The recognition dizzies her, but she suppresses the memories instead of letting them stir. She's less than four miles from the impossible privilege associated with the university, but this place feels a world away.

And like home.

Near a dumpster, a group of three teenagers in hoodies convene. One rests against a rusted green truck with two flat tires. They throw rocks into the woods, harmlessly enough, she thinks, even given the vape mist rising above them every few seconds. Their movements stop as she approaches. The cruiser is unmarked, but they watch as if POLICE is written in neon across the side. From the corner of her eye, she sees one of the boys—it's always the youngest who runs first—dart across the back of the lot, probably headed to warn someone that she's arrived.

This is one of the elements of police work that took getting used to—staying on task, not getting distracted by whatever crime, petty or not, may be going on in the apartment the boy just entered. Larson circles the parking lot once, then backs into a space nearest the road. Even if the kids know she's a cop, it's not a given that the car will be intact when she returns, and there's no time to handle a vehicle break-in today.

A streetlight blinks overhead against the iron gray sky. She takes a second to look over what King has sent her. Tom Campbell had been arrested twice already that year, once for shoplifting, once for trespassing. Attached to the records are copies of his mug shots. He stares defiantly into the camera each time: somewhere between bold and ignorant. Larson wasn't sure what kind of screening tool Robert and Scarlett had been referring to when Lyons admitted Tom into the study, but one look at Tom Campbell reminds her of the goofy but toxic bros she'd watched file in and out of fraternity houses—the same now as when she'd been in college and, she imagined, as long as colleges had existed.

Except most of those guys seemed to come from money; they walked around campus in sweatpants and backward baseball hats like they owned the place.

What is Tom Campbell doing living in a place like this?

Larson exits the car and locks it, shivering as cold air penetrates her thin athletic jacket. The stairs are littered with stray cigarette butts and scraps of paper. A child's shoe rests on the landing, and the hallway has the flickering bulb of some cheesy Rick Plummer horror movie.

She sets her jaw before knocking on Tom's door, and she can hear shuffling inside the apartment immediately. "Shepard Police," she says.

The peephole silently darkens. Larson's impatience begins to gather. She's about to knock once again when she hears a chain slide.

A wide-eyed face appears in the slim door gap, complete with a backward baseball cap like fraternity cosplay. She recognizes the face from the mug shots. "Tom, I'm Officer Larson, I need to speak with you about a death that occurred on campus early this morning. May I come in?"

He glances behind him, and for the first time it occurs to Larson that he may not be alone. Wordlessly, he opens the door and steps back, clenching and unclenching his hands in a sort of rhythm as Larson steps inside and closes the door. He's wearing designer sweatpants and a black Patagonia jacket but looks as though he hasn't shaved in a week.

The relief from the cold Larson had anticipated is slight; if Tom's heat is working at all, he's barely switched it on. Her breath forms in front of her as she surveys the disastrous living room. Beer cans are everywhere, some stacked in what looks like a pillar on the countertop. Takeout cartons have accumulated above an overflowing kitchen trash can. She'd seen fraternity basements that were worse, sure, but the only living room furniture is a beat–up couch and a few plastic milk crates used as de facto shelves. Larson motions toward a small table beside the kitchen, which luckily has two chairs, and they sit.

"What can I do for you?" Tom asks with a leering grin.

Larson shakes off his creepy vibe. "I'm investigating a death that occurred in Hull Hall early this morning. You may have seen something about it in the news. Can I…?"

"I was nowhere *near* there when it happened," he erupts, so immediately that Larson's hand moves closer to the Taser on her belt. "All I did was what they asked me to. What *Elizabeth* asked me to. I didn't know something was going to *happen* to her. I was going to get her number after the experiment or whatever that was, but there was some kind of screwup with my grades that put me on edge. Sue me."

The barometric pressure seems to drop by the second.

"Let's take this one step at a time, okay?"

"I actually called this, you know, I just texted my old roommate, Speedo. I *knew* the police would think I was involved," he says. "I mean, Speedo's not his real name."

You don't say, Larson thinks. "Tom, what do you know about what happened?"

"What I saw on Insta and Twitter, what everyone away on spring break knows by now: Elizabeth Ann Colton was killed in that building. Stabbed."

Larson's positioned herself between Tom and the door but feels herself glance toward the exit anyway. The flimsy kitchen table won't be much of a barrier if he happens to lunge at her. She thinks back to the boys in the parking lot and wonders if she should have asked for someone to come with her.

Larson gestures for Tom to lower his voice. "What makes you say you knew the police would want to talk to you?"

No answer. Then, a smile. "I'm not stupid. I yelled at her yesterday morning in front of a bunch of people."

Larson stops herself from shifting in her chair. "And why were you so upset?"

He pauses.

"Tom?"

"Do you know how those grad students get people to do that experiment? They get a hot girl to offer you extra credit if you'll participate; then someone calls right before you start and tells you you're in academic trouble."

"I heard a little about that. And if that's true, I see why you'd be frustrated. I don't think I'd appreciate being tricked that way either."

Tom's head droops.

"You're saying you found Elizabeth Colton attractive?"

"Does that matter?"

You're the one who brought up her appearance, Larson thinks. "It might, if that had something to do with why you were so agitated around her."

He shrugs. "I don't like being messed with. Girls like that think they can do whatever they want; nobody ever puts them in their place. They act like they have *all* the power. She was hot, and she knew it. But I liked her style, maybe until it turned out she was just another tricky…" Tom stops abruptly, recognition that he is *talking* to a woman flashing in his eyes.

Larson watches his Adam's apple bob. "Did you ever follow her?"

"Not really," Tom answers sheepishly.

Which means yes, Larson thinks. "Ever to where she lives?" she asks.

"No! I mean *no*. Just on campus. She lied to me!" Tom bolts up from his chair again.

"Tom, sit."

He sits.

"Listen, I get it. I'm sorry if you felt upset by the experiment. I won't play games with you, you have my word. We'll be straight with each other, deal? You left the hospital last night around five p.m., right? I need to know where you went after you checked yourself out."

"Campus. The library I like stays open even on break."

And is probably warm, Larson thinks. "Did you go by Hull Hall?"

"It's on the way."

"Did you see Elizabeth Colton?"

Tom shakes his head.

"And did you go inside?"

Tom hesitates again. "The door was locked."

Larson keeps her voice as gentle even as her heart speeds up. "So you tried. Even though you knew there was a chance you'd probably get arrested if someone saw you?"

He stands again and faces the kitchen. The way he scratches the back of his head beneath his cap makes him seem very young suddenly. "I left my backpack in the experiment room. It had... some of my things in it."

"Like your camping knife?"

"I...bring that everywhere. It's just for... It comes in handy for stuff. I wouldn't *pull it* on anyone! I...didn't realize I didn't have the backpack until I got to the hospital."

You must have taken quite a punch, Larson thinks. "What time did you go back by Hull Hall?"

"Just after seven. Then...then again around ten. But really, I was just going to get my bag and go."

A lot of things being forgotten at Hull Hall, Larson thinks.

"But I ran and hid when he pulled up."

Larson looks up. "Who?"

"The professor, the 'famous' Doctor Lyons, came in his car but didn't go inside. He just sat there in the parking lot across the street, then left. Stayed about ten minutes."

"You're sure it was him?"

"I'm *not* a liar," Tom says evenly.

Larson makes a note. Lyons hadn't mentioned anything

about going back to campus. Maybe he wasn't thinking clearly because he was in shock, but he definitely left that detail out.

"You didn't think the cameras would see you hiding?"

"Cameras?"

"The security cameras. The building has two."

A look comes over Tom's face. "It does?"

Larson stands. "I'll be in touch, Tom."

LARSON

Larson pulls out onto the main road, her windshield wipers scraping away the sleet that accumulated while she was inside. She calls King, who answers on the first ring. "Our friend admits to going to the Psychology Department last night. He says he left his backpack there."

"It's on my desk, knife included. I was going to hand it back to him when I went to check on him this morning, but obviously, priorities changed."

Agreed, Larson thinks. "So, listen to this: Tom says he went back to Hull Hall at seven p.m., then again at ten, and claims he saw Joe Lyons pull up in his car, sit there, then leave. *And* he's essentially admitted he'd stalked Elizabeth Colton. He isn't even shy about saying he found her attractive but was angry with her, then started going on about pretty girls and their power."

King whistles into the phone. "That's more than enough to get a warrant to search the kid's apartment, so why does it sound like you don't want one?"

"I'm that transparent, huh? Since the most obvious suspect just put himself at the crime scene? I guess it feels like he's being too honest, like he's not trying to cover anything. Maybe if he was guilty, he would. And we can forget about him being the one who disabled the rear camera. He says he didn't know they existed, which I believe."

"Maybe he's hiding in plain sight, hoping we'll overlook him."

Larson reflects. "He's got that bro persona down pat, but I think he's scared."

"We're reading this the same way, but I have to say I'd be scared too, if I were him."

"It's kind of amazing he's making the grades to stay in that college. This isn't a clinical term, but he has a few screws loose."

"Fact of life now. I sit in on some of the meetings at the counseling center. On the right medication, some students can be high functioning and low functioning at the same time, till something stressful makes whatever demons they're struggling with come out."

"Something stressful, like thinking you're getting expelled?"

"Bingo."

"That department seems like it can do more harm than good." If the purpose of studying psychology was to help people, then psychologists were zero for two in her mind. "I'm wondering what Lyons was doing by driving back to the department last night."

"How much do you believe the kid about that?" King asks.

"Enough to find out if it's true." Larson nudges her turn signal.

SCARLETT

Scarlett reenters her apartment after Robert drops her off, scanning the living room and kitchen adorned with shadows. Had she not left a light on? She can't remember now—the horrific news about Elizabeth has hollowed her, and she easily could have forgotten. She flicks the switch beside the door, makes her way into the quiet, and checks the time. It's before the time that Mark said he would have Iris back to her for the evening, but wanting Iris close feels instinctual.

Just a little longer, she tells herself, glancing out at the apartment's snow-covered driveway. The murder's randomness made the whole world seem more uncertain, the reality of what's happened coming over her in waves. The chaos feels sinister, like something wicked blew in on the wind. It's a silly idea. Life can be maddeningly chaotic, she knows, but the aftershocks make her feel vulnerable in the silent apartment.

She sits to take off her boots, her fingertips slightly numb, and considers texting Mark for an update when headlights flash in the sliding glass door. She bolts back over to the window and sees Mark lifting Iris from the back seat of his SUV, her voice rolling with the same carefree chatter as this morning. As Iris's shoes pound the stairs, Scarlett's chest draws a full breath for the first time in hours. She turns on the other living room lights on her way to the front door.

"Mom! Did you know that pools can go down twelve feet at the deep end?"

Scarlett wraps her arms around her. The dampness of her hair indicates that they indeed did go swimming.

Mark follows, gently shaking his head. "No one went near the deep end today." His expression changes as he catches Scarlett's eyes. "What's wrong? I didn't think we were late?" He glances at his own watch.

Tears form as Scarlett's voice breaks. "Come inside, something's happened. Iris, honey, let Dad and I talk for a second?"

Iris retreats to her room as Scarlett and Mark sit at Scarlett's kitchen table. She can feel that the cold has clung to him as he touches her arm. "Is everything okay?" he asks.

Scarlett presses her fingers to her temples as she says the unimaginable. "A woman in my department was killed last night. Robert and I were on our way in, just after we left here, when we found out. The police are investigating it as a murder."

"*What?*"

She reaches for Mark's hand and squeezes it. "I can't believe what I'm saying either, but it's true."

"Have they arrested anyone?" He looks down the hallway in the direction of Iris's room.

"Not yet, as far as I know. We just… Robert and I just talked with a detective this afternoon."

The crisp citrusy smell of his aftershave touches her nose, reminding her of hurried weekday mornings as they dressed for work at the same time, sunlight streaming in their bathroom window, making the white subway tile gleam. She could always sense his ambition, like a road that somehow kept extending in front of him; his energy and intelligence would take him as far as he wanted to go. "God, I'm sorry. I was going to go back to the hotel, but now I don't know how safe I feel leaving the two of you here."

"Part of me can't actually even believe it. We talked almost every day."

"Damn right you can't believe it," Mark says. "I can't either. Was it a robbery or something?"

"I can't see how. What would anyone be stealing from her?"

"Maybe they weren't stealing from *her*?" Mark lowers his voice. "Either way, I should stay with you guys. Here. I know it's not the time to ask, but as long as I'm offering to stick around, is…that guy Robert…?"

Her expression melts into a momentary half smile as she shakes her head. "Just a friend. I knew how it looked, and I knew you'd ask. But he's a friend. Nice guy."

Mark leans back. "He seemed nice, and that's great. But if the situation was reversed, you…"

"I'd be curious too," she finishes, her eyes meeting his. She knows Mark's more than right—she'd likely be flat–out jealous. In the past two years, she's actively pushed away thoughts about him dating other women so they don't bloom into painful fantasies that hijack entire days. "Have you been seeing…?"

Iris appears in the hallway, cutting off her question. Both Scarlett's and Mark's heads turn. "Are we having dinner? Can Dad stay?"

She glances at Mark, who shrugs but is clearly pleased with Iris's request. "Do you want to?" she asks.

"Maybe it's a good idea under the circumstances."

Iris lets out a whoop of approval before disappearing back into her room. Scarlett does her best to not roll her eyes as she shuffles into the kitchen, locating the cookware necessary for making dinner. Even in a moment like this, she knows to keep her guard up about getting used to the three of them together. She knows what it took for them to adjust to the divorce and tightens with the thought of having the Band–Aid torn off again. They've entered dangerous territory—lesson number one in every book she looked through on divorce is about consistency—making a plan, then sticking with it. Kids, the data concluded, appreciate the structure.

Except that life is nuanced. And there's more than one kind of vulnerability.

She fills a pot with water, then lights a burner. She glances over her shoulder as Mark unties his shoes, then slips off his jacket and sets it on the back of one of the kitchen chairs. She notices his hesitance as he moves, the curious way he inspects the furniture. It's all unfamiliar to him—the space, her and Iris's routines—all markers of their new lives. Lives that were hard to build, that she had been frightened of, but she'd done so with determination and the resolution that getting divorced was actually the best thing for them and for Iris. Now, this murder, on this day, makes that hard–fought progress look like a flimsy house of cards.

That's just fear, Scarlett tells herself, a worry for another time.

Mark being here tonight is lucky.

We're all together right now, she thinks.

Maybe a little safer from whoever is out there.

ROBERT

Robert calls Joe around four in the afternoon. Any other day, he'd either have texted or gone into the small skit–like inside joke that usually began their calls, but neither seemed remotely appropriate under the circumstances.

"Hi, it's…I'm glad you called, Robert. I don't know what to say. I'm beside myself."

"You don't have to say anything," Robert tells him, thinking it was actually *him* who doesn't know the right words to express what he's feeling. What *does* one say to their mentor when the woman with whom he'd been having a scandalous affair was murdered in his office? Certainly no greeting card for that. "I'm here for you if you wanted to talk or something," Robert says.

He had been there for Joe before, actually—two and a half years earlier, when someone reported to the dean inappropriate remarks that Joe made during a class Robert was TAing. Robert had clearly heard the comments; he had watched eyebrows rise around the room—Joe was tenured by then, sure, but the remarks were careless and made from poor judgement. Something about how if a person was outraged, they were missing information, even in the #MeToo era. Nothing sinister, but not tactful either. When the dean had called Robert to his office to be interviewed, he'd looked the man directly in the eyes and told him that whatever the student had walked away with must have been misheard.

Neither Joe nor Robert acknowledged it afterward, not out loud, but thus began the expansion of Robert's responsibilities.

Now Robert hopes the offer to talk comes across as decently as he intends it. Halting the experiment, the perceptions of faculty, even Joe and Elizabeth's affair itself seem miniaturized, as if suddenly they were observing the situation from the window of an airplane.

"Has the detective contacted you?" Joe asks hurriedly.

Robert swivels in his desk chair to look at the bare branches outside his window. In early spring, North Carolina still had a starkness that made it seem like the temperature may never rise again. "She interviewed Scarlett and me earlier. Do you think she has any idea who might have…?" His voice trails off.

"No," Joe interjects. "At least not yet. I think she questioned me first because of, you know, how it looks."

How it looks for Joe, Robert has to admit to himself, is dreadful. He thinks of a time Elizabeth screamed at Joe from across a hallway before throwing a stack of papers in his direction and storming away. Numerous office doors had opened up and down the hall. As Joe began calmly picking up the mess, it had been Robert who'd stepped forward, neither speaking of what happened except for Joe simply telling him, "Thanks."

"I'm sure the detective is on it," Robert says. "But in the meantime, if there's anything I can do, don't hesitate."

"I may need some help, actually, digging through…" His voice trails off.

"Through…what?"

Joe hesitates. "I'll let you know, man. And Robert?"

"Yes?"

"Watch your back."

SCARLETT

After dinner, Mark stays for a while, perched awkwardly on the sofa while Iris shows off to him the coloring book she's working on and her modest rock and fossil collection. Scarlett sits on the floor across the coffee table she bought at a garage sale, watching them interact. How strange it feels to be so open with Mark, and yet, with whom else would she let her guard down? The familiarity of his presence, the expression in his smile, soothes her tonight.

It's as though they've entered some alternate branch of the multiverse where the three of them are still a family but gone are their house and leafy old neighborhood.

When Mark stands to take his glass to the sink, she follows him. He faces her and stifles a yawn before putting his hands back into the pockets of his jeans. "I can stay," he says.

"We'll be fine," she says, which means: *we both know you'd better not.*

"You know, that couch is just as comfortable as the bed in my hotel."

He's being chivalrous and is probably anxious about leaving them, but truthfully, Mark being with them tonight would be a comfort. "I'll get the sheets and a blanket," she says.

SCARLETT

Later, Scarlett lies in bed, her heart knocking around in her chest. Part of her expects to wake the following morning to a message saying it had all been a dream or a mistake, and that Elizabeth is safe and sound, acting like her usually crabby self.

Scarlett has become so skilled at playing a part—one that everyone likes and *trusts.*

The moral compass of the department, as Robert put it.

But the truth is that she's also a thief, and a skilled one at that.

She pushes the word from her mind, but as always, it reappears, stubbornly. Even now, which makes her feel even *guiltier.*

She's been lifting items here and there since the semester she arrived, and told herself each time would be the last—except that it never was, and now the number of things she's taken is substantial.

The thing was that the *wastefulness* of the place, she'd thought at various times, might actually drive her insane. The university had so much money! There were matching polo–shirt–wearing attendants working in a rec center she'd had no time to visit, box seats in a football stadium she'd never set foot inside, not to mention the marked-up socks bearing university logos she'd overpaid for as a Christmas gift for her father.

All while she, Scarlett Simmons, worked steady sixty–hour weeks but couldn't manage to afford school supplies for her daughter.

So, she bent the rules sometimes.

Well, more than bent. But *bent* was the word she told herself when she did it.

Her mother, of all people, had taught Scarlett how when she was a kid—collecting droves of mini shampoo bottles from housekeeping carts on the family's occasional vacations, or pocketing packets of condiments any time they visited a restaurant. Wasn't it more ethical, she'd reasoned, not to let useful items be discarded? When Scarlett worked in a sandwich shop through high school, her mom had flat–out encouraged her to make herself to–go meals and help herself to produce that might otherwise go bad.

The shreds of deceit made Scarlett's stomach ache as a kid, even if she was fully aware that raising seven kids on a pastor's salary required strategic resourcefulness.

Was lifting a few to–be–discarded vegetables really any different from nabbing a few office supplies or a spare box of tissues here and there from the department? And was that any differ-ent, in principle, from repurposing an outdated laptop so that Iris might have an easier time with schoolwork? Even if Iris had *needed* it and the net result of the theft had been *positive*.

Probably.

No, it *definitely* was.

But the petty cash she'd taken from the office drawer had been pure stealing—only twenty dollars so far, but still. *Still.* What was she doing?

Except that at a university like Dorrance, where the parking garages were lined with students' luxury vehicles, no one seemed to notice. *Ever.* And would anyone even care, if they found out?

Maybe, maybe not.

But *Scarlett* knew, and knew that she had to stop before it cost her a position on the research team. Even if the stealing was functionally harmless, the decisions weren't hers to make. The night before, she'd made up her mind to set things right. She mentally retraces her steps, just before Elizabeth was killed, as her phone dings on her bedside table. She reaches for her glasses and sits up. It's late, but not so late that someone wouldn't be reaching out—especially on a day like this.

When she sees the text is from Robert, she realizes part of her had been waiting to hear from him, and that dinner with Mark, pleasant as it was, had left her feeling vaguely disconnected.

I still can't believe it. You ok?

Scarlett settles back against her pillow and moves her finger-tips across the phone screen.

Okay enough, if okay means terrified and sad. I don't even know what to say. Is there a funeral? Are you in touch with the detective, Larson? It all seems too surreal to type.

Across the bottom of the screen, an ellipsis waves as Robert types.

I know what you mean. I haven't heard anything more from Detective Larson. And no word on a funeral yet. Joe apparently was in touch with her mother. He thinks Elizabeth will be cremated and the service will be in her hometown.

There's a pause, then he continues:

And yes also to this being surreal. I can't believe I just typed those last few sentences.

Scarlett's fingertips tap the screen. What about you? You haven't said how you're holding up.

He texts: Beside myself, same as you, I'm sure.

Is she imagining it, or is Robert being more distant than normal? More stilted? But why wouldn't it be? Probably unrealistic to expect Robert to be his charming, loquacious self under the circumstances.

Scarlett considers what it's like for Robert to be alone tonight, then wonders, briefly, *is* Robert alone? She'd been by his place only once, maybe two years earlier—a group had picked him up on the way to a dinner—and was struck by how little he'd settled in. He was the most senior among them, which made his lack of décor seem even more out of place. He'd deflected some mild ribbing from the group, saying he'd been saving for his dream couch, and that living as a ski bum for a year had gotten him used to sparse furnishings. "It's like you could pick up and move at any time," someone had observed.

Was he even in the same apartment now?

Do you live by yourself? Never asked.

A pause, just long enough to notice. Yeah, it's just me.

It'd been a horrifying day but the lack of elaboration seems odd, Scarlett thinks. She types: Well, thanks for checking on me. I suppose we'll touch base in the morning?

Straight away. I'll message you when I hear about a time for that meeting. Night.

She texts, Night.

She checks the volume on her phone to make sure the ringer is set loud enough to wake her should there be some emergency, then realizes how low the battery is.

Oddly low, actually—she must have used the phone more than she'd realized.

She pads out to the living room, which is dark now, and glances over at Mark's shape asleep on the couch, then plugs in her phone and returns to bed.

Outside, the wind howls again.

Texting with Robert should have settled her, but she finds

herself even more wound up. Scarlett adjusts her pillow and tugs at the collar of her T–shirt in response to the lump in her throat. When the office manager had called with the news about Elizabeth, her first thought was that they'd somehow found out what she'd been doing.

Which is *awful* of her, she thinks.

She forces her eyes closed and begins to pray.

At any moment, everything will probably come out.

BRITT

Britt sits on her bedroom floor, legs folded under her as her tortoise-shell cat weaves under her outstretched palm. The electronic group Daft Punk plays from a speaker in the other room, the repetitive clicking of their drum machine a salve for her nerves and a cover for the abyss of a quiet evening where there's too much space to think. Her bedspread is black, as are her walls and curtains. Anyone else might consider her decorating choices morose, but what did that matter when no one but she and Chris had ever seen her bedroom, and Chris had only poked his head inside and then whistled?

The thumping bass coming from the living room sounds cardiac. She dials Chris's number now as she weaves her fingers through the cat's soft fur.

"It's late," he says as he answers. "You need to get some sleep."

It doesn't feel late—in fact, the day has felt like one perpetual moment since she saw the police officer earlier, like the morning never ended. "You're still up?" she asks.

"I am now," Chris answers. The silence that follows on his end of the call is his way of asking, "What do you need?"

"What do you think is going happen now?" she asks.

No answer.

"Chris?"

"Get some sleep," he tells her. "We need to meet with the detective in the morning."

"You…talked to the detective? You didn't tell me that."

"She called and I said we could both meet her at my condo tomorrow morning at eight. You can come over here for it. I was going to text you in the morning."

Britt contemplates this.

"Because you're always up before everyone else, weirdo. And I didn't want you worrying about it all night. Go to sleep, you need to be clearheaded."

"Fine," Britt says.

They hang up without saying anything more, Britt's mind drifting back to how she came to Dorrance University in the first place. She'd been a stats analyst at a university in Texas when one of the famous Joe Lyons studies was published instead of her team's work. Annoyed, she'd picked apart the study's statistical methods, then emailed Joe about how they could be better run. Then, since truly Britt really never slept, she began a Diet Coke–fueled analysis of the rest of Joe's published work and emailed him a massively long critique of his approach to each study. When Joe Lyons called her later that afternoon, it was to offer her a role on his research team. Britt accepted on the spot, under one condition: "You've said you want your research to dig into the core of human nature."

"That's exactly what I want to do," he'd said.

"If you *promise* the experiments will focus on understanding the root of aggression and violence, I'll work harder than you've ever seen someone work before." When Joe agreed, she hung up on him, then drove through the night to North Carolina, where she appeared at his office door the following morning, dark circles under her eyes. "My cat's in my car. The windows are down, but it's hot and I'm double parked," she'd said. "And have to find an apartment."

Lyons had pursed his lips, steepled his fingers, and then welcomed her. He then called a pet–friendly hotel and paid the tab for a week. Britt said little about herself but indeed outworked the rest of the department with the exception of Robert—the only one who could match her focus. She was early to every meeting, did more than what was asked of her, and never complained. And after she'd convinced Joe to take on Chris the year before, everything, for once in her life, seemed complete.

As Britt readies herself for bed, she wonders if Chris had been right in waiting to tell her about the meeting with the detective the following morning.

He knew her better than anyone.

She would need to be sharp when talking with the detective.

LARSON

Officer Larson enters the small house she rents, drops her bag on the floor beside her sofa, and then collapses onto it. Her house is the smallest in the older, quiet neighborhood, close enough to downtown that she can walk to a coffee shop on a morning she's off. And aside from the occasional blast of loud music from a passing car, it's exceptionally quiet with well-kept sidewalks and shady, mature trees.

She looks up at the dark splotch where her landlord fixed a water leak last year. *A bit like a Rorschach test,* she thinks as her dog, Oscar, nudges her hand with his cold nose. "Just let me lie here for a minute, bud." She pets the lab's head as it brushes back and forth beneath her fingertips.

When headlights flash in the living room windows, she jolts up to look out at the dark street. "We'd better put on some music, Osc. The quiet is making me jumpy." Oscar nudges her hand again, and Scarlett scratches the fur behind his ear. "Think it's time to act like a city cop? Think this is what I signed up for?"

Larson shivers as she pushes away the image of Elizabeth Colton's dark blood spilled across the floor. She opens her phone and texts King: We'll need the phone records for Lyons plus all the grad students: Robert, Scarlett, Britt, Chris, and Veronica, the new student. Also, need cell phone data to verify their locations from last night until present. She hesitates. And Tom Campbell.

Her phone dings within seconds. On it already.

Impressive, she thinks, remembering the tremor in his voice earlier that day. King may be close to retirement, but he's as serious about this case as she is.

She feeds Oscar, finds a seventies rock playlist she likes, opens a beer, and makes herself a turkey sandwich. She opens her laptop on the kitchen table. There's too much information floating around already; she needs to sort it before taking in any more, block out all the emotion and swirling questions, then focus on the facts.

Each of the other five students had access to Hull Hall

around the time Elizabeth was killed, and none, aside from Scarlett Simmons, seemed to particularly like her. Could one of them have had words with her—an argument that quickly turned heated, then hastily committed the crime? And then fled?

Among the group, the two most interesting are Britt and Chris. She'd obviously met Britt earlier that morning—Britt having been lucky not to be arrested on the spot for tampering with evidence—but she'd only spoken with Chris on the phone. She'll find out more about them tomorrow morning. Why Chris insisted on being interviewed alongside Britt, and what either has against Elizabeth, is unclear. Larson considers what Tom told her—that Lyons showed back up but never even went inside the building.

Then there's the cleaning crew, who either she or King will talk to tomorrow, and on whom King is already running background checks. But, barring any new information, their association with the murder seems like a reach.

Larson's phone rests beside her, her messaging apps showing notifications—no doubt from friends or family who've seen the news. She eyes the dating app that seems to crowd her home screen, then takes a sip of the beer. Even if she were interested in checking for messages there, there would be no point. "Prime example of why it's just you and me, Osc. How could I explain any of what's going on to anyone but you?"

Ten minutes after eating, Oscar has resumed his slumber.

Enviable, Larson thinks.

LYONS

Morning arrives and Lyons never really slept.

He needs some time to himself before he can handle more phone calls with administration or another curious colleague. Word certainly travels fast, even if Shepard feels deserted.

He'll go for a drive, he decides; it used to relax him. He can only pace for so long.

He unlocks his Saab, cuts the radio off, and motors aimlessly around the quiet streets, the engine's hum vaguely soothing. He chews his cuticle at a stoplight, glancing at himself in the rearview mirror. His expression is that of a ghoul, he thinks, edginess having paled his face, making him look haunted.

When his gaze returns to the road, his eyes widen. An urgent pulse throbs in his throat.

It was just a flash, too quick to tell anything, but enough to foster the thought: *Did I just see what I think I did? Or has fear dredged up a hallucination from my subconscious?*

A horn blows behind him, and he looks up to see the light has changed. Lyons nervously grips the rigid steering wheel.

Could there be a connection? He hopes to God no, even as his mind begins fitting together fragments.

LARSON

At 8:00 a.m., Larson arrives at Chris Collins's condominium and is greeted by him at the door. The interior smells vaguely fragrant—sandalwood or pine, maybe—as Chris opens the door. He smiles charmingly, incongruent with the circumstances, Larson thinks, but not quite odd enough to make the hair on the back of her neck stand up. She'd felt more unease at Joe Lyons's house the previous morning—that was a man who seemed like he was hiding…something.

Chris, on the other hand, acts like a student–athlete with a few years on him, but with the poise Larson associates with money. Art books and trinkets are arranged on the sleek coffee table.

"Detective, come in. Can I take your coat?"

"I'm fine, thank you." She folds the coat over her arm.

"Coffee? Tea to warm you up?" he practically croons.

"Water will be fine." Larson follows him inside and glances around. She had no idea what the condo is worth, but the décor looks like a *GQ* photo shoot inside a Pottery Barn sponsored by an art gallery.

When Chris turns toward the kitchen, Larson sees Britt is seated on one of the brown leather sofas in the living room, leafing through a magazine. She looks up at Larson and gives a curt nod. From the distance she's standing, Larson can make out Britt's black nail polish. When she turns a page, the dark shape of a tattoo is visible on the inside of her forearm.

Chris's voice echoes over the sleek surfaces in his kitchen. "Detective, you've met Britt Martinez? She's a second–year PhD student in our department."

"We met briefly yesterday morning, yes," she answers, aware of how different these two are acting compared with Robert and Scarlett, who had seemed shell–shocked.

Chris returns and hands Larson a heavy glass of water that's cool against her palm, and sits beside Britt, while Larson sits facing them on the opposite couch.

The energy between the two of them is peculiar, Larson thinks, as if they're resigned to be in each other's company. She remembers what Britt asked her after learning there had been a murder: all she cared about was whether or not the person killed was Chris. Larson's mind flashes to something Joe Lyons said the day before about the grad students: *"I trained my team to deceive people."*

The possibility alone can get in your head, which, along with Chris's megawatt smile and Britt's CBGB outfit, adds to the dreamlike feel of the interview.

Easy, Larson thinks, reminding herself she has the upper hand.

"Any trouble finding the place?" Chris asks.

Cut it, Eddie Haskell, she wants to say. "None at all," she answers, opening her tablet. "Thank you both for meeting with me. Time is important in this investigation, and I need to get as much relevant information to the case as I can. Can you both tell me where you were on Thursday evening?"

Chris glances at Britt, then leans forward. "I'll go first. I was at Hull Hall around seven thirty and left around nine. It was pretty quiet, but it usually is that time of night."

Larson sips the water, which is pleasantly cold. "Did you see Elizabeth Colton?"

"I ran into her in the hallway. I asked her if she knew where Joe was. I'd tried to reach him earlier, but he wasn't answering his phone, which isn't unusual. He's extremely busy."

Larson makes a note. "Do you remember what Elizabeth said when you asked?"

"I believe she told me to fuck off," Chris answers bluntly.

Britt smirks, and Larson has to sip the water again to keep her blood from boiling. Chris's candor is brash but makes an impression too—it feels like the unabashed truth. "I take it you two didn't have a good relationship?"

"With Elizabeth? I had no problem with her, really. She couldn't handle any teasing, I can say that. I think it was *her* who would have said she didn't like *me*."

"You just liked to piss her off," Britt says.

"Probably right." Chris shrugs, then another smile. "I come across as kind of a jerk."

A jerk, indeed. Larson stifles an eye roll and turns her attention to Britt. "You were in the department last night as well. How would you describe your relationship with Elizabeth Colton?"

"She wasted time playing her games with Joe; she was late with all of her work and held the team back."

Larson makes a note. "I'd like to talk about your impressions of the other members of your teams, and specifically how they got along with Elizabeth. What can you tell me about Veronica Haskins?"

Chris and Britt exchange a quick glance. "She has a legal background and is supposed to keep us in check, I guess," Chris says. "Beyond that, I only met her during the Zoom interview. Nothing to tell, really."

"Except that she showed up on the day one of us was murdered," Britt says flatly.

Larson feels her cheeks flush. Britt's right: Veronica had no apparent motive to kill Elizabeth Colton, but the timing of her arrival is conspicuous. She needs to be interviewed as soon as possible.

"And Robert?"

"The loyal lieutenant?" Chris asks. "He's kind of the over-bearing camp counselor type."

"He had no apparent tension with Elizabeth?"

Chris snorts quickly. "Not that I ever saw, except Elizabeth probably resented his closeness with Joe. He's always first in line to smooth things over, even after Elizabeth caused scenes over her and Joe's forbidden romance."

"Robert cleans up Joe's messes," Britt adds succinctly. "It drives the rest of us a little crazy."

"Noted," Larson says, recalling Joe telling her to talk with Robert first. Was that because he knew Robert would cover for him? Help to conceal something? "And Scarlett Simmons?"

"Girl Scout. Room mom," Britt says. "Talks about her kid a lot. She's probably in love with Robert but is all *Sense and Sensibility* about it. Always nice to me, though."

Chris shakes his head. "Always nice to *everyone*. She's the kind of person who drinks milk with dinner."

Larson leans forward, her elbows pressed into her knees. "But in the experiment everyone keeps talking about, you're all acting, correct? How do you interact in front of the participants?"

"In that room, we're supposed to give the appearance of complete cohesion. All of our personalities turn off," Chris says. "The uniformity is supposed to exclude the subject. It adds some stress for them to feel like they're on the outside."

"So, we just act like we all get along." The side of Britt's mouth curls upward. "We become office furniture."

Larson makes another note and asks several more questions, gathering information she plans to confirm with the cell data and camera records she hopes to have later that morning. Later, it should be easy to see if each suspect is telling the truth about where they were at the time of Elizabeth's death.

She closes her tablet and slips it into her bag. "Thank you both for your time," she says, standing. Chris and Britt are curious but not particularly likable—which is fine—they're not her new friends; they're suspects.

Chris starts toward the door to show her out. When Britt stands, Larson stops. "I noticed the tattoo on your forearm."

"It's there, yeah," she says, making no effort to elaborate as Chris returns to her side.

It's going to be pulling teeth at every turn with her, Larson thinks, bending to observe what the tattoo is: a semicolon, black and bold.

"May I ask what it means?"

Britt stares into Larson's eyes for what seems like forever before her lips purse into the prickly expression she's clearly practiced. "You don't know?"

"I'm familiar with the punctuation."

"It can mean a lot of things, usually a change in life. The tattoo is about moving forward. For me, it means I attempted suicide about four years ago. I cover it up most of the time, especially during the experiment and when I teach my class. Here." She jerkily rotates her wrist so Larson can examine the mark more clearly.

"I see," Larson says, reminded of how people are often drawn to psychology as a way of trying to understand themselves more fully. They've had experiences that they need to process and explore.

Maybe that's why she's here, part of Lyons's research, Larson wonders fleetingly.

Britt holds her gaze until Larson feels hers drop.

Chris pipes up, his voice returning to its mannerly cadence. "Will there be anything else, Officer? Sure you wouldn't like some hot tea to go?"

"No, thank you," she says, and then sees herself out, her mind full of questions.

LYONS

Joe Lyons kneels beside the filing cabinet of his home office, his hands quivering as he flips through file folders of documents. The old paper smells musty and like vanilla, like a library. There's no sound aside from the sluggish ticktock of the grandfather clock in the hall. It's nearly 7:00 p.m., and he's on his knees with a sheen of sweat on his forehead, wearing the heather–gray university logo T–shirt he's worn all day.

It had been just a passing glimpse on the road, but he was sure...

...sure *enough*, at least, that he needs to dig up the records.

He wipes his palms over his shirtsleeves. Shock should have tied everything immediately together in his mind, but instead it numbed him until this morning. He'd burst in the door upon returning, his vision or hallucination just a jagged fragment of a thought. *Of a panicking nightmare.* Not some watered–down version of discomfort engineered in a psychology lab.

Life and death.

His urgency confuses his search. He hasn't seen most of the

records in years. He'd meant to be more organized than this. Damn the experiment and everything that has taken his focus away from what was really dangerous all along.

What happened was *years* ago, and why would it have anything to do with Elizabeth?

But the chances were too small to be a coincidence—he sees that now. Was his insight delayed because of his own sense of guilt? Or worse, his own self–protective instincts kicking in because of how guilty he knew he suddenly looked?

Elizabeth had threatened to end things, and maybe wouldn't have minded exposing his dirty laundry to the university as she did. He'd already dodged one inquiry a few years back because of those careless comments he'd let fly out of his mouth during class.

He didn't want to withstand another scandal.

Had he been using her? Leading her on? It didn't feel like it, but that's certainly how it looks.

He stops. *Looked.* Past tense. Now, he doesn't have to worry about Elizabeth spilling the intimate details of their relationship, does he?

Joe's eyes fly across names, read page headings, scan opening paragraphs. He shakes his head as his fingertips move from folder to folder. He'd been way behind in terms of digitizing everything, and now he's paying the price. A more astute professor could have found this particular file with a few keystrokes. Some of the guiding principles about record keeping he knew were myths—records have to be secured behind three locks—but the one he *always* followed was keeping records for seven full years.

Thank God.

He's been a professor for nearly two decades, and his files go all the way back to the beginning of his career.

"Come on, come on," he says to himself.

Grief over Elizabeth is a pit in his stomach. He hasn't eaten since hearing the news, which means he's had nothing but black coffee since the day before yesterday. He hasn't tried to force himself; his throat is still vaguely bitter after losing his breakfast by the side of the road the day before.

He slams the drawer closed and opens another. What he's looking for has to be here somewhere. It has to. Unless it's…in his office.

Where she'd gone.

He's always kept his records in two places on purpose, the most sensitive ones close to him. Easily accessible, hypothetically. Only *to her*. "Shit," he says, out loud.

She was the only other person with access to his things.

He pictures his office window. Had Elizabeth been looking for something other than a routine file in his office last night? Something unrelated to their experiment?

She'd read *the report*, he was sure of it, but would she have had any reason to suspect…?

Or to put everything together herself?

Surely, no.

Except that nothing feels for sure now.

Joe wobbles as he stands. He reaches for the corner of his desk to steady himself, nearly knocking over his emerald-green lamp.

He needs that file.

Maybe they all do.

He jumps as his phone rings, knocking his head against the side of a bookshelf. His scalp smarts as he staggers toward the chime's general direction. The cloudy afternoon hastened nightfall, and his reflection appears starkly in the glass. When he sees Larson is calling, a vague hopefulness rises in his chest—it reminds him of the dependent feeling he had toward nurses, following various emergencies in the past.

Larson is like that for him now, a source of stability amid the swirling insanity. Maybe she's learned something; maybe she's about to tell him that what he's begun to suspect can't be true.

He hopes to God it isn't.

Except the tenor of her voice is not what he'd hoped for. "Dr. Lyons, it's Alana Larson, do you have a few minutes to chat?"

Just tell her, he thinks.

Except if he's wrong, if he's dreamed up a false connection, he'll break confidentiality laws and throw off the entire investigation.

Joe sits and extends his arm to check the time on his phone—nearly 7:00 p.m. Larson works just as hard as he and everyone on their team, evidently. "Now's fine, I was just doing a little digging, just…looking deeper into something from a long time ago."

Larson seems to hesitate. "Anything you want to share?"

"I'll…let you know if it's anything."

"I'm calling to ask you about Thursday night. I have a witness who can place you at Hull Hall around 7:00 p.m. They said you stayed in your car and left without going inside. Did you go there to see Elizabeth?"

He finds it hard to draw a full breath. His heart skips a beat. "I don't suppose I'm allowed to ask who saw me?"

"Was it you?"

"Yes. That was me."

"Why were you there, Professor? To see Elizabeth?"

"No, I didn't think she'd be there, I thought she would have gone home when she left here." His voice is shrill.

"But you didn't contact her?" Larson presses. "The last text between your phone and hers was at 6:16 Thursday evening."

The truth feels like an accusation. Of course a detective has pulled phone records, but it's unsettling to know he's being investigated. He hasn't slept in thirty–six hours; he feels dizzy. Joe pinches the bridge of his nose and stammers, "I…was just apologizing in that text."

"We're looking at everyone near Hull that night, Professor. You hadn't mentioned earlier that you were there. It's curious."

"It seemed irrelevant. I know how that sounds, but it's true. I never went in, I didn't see anyone, and I left," he says.

"Did you intend to end your relationship with Elizabeth?" Larson asks.

He looks over his shoulder in the direction of his file cabinet. She certainly doesn't beat around the bush, Lyons thinks, and she's stunningly intuitive. "No," he says, eventually. "Actually, I don't know. More like I wanted to make sure she was okay. And maybe make sure she didn't torch my career, to be honest." The truth sounds clear and sharp coming out of his mouth now, self–protective. He sounds like a weasel to himself and he hates it. "Neither of us knew where things would end up between us; she was going to graduate next year, and I know she…wanted to get away from here."

"Did you sense that *she* wanted to end your personal relationship?"

"I don't know, maybe. Or go forward. We were at a crossroads." Joe stops, the hardwood floor cold beneath the soles of his bare feet. "Detective, how long before I can get back into my office? I need to dig into my files there, I may have something that…"

"Files?"

The files are in one of two places, he knows, and his search of his home files is nearly complete. With what he's looking for in hand, he'll know enough to tell Larson everything he suspects in the morning.

The glare of headlights flashes across the front windows, and Joe squints in their direction. A vehicle has pulled in to the driveway.

"Professor?"

"Just a second, someone's here." He strides toward the front door, an irrational part of him expecting to see the unmarked police cruiser that Larson had arrived in that morning, or even Elizabeth herself—the denial element of grief such a skillful conductor of daydreams.

"Did you say someone's at your house?" Larson asks.

Lyons raises his hand to block the light before the headlights go dark, then the door closes with a metallic thud. Soon, the sound of footsteps crunching through snowy pine straw emerges from the dark.

"Yes. Oh…it looks like…it's just her."

Lyons opens the door. The night air wafting in smells clean and sweet.

"Professor, you were saying something about looking for a file? To answer your question, we can go together to your office as soon as you'd like."

He considers the time it may take to find what he's looking for, let alone make sense of it as footsteps brush toward him. "Fine. Tomorrow morning, then. Let me handle whatever this is about and…"

"First thing? Meet at your house at eight a.m.?"

"See you then," he says, knowing there's no way he'll be able to sleep again that night. Not that sleep is important now. Piecing together what happened to Elizabeth and protecting everyone else is all that matters.

The line goes dead as Larson ends the call. Lyons leans out into the night, the slight breeze frigid against his cheeks and neck.

He tugs at his shirt collar and forces a smile.

"I didn't expect to see you here," he says.

LARSON

Snow fell overnight. The ground and branches are so white, they glimmer pink.

The engine of Larson's Tacoma revs as she climbs the hills leading to Lyons's house. The truck's body is scarred with scratches, but its four–wheel drive is unrelenting, its tires bearing down as she winds through the pines.

There's something magical about the untouched snow, the sense of newness or possibility. The night before, Lyons sounded like he was onto something. A murder so gruesome requires intentionality that would be impossible to hide for long. One solid lead is all that's needed to uncover it.

Larson crests another hill, then ascends Lyons's steep

driveway. She slides on her sunglasses to block the glare and checks the time—still a quarter to eight, not that she minds arriving early.

He'd said someone came to see him as their call concluded, but a scan of the driveway shows no tire tracks—maybe the snow froze overnight, she considers, covering whatever marks were left.

Larson climbs out of the truck and approaches the house, noticing barely visible indentations leading to and from the door.

She steps around them as she climbs the steps, then rings the doorbell, activating a chime inside. Silence follows. Wind cuts through her jacket as she glances down the steep slope down to the road, the air bringing forth the faint scents of pine and woodsmoke—something burning in the distance.

She rings the doorbell once more, then knocks.

Another few more seconds of silence before she finds her phone and calls King.

He answers immediately. "I was just about to call you. You're on your way to talk to Lyons?"

"I'm here," she says, teeth chattering as a gust of wind reminds her of the ridge's steepness. "I'm ringing the bell, but he's not coming to the door."

"You think he forgot?"

She wipes the back of her wrist beneath her nose, then takes a confirming glance at the bumper of his gray Saab. "No, his car's in the carport. Something's wrong."

"I'm on the way," King says before hanging up.

Larson calls Lyons's name as she tries the front door, which opens. Her pulse speeds up. Warm air rushes out, carrying a sour, metallic scent.

"Lyons?" she calls again, but her stomach is already plummeting.

The door creaks lightly as it swings fully open. A wooden chair lies on its side. Beside it, a potted plant is broken, black dirt sprayed across the floor in every direction. Dark droplets are everywhere. Closer to the kitchen are smears of crimson–purple handprints.

Larson's breath catches as she finds her phone and calls King, shouting before he can speak. "It's a crime scene, Patrick. He's dead. I'll make the calls! Hurry!"

CHAPTER 6

LARSON

The snow is soon awash with red and blue reflected lights. King sits beside Larson in the Tacoma, the engine rumbling as warm air rushes through the vents. Larson wipes her sleeve across the windshield to clear away the condensation, while crime scene investigators file in and out of Lyons's front door, carrying marked sample baggies, white paper booties covering their shoes.

"Thanks for coming out here," Larson says. "I know we're not on university grounds."

King shakes his head. "Here is where I should be, this thing is getting worse by the second. And nobody's on campus now except for the squirrels. I don't know how to ask this, but are you okay?"

"Dandy," Larson says succinctly.

King raises an eyebrow, stopping short of saying anything more.

She picks at some lint on the dashboard and clears her throat. "I don't mean to be rude, sorry, I'm just trying really hard not to be upset. Patrick, he and I were *on the phone…*"

"You're fine," King says.

The investigators' shapes move through Lyons's living room as Larson taps her fist against the steering wheel. "My call with him ended around 7:09. He told me before we hung up that someone had just arrived, and used female pronouns. He said, 'It's just her,' or something like that. Whoever came to the door was female and was familiar enough that he was surprised but not alarmed. That's not airtight, obviously, but it's a start."

"You couldn't have known. Hell, he may have looked right at whoever did this and didn't know what was going to happen. We'll have a location on the cell phone of everyone related to this case last night anytime now, but what's your gut say?"

Larson bites the inside of her cheek. "Britt, the grad student, is the first person I think of. Female pronouns, angry, peculiar affect."

King nods. "She's the one who contaminated the crime scene Friday morning?"

"One and the same, possibly returning to the scene of the crime the morning after? I have to wonder. She was at Chris Collins's apartment when I went to talk with them yesterday." Her memory flashes back to the semicolon tattoo on Britt's forearm, and the confrontational way she went about explaining its meaning. "The other person I think of is Veronica, who I haven't even interviewed yet. We played phone tag a few times yesterday, I was planning to talk to her after I met with Lyons."

A man in a dark jacket and black cap emerges from the front door, makes eye contact with Larson and King, and waves them forward. Snow crunches beneath their shoes as they make their way up the sloped yard, steering clear of the area around the door.

The officer extends a box of the white booties to Larson and King, who slip them over their shoes and follow him inside. In the yard, another investigator kneels over the footprints Larson passed earlier, his camera flashing over and over like miniature lightning.

The living room is warmer than the outside, but barely, a breeze wafting in through the open front door. It's the same space where she went to see Lyons the day before—same modern furniture and stacks of books—but now movement is everywhere. Every crime scene is different, but the smell of blood is the same, Larson thinks, animalistic, metallic. She hears the click as a device is waved over an indentation in a sofa cushion, then a whir as white measuring tape is stretched between the hallway and the overturned chair.

Joe Lyons lies on his kitchen floor, arm extended over his head as if he were reaching for life as it fled his body. Blood has pooled around him, its volume inconceivable. Larson blinks at the dullness in Lyons's eyes, gritting her teeth to stifle a wave of nausea. She shifts her gaze to a quilt folded over the back of the couch—anything to anchor her attention so the moment can pass.

"That's the same kind of cut that went through Elizabeth Colton's throat," King observes. "Our killer likes using a knife."

"Yeah," Larson mutters, swallowing her feelings.

A grandfather clock near the front door ticks, its gold pendulum swinging rhythmically. The investigator who led them inside circles the kitchen table with a discerning squint. "It looks like Lyons was sitting here, and someone else sat across from him. Maybe they were having a conversation, facing each other. Then, maybe something changed. An argument, maybe? The splatter patterns indicate Lyons was headed this way," he points through the kitchen.

Larson steps toward the round wooden table, trying to picture the scene from the night before. "His chair was knocked over, but there was a coffee cup beside the place mat where he sat. It looks like he was working when company arrived. The footprints through the blood go in the opposite direction, back out the front door. Maybe Lyons trying to run out the back."

King motions toward the woven place mat. "Was there a laptop or a tablet there?"

"If there was, it's gone now, but we can find out. No way this was a robbery, though. He knew whoever came to visit. No struggle at the front door."

King crouches beside the chair opposite where Lyons had been sitting. Turned at a slight angle, it looks like someone sprang from there. Larson replays their conversation in his mind; he sounded ready to allow in whoever had shown up. She leans toward King, speaking slowly to keep her voice from shaking. "That cell data is...?"

"Coming today."

She nods. "There are three women in Lyons's circle who also knew Elizabeth Colton: Scarlett, Britt, and the new student, Veronica. I'm going to see her first."

———

Larson starts toward the door when her phone rings, the incoming number one she doesn't recognize. She steps onto the porch to answer. "Detective Larson."

"Hi, I'm… This is Veronica Haskins."

Larson's eyes widen as she snaps her fingers to get King's attention, but he's angled away from her, hands shoved into his pockets as he studies a mark on the floor. The call is timed as if Veronica had been reading Larson's mind—or listening in. Larson turns, angling her body to block the breeze buffering the audio.

"I wanted to tell you I'm leaving," Veronica says. "I'm packed up. Coming here was…a mistake." As she pauses, Larson can hear that she's crying. "Too much has happened, I just can't… I told Dr. Lyons last night that I have to…"

"I trained my team to deceive people, Detective. You can't think you're the exception to anyone's rule," Lyons had said. Veronica either doesn't know or is an incredible actress. "When did you speak to Doctor Lyons?"

"When? Last night," Veronica says, sounding too dizzied to recall the precise time. "I went to see him at his house. I wanted to do the responsible thing and not just disappear."

"Oh, it's her," Lyons had said.

Larson leans inside the doorway, finally catching King's eye. He stands. "Are you at your home now?" Larson asks Veronica.

"Yes, but about to get in my car. I'm going."

"Stay exactly where you are,"

"I'm…"

"You aren't going anywhere, wait right where you are. I'm on my way to your apartment. Do you understand?"

Veronica mutters, "Yes," as Larson ends the call, booties slipping slightly on the hardwood as she strides back into the living room.

"What is it?" King asks.

Her pulse throbs in her neck as she looks up the list of addresses King sent her the day before. "Tell me if you think this is suspicious," she begins.

LARSON

"The call's timing is remarkable, I'll give you that." King's facial expression is steady as they rush down the highway.

"The only one of the grad students I haven't talked to yet calls me *at the crime scene*? Someone who arrived the day before last, and now two people are dead? *And now she plans to leave the state*? I should have talked to her yesterday."

"How did she take the news?"

"She didn't, I didn't tell her yet."

King grasps the handle above the door. "You want to see her face when you tell her," he says.

It had been her strategy with Lyons a day earlier, and look how that had turned out, she thinks. But Lyons was a man dizzied by guilt. He'd been beside himself during and after identifying her body.

He'd wanted to tell Larson *something* this morning.

Something he never got to say.

The truck tires spin in the icy gravel as Larson leans on the gas. They take the hills toward town, the engine growling as King verifies the address. Five minutes later, King and Larson question Veronica in the nearly empty living room of her first floor apartment, standing beneath bulbous gold light fixtures from the nineties because there's no place to sit. True to her word, she appears to have repacked her things.

King's boots make triangle–shaped indentations in the carpet. He glances up at a vent expelling warm air.

Veronica hasn't turned off the utilities.

Maybe she's in a hurry to leave, Larson thinks.

When King breaks the news about Lyons, Veronica leans slightly forward and buries her face in her hands, holding the position long enough for Larson and King to exchange a glance. Her back heaves as she begins to sob. "It's too much, all *way* too much," she says, now pacing the room. "What's *happening*?" She runs her hands up and down her arms, her voice crackling with emotion. "What *happened now*? To Professor Lyons?"

King laces his fingers together in a way that looks pastoral. "The investigation is just getting underway. On the phone, you said you went to his home last night?"

"Wait." Veronica stops. She pushes her hands through her hair. "Am I being *questioned*? In a *murder case*?"

"We need to gather as much information as we can," Larson says. "Can you tell us what time you were there?"

"I *know* my rights," she says. "And I'm not saying another word until I have an attorney present. You can't keep me here in Shepard without arresting me, and there's not enough evidence for that."

The thermostat clicks as the air ceases flowing through the overhead vent. "You're correct," Larson says calmly as she takes a step in Veronica's direction. "It's your right to be represented by counsel before any questioning. But you're wrong about our needing to arrest you to keep you in Shepard. With any evidence at all, I can get a court order to keep you here, especially at this stage of an investigation. And I have to say, it's pretty interesting that you're refusing to answer questions about your whereabouts last night immediately after placing yourself at the crime scene."

Veronica glares at the two officers and folds her arms over her chest. "I *know* my rights," she repeats, defiant.

"Talk to you outside?" King asks Larson.

Larson nods, and they reconvene in the parking lot, where patchy ice covers the new asphalt. Wind gusts icily against Larson's cheek.

"Want to make a call for that judge's order? What are you thinking our move should be?" he asks.

Larson's cell phone is already in her hand. "If she knew Lyons was dead or had anything to do with it, she should get an Academy Award. I really don't want it to get to asking for court orders, but it'd be irresponsible not to since she's trying to bolt. My gut says she's scared, but the clock is ticking and I need her to talk. Maybe she at least saw something that could help."

King glances at the clouds. "That sky looks ominous. And I'm with you. If Veronica was guilty, she wouldn't be so obvious about it."

"And she might have seen something," they both say in unison.

"I'll let Veronica know she's not going anywhere, then make the call about the order," King says. "And I'll check again on that cell location data."

"Thanks. I need to get to Britt Martinez and Scarlett Simmons," Larson says, and then climbs into the truck cab as King disappears back into Veronica's apartment. Everything is unraveling so quickly, the sensation is dizzying. She got the first call related to this case less than three days ago—an undergraduate named Tom had caused a disturbance at Hull Hall.

That quick exchange feels like the clicking of an ascending roller coaster now.

She rubs her eyes with the heels of her hands.

Had she been tired from sleeping so little the night before?

Or was the truth far worse?

Had her antipathy toward psychologists carried over to Lyons? Maybe a small part of her thought, *Let him fend for himself.*

No, he'd *known* whoever had come to see him while she was on the phone.

She could hear the familiarity in his voice. He didn't sound frightened.

No, he actually sounded irritated, like dealing with whoever had come by was an interruption.

Larson's eyes rest momentarily on the apartment door as she imagines what Veronica's process of finding representation will be like after having lived in North Carolina for only two days. She's tempted to stride back inside and tell King not to bother with the court order. Except maybe by now he's got her talking.

King's so good at setting people at ease, making them comfortable enough to open up.

She opens her phone and calls Britt Martinez, whose phone goes directly to voicemail. Larson leaves a message, hangs up, then calls Scarlett Simmons, who answers immediately.

Her voice sounds sleepy. "Detective?" Scarlett asks.

Larson checks the time. It's just after 9:00 a.m., but Scarlett probably didn't get much sleep last night either. "Ms. Simmons, I need to talk with you about where you were last night."

The rustling of sheets comes across the line. "Is something happening with the investigation?"

"May I ask where you were last night?" Larson repeats.

"I…was here," Scarlett says reluctantly. "Will you hold on, Detective?"

Larson hears the phone being set down, then what sounds like the rustling of sheets. She hears Scarlett's muffled voice asking a question, then another. A few seconds pass, then the phone is picked back up.

"Sorry, I needed to see where my daughter was."

Larson can hear the nervousness in Scarlett's voice—and the news she was about to get was only going to set her more on edge. She has little reluctance in questioning Scarlett. A single mother in grad school—not only did she have no obvious motive to murder either person, she's probably too sleep deprived to have planned out either crime.

Larson glances at Veronica's door—still shut. Maybe King has convinced her to cooperate after all. She switches the phone from one ear to the other. "Scarlett, you said you were home. You were there the entire evening? Was anyone with you?"

"My daughter was here. And my ex–husband, he spent the night."

"Scarlett, I'm sorry I didn't tell you this sooner, but I have some terrible news. Joe Lyons was attacked in his home last night and died as a result." She pauses. "I know he meant a lot to you, you said as much yesterday when we met. The police are going to work until we find who's responsible, I promise."

"I…I can't… He's *dead*?" Scarlett's cry sounds like glass breaking, pain and surprise so sincere it's infectious—Larson's

eyes begin to well up as her sobs come through the line—
another part of her mind focusing on facts: Scarlett has an alibi,
two, in fact, who were with her the night before.

After answering a few of Scarlett's questions—the ones she's
able to address—about Lyons's death, she ends the call.

King emerges from Veronica's door.

Larson tries to read his expression, but it's hard at this distance, him squinting in a gust of wind. He frowns slightly as he
approaches, rubbing the back of his clipped hair.

Larson opens her phone, her fingertips shaking as she
searches for Britt Martinez's number. Just as King opens the
door, her email refreshes and her phone dings as a new message
appears.

When Larson looks back down, her pulse begins to pound.

There is an email from Joe Lyons.

She brings the phone closer to her face to make sure she's
not reading it wrong.

The message is time–stamped fifteen minutes after their call
ended the night before.

SCARLETT

Scarlett's first impulse is to call Robert, to let him know. Her
phone lights up the bedroom when she opens it, and then she
hesitates. Friday morning, beneath the fluorescent glow of the
diner's window, Larson had said that Joe had told her to talk
with Robert first—but she'd never clarified why. He'd answered
her questions accurately but so succinctly his responses seemed
rushed—a stress response, surely, but it felt odd.

But what *didn't* feel odd anymore, she considers. Robert is the person she trusts most in the department, and he'd been nothing but consistent and kind in her presence for more than two years. He's watched over Iris—a task she'd allow few people to do—who positively adores him.

Psychological assessment, Joe Lyons had said numerous times, *is just an expedited way of getting to know someone. Tests are designed to gather large amounts of information quickly—the same as you would by spending longer stretches of time in someone's company.*

How many hours had she spent in Robert's company? Too many to count. No, his track record was impeccable. The trauma was pushing her into paranoia.

She texts Robert: Call me ASAP. Then, she calls Chris and breaks the news about Lyons. He listens before telling Scarlett that he'll call Britt. His tone is hurried as she rushes to end the conversation, his emotions always so buried beneath layers of polish.

Scarlett overhears Iris asking Mark about the day's plans as she emerges from the bedroom. She can smell brewed coffee that she hasn't made. It's a different, more innocent world fifteen feet away, she thinks, hearing Iris's laugh followed by Mark's guiding voice. "That's great, but here, look, the curl tucks in like this. Like a tail."

"Like a tiger's tail," Iris says, intent.

"Sure, a tiger…or even a leopard," Mark agrees. She finds them leaning over a beige sheet striped with green and pink lines at the kitchen table.

Mark's eyes twinkle as he looks up, but darken as he notices her expression. "Babe, what's wrong?" He hasn't called her a pet name in several years.

Iris sets her pencil down and lets it roll onto the carpet as she stands too. "Mom?"

"Baby, just hang on for a second, I need to talk to your dad."

Iris's eyes flick up to meet Mark's gaze. "It's okay, kiddo. Sit tight."

Mark follows Scarlett into the dark bedroom, where she sits on the side of her bed, her legs buckling from the weight of what she's learned. It feels almost as though the bed catches her, as if she couldn't have walked another step. The mattress shifts slightly as Mark sits beside her, then his warm hand finds her bare upper arm. "You look like you've seen a ghost," he says.

"I just got off the phone with the detective." Her eyes meet his. "Mark, Professor Lyons is dead."

"What? What are you talking about?"

"She didn't say the word, but he was *murdered*. Attacked, she said. She wanted to know where I was last night. I don't even… How can this be?" Scarlett leans forward and rests her elbows on her knees. She looks at him, a twisting spiral of confusion in her eyes. "How are they *gone*? And *why*?" The word catches in her throat, then becomes a sob as she leans into Mark's chest. His smell is so familiar, she forgets for a moment where she is, what's happened, that they ever divorced. "I need you to be here right now," she says.

"I…was happy to stay. I *am* happy to stay." Mark hesitates, like he's unsure what to say. "Scarlett, this is crazy."

Tears streak her cheeks, and Mark wipes them with the back of his sleeve.

Scarlett's head tilts up just as Mark pulls her into a warm embrace that makes the room stop spinning for a moment.

CHRIS

Chris Collins brushes his teeth furiously over a rushing tap, Scarlett's tearful voice still echoing in his mind. He throws on a sweatshirt and baseball cap as the woman who spent the night leans against the bathroom's doorframe. Her name is something like Carissa, he thinks, but can't remember at the moment. She wears his gray heathered SMU tennis T-shirt, which hardly covers her legs, and then frowns as Chris hardly glances at her as he heads to the front door.

"Is everything okay?" she asks, tugging at the T-shirt hem.

But it's not, no. Everything is far from okay.

"There's food in the fridge and coffee in the cabinet," he manages to say. "Stay if you want."

He rubs his hands over his face as he heads down the stairs. They've gone white and cold the way they always do when he's agitated. A minute later, he curses under his breath as he speeds across town in his black Tesla. The windshield wipers brushing away the sleet, which falls steadily from the low clouds. It's his first spring break in Shepard—a far cry from Punta Cana, where he spent half of last March—and like Britt had warned him, the place is positively deserted.

He'd never envisioned himself in a graduate program, much less on a research team like Joe's. His plan had been to become a tennis pro after college. He'd walked cockily onto his undergrad court and beat the coach on a bet, then proceeded to play three seasons so intently, he injured his Achilles and developed a limp to show for it.

"You don't know when to stop," Britt told him at the time.

"No, I don't."

"That's a difference in mindset," she'd told him. "You think that makes you sound tough. I think it makes you seem stupid."

"Touché," he'd acknowledged.

When there was an opening on Joe's team the year before, Britt told Joe Chris was taking it, just like that. And Britt was irreplaceable. And so with a stiff left leg and a passable understanding of research technology, he'd joined—a fish out of water in a North Carolina college town.

He pauses at a red light, then looks both ways before punching it across the intersection. It's hardly a time to get stopped by a cop, but no one's visible in either direction.

He texts Britt as he pulls in to her apartment complex—she's standing at the door when he reaches her place, dressed in a black sweater and jeans, her cat weaving between her shins. Britt's hair is spiked into a kind of mohawk as if she's headed out to a punk show—it's hard to believe, but Chris knows from experience that this is how she dresses even when she's by herself at home.

"*What?*" she demands, her voice throaty. "*What's going on now?* The detective left me a voice message just now."

Chris pushes past her into the apartment and closes the door once she's inside. Her place looks something like a coffee shop mixed with a used electronics store. Wires are plentiful and the shades are drawn. An aluminum baseball bat leans against the wall beside the front door. "Did you listen to it?"

"Uh, not yet? I saw you pulling up."

"Sit down," Chris says, and they sit on Britt's firm couch. When her cat jumps on his lap, he gently sets it back on the floor.

"Are you going to tell me what's happening, or do you need me to ask a few more times?"

Of course she didn't answer when the detective called, so she has no idea, he thinks.

"Scarlett called me. She told me Lyons was killed last night."

Britt covers her mouth with her hand. Her eyes pinch closed.

The silence in the apartment is a buzz.

"She said the detective wanted to talk with you," Chris says, leaning toward her. "You. Specifically."

Britt opens her eyes and wipes away the tears that have formed. Her gaze refocuses on Chris and she frowns. "Why are you looking at me like that?"

Chris's eyes narrow.

"After everything we've been through," she says.

LARSON

Larson turns to King. "You've got to see this."

She angles her phone toward him, the morning light reflecting dully off her screen. Her finger hovers over her phone screen as her mind arranges the facts of what's happened into a narrative that makes sense. The email sits at the top of her inbox, its presence seemingly impossible. As she arranged with Lyons to meet this morning, someone he was familiar with—a female, based on his pronoun choice—had shown up at his house. Based on what little Veronica has said so far, that person was her, which makes some sense, even if her reasoning for going to see him isn't fully clear.

About fifteen minutes after her call with Lyons ended, he'd sent her *this* email. Based on the state of his body and the initial chemistry read on his blood, the medical examiner placed the time of his death around that same time.

Larson's memory flashes to his blue bare foot extended at an unnatural angle, the blood on his kitchen floor, the desperation of his outstretched hand. Sending this message is likely the last thing Joe Lyons ever did.

"Forward that to me," King says, gravely, reading glasses dropping from his forehead to his nose. "Just as a backup."

She forwards the email, then they lean over her phone, open the attachment, and read.

———

The subject line reads: *Prime identifier is Ani*

The document below is highly redacted.

PSYCHOLOGICAL ASSESSMENT (Part 1 of 3)

Confidential Material

NAME: XX

DATE OF BIRTH: XX

DATES OF ASSESSMENT: 3/13/2013, 3/22/2013

IDENTIFYING DATA AND REASON FOR REFERRAL

Patient is a XX-year-old Caucasian XX, referred for a psychological evaluation to determine their current cognitive and emotional status involving XX.

**During the course of researching this evaluation, information became available that Patient had attempted to conceal. The evaluator's awareness of this information was not revealed to Patient until the feedback session at

the evaluation's conclusion. An armed off-duty police officer was present outside the building for security purposes because of the report's implications.

FORENSIC NOTICE AND INFORMED CONSENT

At the outset of our first meeting, I clarified my role as an independent medical expert who would provide opinions about this case. We discussed the possibility that my evaluation could be beneficial, neutral, or detrimental. I explained that I would not be providing treatment and that, with their permission, I would send their lawyer a copy of my full report. I also told them that the report and anything they told me might be relayed to the court and the prosecution. I also told them that they were free to refuse to answer any of my questions. After my explanation, XX was able to say that I was on "no one's side" in this case. When asked who would get a full copy of my report, XX said their lawyer. XX also recalled that a copy might be given to the judge. I reminded them that they were free to decline any or all of my questions. XX expressed understanding and gave consent.

When we met the second time, XX remembered that I was doing a psychological evaluation relevant to their legal case. XX recalled that I was a neutral party. When asked who would get a copy of my report, XX said "my lawyer." I reminded them that they had only given me permission to share the report with their lawyer but that a report might ultimately be given to the judge. I also reminded them that I might be called in to testify if their

case went to trial and could be asked to talk about anything they and I discussed.

BEHAVIORAL OBSERVATIONS

Patient was polite and cooperative during the scheduling
of the evaluation. It was explained to Patient that the evaluation would last approximately five hours, including two
thirty-minute breaks. Patient subsequently made adjustments to their schedule and arranged a time to meet.
They arrived on time for the examination and presented
as polite and cooperative. They willingly accompanied
the examiner to the testing room, which was clean and
well-lit, and free of distractions. They were dressed
casually in jeans and a sweater, appropriate for the cool
weather, and their hygiene appeared to be appropriate.

They demonstrated good posture, appeared to be in
good health, and showed no difficulties with ambulation.
Patient was of average height and weight. They were oriented to person, place, time, and purpose, and maintained
good eye contact throughout the evaluation. English is
their primary language, and they are right-handed. They
spoke with normal volume, rate of speech, and voice tone.
There were no signs of incoherence, blocking, circum-
stantiality, or loosening of associations. Their thought
content was logical and was consistent with the topic of
discussion. There were no indications of hallucinations or
delusions. Their attention span was excellent, and they
exhibited a pleasant, if not charming, mood.

During the exam, they answered the questions that

were asked of them and elaborated when appropriate. Rapport was easily established, and Patient appeared to give full effort on all tests. Therefore, it appears that this evaluation is a valid indicator of Patient's background and functioning.

The information collected during the assessment should be considered a reliable representation of Patient. It should be noted before elaborating further that Patient knowingly provided incorrect and misleading information. This was confirmed by the accuracy of outside records and by the indication through several assessments' validity indicators that Patient was willfully lying.

SOURCES OF INFORMATION

Background information was obtained from interview, developmental history and rating scales, as well as medical records. This information appears to be from reliable sources and valid. Information was also obtained from two previous psychological assessments conducted when Patient was a juvenile.

Current status of their learning and behavior was obtained from observation during testing and from standardized psychological tests. The validity of their performance on most tests was deemed to be accurate due to their cooperation, apparent motivation, and validity indicators on the assessment measures themselves.

BACKGROUND INFORMATION
Emotional/Psychological History

Patient reported that they are typically in a happy mood. They stated that they are proud of themselves and their accomplishments, as they have adjusted well to adult responsibilities. When asked how a friend would describe them, Patient replied, "Friendly, reliable, and optimistic."

Patient stated that they have never received therapy or been hospitalized and reported no history of abuse. Upon direct questioning, Patient denied any current or past suicidal ideation.

Patient reported no family history of mental illness. However, they indicated that their biological father suffers from alcoholism. They stated that he began to abuse alcohol when he returned from the Iraq War and continued through Patient's adolescence. Patient denied that their family has any other history of substance abuse problems. **Records indicate that this was false. By all accounts, Patient had no relationship with their biological father.*

Alcohol and Drug Use

Patient reported no history of significant alcohol abuse. They agreed that they had engaged in modest experimentation with alcohol as a teenager and that they typically consume 1–2 alcoholic beverages per week, on average.

Likewise, Patient reported no difficulties with marijuana or illegal drugs. Patient noted that marijuana was tried on several occasions, but that the effects were disliked. "It was not my thing."

History of Behavioral Disturbances

The first account of Patient being physically aggressive was when they were in the fifth grade. By all accounts, they were spending the night at a friend's house when another guest began "roughhousing" during what began as a pillow fight. Interviews later indicated that Patient went through the motions of pillow-fighting at first, but shifted into maneuvering their body to shove their knee onto the other child's chest, then leaning their forearm onto the child's throat until they began gurgling and gasping. "I turned their head to the left and could see them straining the ligaments in their neck. XX opened their mouth to scream but of course could make no sound."

The parent who broke up the encounter described seeing "an eternal blackness in Patient's eyes."

The scene was broken up as the others rushed in.

(CONTINUED)

END OF PART 1 of 3

———

They read the report in silence except for the truck's windshield wipers occasional scraping and the sound of the train in the distance. Larson has nearly completed a second pass through the document when King rubs his hand over the two-day stubble on his cheek. His brow is knitted heavily together. "It feels like I'm reading a puzzle. I assume he made it like this so members of the court couldn't identify a witness or something. Confidentiality?"

"Probably," she confirms, but she's really just speculating. She's never read a report as heavily redacted, and Lyons's motivation at the time is anyone's guess. *Now* truly *a guess*, Larson thinks, finally tearing her gaze from the screen. "He ran a forensic practice but told me yesterday he didn't do assessments anymore. So why would he send me one?" She glances down. "From 2013?"

"I thought they gave one to everybody who participated in their deception study."

Larson's head cocks. King's right: which is it?

She glances again at the report and the answer comes to her. "This looks like more like a complete *assessment*. What they gave those kids before the study was just a screening. What we're looking at is part one of three, and there's almost four pages. He spent hours with whoever this person is."

She stops.

King senses she's realized something. "What?"

"We're assuming Lyons was the psychologist who conducted the assessment—but what if he wasn't? It's unlikely he would have evaluated any of his current grad students, right? If he hadn't been the practitioner, the report could easily be about any of them: Chris, Britt, Veronica, Robert, Scarlett, or even Elizabeth."

King nods. "There has to be a version out there where everything isn't x–ed out or has the details changed."

"Agreed. Lyons, or whoever redacted this, obviously wanted to protect the identity in this draft, but there have to be some clues in here," she says, nearly adding, *The clock is ticking,* but there's already enough pressure.

"If Lyons been *trying* to play a game with us, he couldn't have done much better," King complains nervously, the tremor in his voice from the day before returning. "What do you make if the subject line? 'Prime identifier is Ani.'"

"A name, maybe?" Larson guesses. "The start of a word? Maybe professional jargon?"

Ani.

Larson bites the inside of her cheek. King's agitated, she knows, eager to make an arrest. But Lyons wasn't playing a game; sending this version was the best he could do. And for all they know, the few seconds it took to send may have cost him his life.

He might have been able to run if he hadn't taken the time.

"All we need is *some*thing, even just one little thing buried in here to put us on the right track." She nods toward Veronica's door. "You were in there for a little while. Any luck getting Veronica to say more?"

King draws a quick, steadying breath, then releases it as she shakes his head. "Just a little. She's being stubborn and is intent on having a lawyer. Like you said, she's placed herself at the murder scene, so we have to hold her. Her story is that she was disoriented by that kid Tom's attack in the department, then by Elizabeth Colton's murder, and decided she'd had enough and wanted to leave." King again lets his reading glasses drop from his forehead to his nose with the fluidity that comes from immense repetition. "She figured she'd hardly unpacked so getting her stuff together would be easy. When I reminded her we knew she was at Lyons's house last night, she shut down again. After a lot of tears, it slipped out that she wanted to tell him herself that she was leaving."

"So why not call?"

"She said he never answered his phone."

Possibly valid, Larson thinks. They'll see soon enough in the phone records. Maybe Lyons didn't want to hear from Veronica right then; he had sounded like he was preoccupied and in the middle of something. "Any details about what she saw at his house, or if anyone else had been there already?"

King shakes his head. "That was when she zipped it. I came out here to let her start her lawyer search. I'll say this: If her internet searches from yesterday show anything other than 'best motels along I-40' or 'best audiobooks,' my suspicions are gonna double."

"You're not suspicious of her now?"

"I get how it looks—she's the new variable in this equation and now two people are dead—but she's too...*official,* or uptight. Something." He motions toward her door. "And if she actually called Lyons repeatedly before driving to his house and doing what we saw this morning, she's so crazy, we should be scared."

You sound plenty scared already, Larson thinks. Actually, King had looked afraid to her since she saw him outside Lyons's office yesterday morning. But her gut tells her he's right about Veronica. Probably, their job is to remove her from the list of suspects— carefully, without missing anything, and while finding out what she may have seen the night before. One advantage of Veronica being so new in town is that her perceptions are fresh.

There was less time for her impressions of the others to calcify.

Larson's eyes drift back down to the report lighting up her phone screen while King flips the screen on his phone, then dials. Seconds later, he's explaining the situation to a judge. His voice slows slightly, and the valleys of his Carolina drawl deepen as he talks. This is his man–to–man voice, Larson realizes—ever so slightly different than how he speaks to her, but the change is noticeable. It's not lying or fake, she thinks, just another side of King.

They talk for less than two minutes. Larson hears the judge's grim chuckle before King hangs up. "If only everything was that easy," he says. "I'll go break the news to Veronica that she's staying put, not that she doesn't know what's coming. Want to come?"

Larson taps her phone screen. "I'm going to think this report over."

"Back in a minute," King says, closing the truck door as a gust of wind rocks the truck. The silence that follows is like a current that carries Larson's thoughts.

If Lyons wasn't so keen on giving assessments anymore, why did he bother digging one up? And sending it, so frantically? Not only was the report more heavily redacted than any Larson had ever seen, but there was an even more unusual part she and King hadn't discussed: the addendum within the text, denoting the willful inaccuracy of the client.

The client lied, and the evaluator had gone along with those lies through the early part of the report. The additions came after they realized the truth.

After they learned they'd been tricked.

Larson rubs her jaw and glances again at the screen. The time she would spend going through later flashes forward to her, like glimpsing the first clue in an intricate crossword puzzle. The assessment was conducted over the course of several meetings. Assuming Lyons wrote the report, if it wasn't for whatever digging he had

done in between sessions, he might have never known the original information was false. Whoever he'd been evaluating had been
convincing in not telling the truth—someone *perfect* to conduct
an experiment where all the participants are deceived, she thinks.

But would Lyons really bring someone like this onto his
staff? Someone with "an eternal blackness" in their eyes?

Larson glances again at the apartment door—still closed,
with King inside.

Lyons had followed Elizabeth Colton to Hull Hall two nights
earlier, then waited in his car before driving away. He'd been
reluctant to admit it when she'd asked, but he hadn't denied it
either. No, Lyons might have been about to explain more about
why, when someone—most likely Veronica, it looks like now—
showed up at his door.

Larson hears ice crunch on the sidewalk and looks up as
King approaches the truck and climbs back inside, a puff of cold
air following him in. "She's making this hard on herself and is a
mess because of it, but nothing I can do about that. She knows
not to go anywhere." He shrugs and rubs his hands together.
"Back to Lyons's house?"

"Why didn't Lyons call for help?" Larson asks as they pull away.

King scratches the back of his head. "His phone was gone this
morning, right? Maybe he only had time to make it to his laptop."

LARSON

At Lyons's house, police tape now lines the edge of the driveway.
Two news crews are now stationed beyond it, both testing lighting for their broadcast.

Larson leaves the truck running as King climbs out. "Not staying?" He sounds vaguely surprised.

She glances at the team of investigators ostensibly comparing notes on the front porch. "I need to dig into some backgrounds, *fast*," she says. "Maybe I can match a piece or two with something in that report, then I need to call campus IT. Lyons's computer may have been here, but I want them to comb whatever server he was using for the rest of it. If that fails, maybe there's a paper copy in his cabinet."

"Maybe a copy that someone wanted to steal Thursday night?"

"Exactly," Larson says.

King hands her a key card. "For all–campus access," he says, scanning the clouds before he stomps his feet. "*Damn*, it's cold. Based on how many on the team are here, this should go pretty fast."

One of the investigators passing King turns his head. "Double time, now. We gotta be finished by two, two thirty."

The man glances at Larson, then back at King. "You two haven't heard? We're getting a foot of snow in the next twenty–four hours that's going to shut the whole town down. It's why everyone up there is hustling."

Larson's pulse accelerates as she opens the weather app on her phone. A winter advisory pops up immediately. She taps the screen and the radar image beside the text shows a map of Shepard, a diagonal blue line approaching from the west. Behind it trails an inch of white that, by Larson's estimation, stretches over a hundred miles.

The investigator's right: it's massive.

And inescapable.

"Shit," she mutters, gaze flicking to check the time on her dashboard.

"Whatever you need done, I'd do it now," the man says. "You know what the plows are like in this town. Not much'll be possible for two, three days."

Shepard isn't Boston, Larson knows. A heavy snowstorm will grind everything to a halt until it thaws. She scrolls to the temperature forecast for the next five days, and her stomach sinks further. Cloud cover will be consistent and not once will the temperature rise above fifteen. Whatever comes down is going to freeze and stay that way.

The description she'd stopped herself from using earlier applies suddenly: *the clock is literally ticking.*

King bounces on his heels, hesitating before closing the truck door. "Those forecasts are usually worst–case scenarios, maybe it won't be as bad as they say."

For someone who's spent as much time in Shepard as he has, he's either being naive or misleading, she thinks. "Maybe, but I better go," she says, sliding the truck into gear.

The second her tires hit the roadway, her phone chirps and she checks the screen.

It's exactly the person she wanted to talk to next.

"Hello," she answers.

"Detective Larson? I'd like to meet with you as soon as possible."

"I'm listening."

LARSON

Fifteen minutes later, Larson double checks the time as she

approaches the police station. A reporter, obviously waiting for some time, practically leaps forward, shouting questions. A light pops on behind him. "Two murders in two days, Detective. What's the connection between them?"

Larson shields her eyes. "We'll get a statement for you guys as soon as possible, okay?"

"Detective…"

Larson turns on her heel, not caring if she's being recorded.

Actually, *hoping* she is. "Listen, this is your job, I get it. I respect it. The best thing you can do for the community right now is to give us some space."

"But…"

"That's all for now," Larson says as she walks inside.

At her desk, Larson opens her laptop as she sits perched on the edge of her desk chair. She estimates she has only a few minutes to herself. Background checks can be labyrinthine or brief depending on the amount of detail needed to identify or rule out a suspect and the time that's available. She's old enough to remember FBI Most Wanted bulletins in the post office and *Unsolved Mysteries* flickering on her grandmother's box television, but young enough to seamlessly navigate databases for leads.

Her screen lights as she touches the keyboard, but before she can begin her search, an email from King appears, subject line: *B. Martinez Background check.*

Britt.

Larson opens the file and reads:

I had a few minutes after you left and started looking into

Ms. Martinez. Not much to find but what came up isn't much of a surprise.

Larson scrolls further into the body of the email. There's a citation for disorderly conduct four years earlier from what looks like a scuffle outside an Austin shopping center, then three speeding tickets and four parking violations. It all seems on brand with the person Larson met; not a squeaky–clean record, but nothing resembling a pattern of serious violence.

And Larson, to her own slight surprise, heaves a small sigh of relief.

Her desk phone buzzes. She springs into the hall leading to the lobby, where she opens the door.

Robert slumps in the brassy morning light, hands shoved into his coat pockets. His eyes are red rimmed and his mouth is pinched into a straight line.

"I'm glad you called," she says. "Come in." She leads him to one of the meeting rooms, which smells like Windex and dust. A conference table sits in the center of the room, and there are gray and red scuffs in the off–white paint.

Robert's hands clench into fists as he paces the back wall in quick, deliberate strides. He's angry, a perfectly natural response, Larson thinks, especially this early after hearing the news about Joe.

"I'm sorry," she offers, measuring her words carefully as she leans against the doorframe, observing Robert's body language. She thinks back to how Veronica acted an hour earlier and wonders if either was inclined to put on a show, except that Robert's neck shows ropy veins from the angry train of his grief.

Hard to fake.

"I was going to help Joe look through some files or something this morning," he says.

"Files in Joe's office?" she asks.

Robert casts a quick glance in her direction. "Yeah. Where are...things? With the investigation?"

"I can't say very much. The CS team is at Joe's house and we're conducting background checks on everyone involved." She tilts her head, speaking gently but directly. "On the phone, you said you wanted to meet. So, here we are. What did you want to say?"

Robert grips the back of a chair and shakes his head once to dispel his tearfulness. "You know how the point of any psych assessment is efficiency? They're supposed to collect the exact data you want very quickly. Joe used to say that."

Larson nods, her recollection of being assessed for duty postgraduation present in her mind. "I'm following," she says.

He wipes his sleeve under his nose, then looks up at Larson. "If you'll take a risk, I have an idea."

SCARLETT

Scarlett answers immediately when Robert's face appears on her phone, part of her wanting to slide into the fantasy that today is a regular Sunday, like any other: when Robert might call to see if she wanted a ride in to the department. In that fantasy world, Elizabeth and Joe Lyons are still alive, and all the grad students would be getting together for their regular Sunday meeting.

"Hi," she answers, closing her bedroom door.

"Hi... You doing okay?"

"Sick to my stomach, honestly. I feel helpless," she says. "I hate it."

"That's why I'm calling. I want to have a Sunday meeting."

Scarlett changes the phone to her other ear. "Now?"

She and Robert had started a Sunday meeting tradition informally over a year ago—just the two of them. Once, Elizabeth joined them, and then began showing up regularly. Chris didn't like being excluded so he also started appearing, and of course Britt followed wherever Chris went. They were usually all in their offices on Sunday afternoons anyway, so putting their heads together could be helpful to strategize about what was upcoming that week.

The meetings felt like the "players only" meetings that the athletes on campus held—no coaches, no trainers, just team captains leading discussions about what went wrong in the previous game and what needed to be fixed.

Joe had never come to one—Scarlett wasn't sure if he even knew they happened—and in those times they operated almost like siblings. Despite all their differences, they were the only ones who really got what being on the team was like.

"Yeah, today," Robert says. "At the regular time. I can't just sit here. I can't *not* do anything. The four of us knew them both."

Robert had acted differently after they'd heard about Elizabeth, but he sounds even edgier now. For the first time, he sounds a little strung out.

Maybe learning about his mentor's death had pushed him too far, she thinks.

"Are we even allowed in the building? Maybe we should let the police work?"

"Detective Larson said we're free to come and go at this point, we just have to stay out of Joe's actual office."

The image of police tape over his door makes Scarlett wince as she digs the side of her heel into the carpet. "Robert, I…"

"One of us had to have seen or heard *something*. I say we stay in the room until it comes out. And if any of us doesn't show up, that would mean something too."

She pulls the phone away from her cheek to check the time, eyes narrowing as a weather alert pops up. A snowflake icon sits beside the number 100% for the next seven straight hours. She pictures the usual local panic under these circumstances: milk and bread vanishing from grocery shelves, lines at gas stations— the sort of behavior that made her interested in studying social psychology.

She normally trusts Robert implicitly; she's followed his lead for two years. But there's a lump in her throat. It's like he's not thinking clearly.

Or not telling her something.

"Robert, have you seen the news about the storm? Is it a good idea to go out?"

"That's why we better meet right away. Do you want me to pick you up?"

Scarlett's head turns as the front door squeaks. Iris's voice floats in from the living room. "Mom, I've scored fourteen goals!" She cracks the bedroom door and sees Iris bounding into the hall, trailing a pink soccer ball. She has a flash of the potential awkwardness of being picked up by wild–eyed Robert. "I'll drive myself," she says. "See you there."

"See you there," Robert echoes.

She grabs a coat and plucks her keys from the ceramic dish on her dresser where they "sleep."

In the front room, Mark notices her keys, and his expression turns curious. "You're going out?" He sounds reluctant, as if inquiring directly is impolite. Under her arm, Iris holds the soccer ball Mark bought for her the day before. They've been playing a one–on–one "game" of soccer in the courtyard for some time, Mark making a case for being the world's best dad.

"I want to show you my new kicking style," Iris says.

"I won't be long," Scarlett says.

Mark follows her to the door. "Hey," he says gently.

"I don't mean to bail on you guys, I just…"

"That's not it. You know I'll eat up the chance to hang out with her all afternoon. It doesn't feel safe, not with what's going on." He reaches for her shoulder, then catches himself, folding his arms.

The resolve from a moment earlier drains from her legs. "I know, I know, but I should. I need to. We really should put our heads together on it. Besides, it's broad daylight, and I think…"

"*You* think? Or Robert thinks?"

"It's not like that," she says, but she doesn't clarify whether that means that Robert doesn't think for her or that they're not involved. She rests her hand on the doorknob, then turns it.

"I'll be back in an hour," she says, the wind frigid on her cheeks as she steps into the cold. Already, snowflakes have begun to fall.

ROBERT

Robert calls Veronica and leaves a message on her voicemail when she doesn't answer.

He calls Chris, who sounds more eager to come than he'd expected, and says he'll be in touch with Britt.

He checks his watch and drives on.

LARSON

At five till noon, the vehicles begin to arrive.

A black Tesla is first. Chris Collins steps out and enters the building through the rear.

Then, Robert's beat-up Civic appears.

Larson leans forward, resting her chin against the steering wheel. She's parked in the lot across the street from Hull Hall— not exactly high-tech surveillance, but she's positioned herself at an angle to best think through Joe's arrival the night Elizabeth was killed. To her direct right is the hedgerow Tom Campbell crouched behind, and it's obvious why he picked this spot—the angle of the hill keeps anyone in the parking lot from seeing her truck.

Within the next five minutes, Britt, Scarlett, and Veronica then arrive in that order, then all go inside.

She'd been wanting some data and is getting more than she'd expected: each of the primary suspects arrives at the scene of the first murder, the sky just dark enough behind Hull to highlight the illumination of any room they enter.

It's like one of the million movies or books based on *Rear Window*, she thinks.

In about three hours, the whole town will be covered in ice.

Whatever they're about to discuss, they'd better hurry.

SCARLETT

Through the courtyard, the wind howls, ripping through the trees and rattling the window. Scarlett swallows as she sees the yellow tape crossing Joe's office door in an *X*, the other doors in the hallway ominously closed. None of the students or staff have been in the normally bustling office for days, the dim hallway deserted.

"In here?" Chris asks.

Robert opens the experiment room door, reaches in, and the overhead lights flicker on, emitting a faint buzz.

"Ho–kay," Chris says as he passes Robert, his eyes cutting him a quick glance that looks like a warning. Chris has always looked gym fit in his tight cashmere sweaters, but for the first time, Scarlett takes in the muscly breadth of his shoulders as he passes Robert and realizes he outweighs everyone else by forty pounds.

Scarlett takes a seat, the chair's metal frame creaking slightly.

The chairs have been rearranged since the incident with Tom, but the energy of his attack lingers in the room, even if it feels like a long time ago.

"I'll just keep an eye out for the others," Robert says from the hall, before pulling his phone from his pocket, light from the screen reflecting off his glasses. "Be right back," he says.

Chris leans forward, his signature grin absent. "What do you think this is about?" he asks.

"Just what he said, I guess. The four of us knew them both, maybe we can piece something together, help the police."

Chris glances at the hallway where Robert lingers. They're only alone enough to whisper. "I guess you were home last night?" he asks.

It feels strange to acknowledge an alibi. "I was. Two people with me. You?"

"Home with a friend," Chris says, then motions toward the hall. "What about him?"

"Home too, probably. *More* than probably. Where would any of us have gone to?" But Chris's questioning Robert gives her a sinking, disoriented feeling, like learning something untoward about a favorite teacher.

"Something about this doesn't add up," Chris says. "I don't like it."

Her eyes have widened, she realizes, as Chris gives his head a quick shake that functions as a subtle warning.

Robert reenters the room and rests his hands on the back of her chair, his knuckles brushing her sweater.

"Why'd you want to do this here?" Chris asks him.

LARSON

Criminals so often return to the scene of their crime—it's as though they can't help it. What's the social psychology behind that phenomenon, Larson wonders. Do they want to look approvingly over their work? Or revisit justifications for what they've done?

Her gaze sweeps from the parking lot to the rear door to up across the second floor windows to the window of Lyons's office on the other side.

That window is dark.

When Joe Lyons sat in this place, he could clearly see whether his office light was on or off. According to Tom, he waited in this spot for ten full minutes before driving away. Elizabeth had left his house only a half hour earlier. When she asked him about the fact that he'd come here after her, he acknowledged that he had, but hesitantly.

Maybe that meant he was reluctant to admit he'd followed Elizabeth, but what if that pause meant something else?

Bits of sleet tap the windshield like a handful of pebbles. Not that investigations are conveniently scheduled, but the timing of this one is abysmal.

And about to get worse.

Larson lets out a deep breath as her thoughts swim. What if Lyons hadn't followed Elizabeth here at all?

What if he'd come here to go to his own office, but stopped when the light told him someone was inside?

Someone he'd assumed was her.

And maybe she *was* in there, but wasn't the first one to arrive.

Yes, Larson thinks, *Elizabeth Colton hadn't drawn Lyons to his office in Hull Hall so much as she'd stopped him from going inside.*

Her chest tightens as she thinks back to what Lyons had said the night before. He'd wanted to meet her at his office the following morning—this morning—before he'd been stopped.

What had he hoped to find? To show her? The same thing that had drawn in Elizabeth?

Another light switches on inside Hull Hall and the window glows a flaxen color.

Larson wonders who among the grad students will stay after the meeting. Who will be drawn here?

And who might stay away?

She opens the truck door, wind whipping her hair. Her heart hammers in her chest as she steps into the cold.

SCARLETT

Scarlett's chair shifts slightly as Robert releases it.

"Where else would we meet?" he answers dismissively, circling the room. Scarlett tries catching Chris's gaze, but it flicks up toward the door just as she hears footsteps.

Her head turns in time to see Veronica march in and then slump down in her chair. She's put her hair up in a high ponytail; the way she folds her arms makes her look like a kid throwing a tantrum.

"You…showed up," Robert says. "I wasn't sure you would."

"I have a right to hear what's said in this room," she says coldly. "Particularly if it involves me. But this meeting *isn't* smart, in case anyone was wondering. I keep getting notifications on my phone that we're about to be buried in ice. It's *not safe* to drive in this. I wanted to go home, but even if I could, we're all going to be *stuck here* in the ice."

"Just wait for it to melt, genius," Chris says. "I promise it will."

Veronica's gum-chewing slows.

It's harsh, but for once Scarlett agrees with Chris. Veronica isn't easy to like. "You're leaving town?" she asks. "Like for good?"

Veronica wipes at her eyes with the back of her sleeve. "Well, I'm not *allowed to yet*, apparently. But I have no reason to be in this madhouse anymore. And exactly *why are* we meeting?"

Robert circles like a child playing duck-duck-goose, deciding who to tag. "Because this is our chance to look each other in the eye and see what we all know. And because meeting and strategizing is what we actually can do."

"What's what we *can do*?" Britt asks, entering last. She closes the door solidly behind her and takes the last open seat at the table. Scarlett smells traces of patchouli and cigarette smoke as she passes.

"Meet, talk," Chris answers.

"And hold each other accountable for where we've been in the last two days," Robert says. "The common denominator between what happened with Elizabeth and Joe is us."

"You're saying you think someone in this room did it? One of *us* is a murderer?" Veronica's eyes dart from person to person.

Britt rolls her eyes.

"Not necessarily," Robert says. "Do I think the obvious suspects are all in this room? Sure. But we've each talked to the detective and not to each other. I'd like to hear what everyone saw Thursday night and yesterday. And personally, I'd like to help catch whoever is responsible."

"Hear, hear," Chris says.

"Have the police told anyone here *how* Joe was killed?" Scarlett asks.

The room buzzes with silence.

"I'll let everyone here speak for themselves, but I personally had no reason to want Joe dead. Or Elizabeth, for that matter," Chris says.

"No *obvious* reason," Robert says. "But what other connections are there between them besides us?"

Scarlett pipes up, "Maybe we should all say where we were three nights ago when Elizabeth was killed. We'll all say it for the record, and then everyone can leave separately."

Veronica sinks back into her chair. "Okay, fine. *I'll* start. I was actually on the phone all night planning my escape from this insane asylum, and if need be, I'm sure the police can place exactly where my phone was." She looks around. "Next?"

Her abruptness leaves a wave of quiet that takes a moment to ebb.

"I'll go," Scarlett says. "Because I actually need to tell everyone something. It's only partly related to what's happened."

"What is it?" Chris asks.

Scarlett looks down. "I've taken things from the department I shouldn't have. I've been doing it for almost a year." She looks at Robert, who pushes his glasses onto the bridge of his nose. "I was here Thursday night, but it wasn't to work like I said. I...stopped in for what I thought would just be a few minutes to return some equipment I'd borrowed. *More* than borrowed, to be honest. It was a laptop I didn't have permission to take out of the building. I was letting Iris use it, but that's no excuse. I'd realized it was wrong and was putting it back. That late on the night before break, I didn't expect to see anyone here." She glances again at Robert. "Even you. But I guess that morning had us riled up, so we *all* were here. We're workaholics, right? Especially Britt?" Scarlett laughs nervously, her feet tucked beneath her chair, crossed at the ankle. "I know we're here to talk about what happened, but I owe you all an apology."

"Things? Taken *things*?" Veronica asks, motioning with her hand for more information.

"The laptop was the main thing. But there've been other office supplies, and petty cash from the office drawer."

"Scarlett," Robert says.

"I know."

A short incredulous laugh escapes Britt. "I wouldn't worry about it much under the circumstances."

"But it was wrong. Taking the laptop was impulsive, and I told myself…"

Chris waves his hands as if clearing away an odor. "Wait, who cares, Scarlett? It's called petty cash for a reason. And you were putting the laptop back, right? So, no big deal anyway," he adds. "Moving on."

"Thank you for that, Chris, but I feel awful about it. And we're all supposed to come clean here, right? I'd started to leave the laptop in the lounge when I heard the back door and ducked back into my office. I saw Elizabeth pass by, then I heard her talk to you, Chris. Then, I saw you leave. And that's…all I remember."

"Well, frankly, I think this speaks to character," Veronica says. "I find it interesting that there's a thief among us."

Scarlett tucks her hair behind her ears. The other three stare at Veronica blankly.

"Remind me who invited you to this meeting?" Robert asks.

"Are you from fucking *Earth*?" Britt asks, eyes narrowed.

Veronica shrugs. "I don't have to accept snide comments from anyone here. I'm only staying till the storm passes and the detectives make an arrest. I'm already packed."

"You'll be missed," Robert says.

"Deeply, *deeply* missed," Britt agrees.

"It's been real," Chris says, peace sign raised. "I'm sure Tulane's not the same without you."

Scarlett looks up. "You were at Tulane?"

"Apparently I'm the only one who remembers the interview?" Chris says.

Scarlett leans forward. Her elbows rest on her knees, her head slightly cocked. "For how long?"

"For some time," Veronica answers, and then purses her lips.

"Tulane was where Elizabeth did undergrad," Scarlett presses, glancing around.

"That…may…"

"Wait, you *knew* her," Robert says. "Didn't you?"

A pause follows that seems like it might expand indefinitely, like the room's parameters might widen, like the air might vibrate with possibility.

"Sure, yes," Veronica says. "But so what?"

A sound escapes Britt that's somewhere between a cough and a laugh, her eyes bugging out.

"I was a senior in the sorority she was kicked out of back in undergrad." She shrugs with a theatricality that makes Scarlett literally nauseous. "And to answer the question that's on everyone's mind: *no*, she didn't know I was joining the team. And, no, I didn't mention the connection to Joe. *I* didn't even know she was here until I was getting ready to move. Elizabeth *wasn't* on the Zoom interview." She nods at Chris.

Scarlett's pulse races as she shifts in her chair. "I'm sure you mentioned that to the detective," she says.

"It's not secret," Veronica answers. "Which is all that I'll say about that henceforth."

"Henceforth," Britt echoes with a snort.

"Maybe we should talk about Tom," Robert says.

"The kid I punched? He has nothing to do with what happened."

"How…can you be so sure?" Scarlett asks, although she senses Chris is right. Tom looked off, sure, but in an impulsive, haphazard way—not at all like a methodical killer. Never mind that none of them seem particularly suspicious to Scarlett. Not even Veronica, despite what's just come out.

"Can't say, exactly," Chris answers. "But I didn't get that vibe. Besides, I think Elizabeth was stronger than that." His lip quivers for a split second before he turns his head and seems to pretend to cough. Is that actual emotion Scarlett hears in his voice?

Britt clears her throat. "As long as we're putting everything on the table, considering possibilities here, should we talk about the *pilot* study we'd started? Since it *obviously* relates? Maybe it was one of them?"

Robert glances at the glass. He shakes his head no.

"One of *who*?" Veronica shifts in her chair, her eyes scanning the room. "What pilot study?" She looks at Robert. "What's she talking about?"

"We agreed not to discuss it," Robert says.

"I'd been asking for it for two years but it was Joe's design," Britt presses. "And we were just getting started."

"*What pilot study?*" Veronica asks.

Chris rubs his knuckle in his eye. "It was only a handful of times, Judge Judy. And we *did* agree not to discuss it, and we *definitely* shouldn't with you in the room."

Veronica stands and puts her hands on her hips. "I deserve an explanation here."

"Sit down," Britt tells her, as she and Veronica lock eyes.

Veronica arches an eyebrow. "You'll tell me about it or I'll disclose it to the university review board."

"Let's everyone take it a little easier?" Robert says, stepping forward. "Britt, you brought it up."

Britt gestures sweepingly toward Robert as if to say, "Go ahead."

"We wanted to learn more about human aggression…to shed light on school shootings and terrorism. Joe thought aggression is motivated by self-concern, that harming other people isn't usually the real goal. He thought people react violently when their statuses and self-concept are threatened, so gossip, spreading rumors, and bullying directed at the self-concept would be most likely to make someone violent. So that's what we did."

Veronica's eyes ask, "How?"

Scarlett says quietly, "There was a separate condition to the study that we'd just started to run. Five times. After the experiment, the second phone call was different."

"It's harsh, I'll admit. The script in that call recommends the student transfer to another university based on their overall performance in school and how they did on the task in here," Robert says. "They were asked to stay in the observation room and then took those calls here, where their behavior was observed for the next ten minutes. We made notes about their facial expressions, measured the amount they moved the furniture and marked up the forms, things like that."

"You bullied them," Veronica says. She pounds her fists on the tops of her thighs. Everyone's heads turn toward her. "This isn't some *experiment*. It's real life. Maybe what we should talk about is how you ran an experiment that drove people crazy. And maybe someone *especially* crazy."

The break in Veronica's voice makes Scarlett wince. It feels like the five of them are carrying on a defensive, suspicious improv scene.

"To be clear, now would *not* be a good time to bring this to the review board," Robert says. "And it's nothing compared to experiments in the sixties. Zimbardo, Milgram, what those studies gave the field is immeasurable. The students were called again after ten minutes. The third call explained that there had been a mistake, that everything was in order, that the student was in perfect standing and had nothing to worry about. But I'm confident none of the five were involved in what happened."

"How?" Chris asks. "Do tell."

"I checked their social media accounts and all five have been out of town since Thursday morning. Two in Panama City, three in Mexico." Robert rubs his forehead. "But getting back to Thursday night, I was here, reviewing the procedures for experiments similar enough to ours that I'd have some suggestions for adjustments we could make. I'd have to check the times I clocked in and out, but I stayed late. I'll concede that's not much of an alibi. Like Veronica, I live alone. I saw Scarlett and her daughter when they left. And I heard Britt come in, and then Elizabeth coming in. Chris, I heard you and Elizabeth get into it in the hall."

"If you can call it that," Chris says. "I was here from about five thirty till nine. I did see Elizabeth, and we exchanged words, but nothing out of the ordinary."

"You blamed her for siding with Joe," Robert says.

"If being frustrated was a crime, we'd all be in jail by now."

His words hang in the air.

Robert folds his arms. "You know what I'm curious about? The little alliance between you two. Britt, you practically made Lyons take Chris on last year. And no offense, Chris, but you wouldn't have made it in without the endorsement. Maybe now's a good time for an explanation."

Chris shrugs, his scowl smoldering like a cologne model's. "We grew up together. Is that so hard to believe?"

"No, but it doesn't explain anything," Scarlett chimes in. "I've been curious too."

Britt's eyes burn as she stares straight ahead. "We don't *have to* explain anything, to you or to anyone," she barks, shoulders swiveling toward the others as if shielding Chris from the questions.

Scarlett raises her palms, then speaks again, slowly. "The police think one of us is guilty. They're looking into everything from each of our pasts as we speak. Anything you wanted to keep hidden, you won't."

"This is a waste of time," Chris says, stirring. "I'm leaving,"

"I thought maybe finding out who killed our colleague and professor might interest you," Robert says.

"Stand down, lieutenant," Britt says.

"Wait, let's finish talking through this," Scarlett says. "Please."

"Come on," Chris says, motioning toward Britt. "I think we're heard all we need to for one day."

When Robert stands, Chris raises his shirt. The handle of an automatic rests against his tanned abs. "Try stopping us," he says.

"Oh my God," Veronica squeals.

A sheen of sweat forms on Scarlett's brow.

"Chris…" Robert says but can't seem to find the word to complete the sentence.

"Before any of you get too excited, I have a concealed carry permit even if I normally keep this locked in my car. I should have known this meeting was some kind of witch hunt, even if it feels more staged than the experiment. Let's go." Chris wraps his arm around Britt's shoulder as they push past Robert to the door.

Scarlett can hear her pulse in her ears, Chris and Britt's exit seeming to send a wake of energy. A moment later, Veronica clutches her purse and strides into the hall. The click of the hall door soon follows.

Robert stands frozen where he'd stepped aside. His and Scarlett's eyes meet, but the look in his is unreadable. She's been alone with him countless times, but they're something mysterious about how he's acting that makes her feel like she's standing on a ledge.

"I should go too," she says to Robert, to which he nods. In the stairwell, she rushes to be outside again, the tangle of shadows and slapping of her footsteps merging into chaos as she jogs to her car.

LARSON

In the darkness of the observation room, Larson lets go of the handle of her revolver. Beads of sweat cooled her temples in warm space. She'd started toward the door when Chris showed his gun, then hesitated as he and Britt had left down the hall. It was Chris who'd felt threatened then, and yet in an instant, she'd seen a flash of how ill-advised her and Robert's plan had been.

Larson swallows the fear in her throat as she closes the tablet on which she'd been taking notes. At the police station, Robert had assured her its glare wouldn't be visible through the one-way glass, but she'd dimmed the screen as far as it would go before the meeting began. How interested would she be in observing the five of them talking candidly about where they'd been at the time of the murders?

"Very," she'd answered.

Now she watches Robert through the glass as his eyes trail Scarlett down the hall. The meeting had been shorter than they'd hoped for but very useful. She'd learned about Veronica's connection with Elizabeth, and that Britt and Chris *really* don't want to discuss their pasts. She also witnessed Chris break the law by bringing a handgun on campus and now wonders if she has a responsibility to stop everything else and arrest him. And if she even should.

There's a short knock on the door, and then Robert opens it, his expression depleted. He pressed his knuckles into his eyes. "Chris caught me off guard with that pistol, but he's mentioned his permit before."

"I started toward the hallway the second I saw it," Larson says. "I was ready to draw if need be." Not anticipating a firearm, even a legally carried one, was a tactical error.

Robert nods solemnly. "*Please* tell me you saw something worth putting all of us in danger. Trust me when I say I take no joy setting my team up to be observed like that. It's just that Joe treated me like a son."

Larson hesitates, her hands making a "slow down" motion. "Let's step into the hall." The observation room feels a little tight with a suspect, even if it's Robert. Larson feels her shoulders relax once they're outside the door. "Look, I can't talk much about my end of the investigation, but I'm all ears if you want to tell me what you saw in there."

Robert rubs the back of his neck as if quelling a surge of adrenaline. "First impressions? Chris was carrying, that's the most obvious thing I saw. You haven't said a gun was used in either crime, and if he's licensed to have it on him, it may not mean anything."

"I'll have his permit pulled and verified," she says. *And make sure he knows the gun laws*, she thinks.

"If Veronica was on the phone all evening, that's got to be some kind of alibi, right? And Scarlett shouldn't even be a consideration. Which just leaves me."

Larson has the feeling that she's missing the obvious, part of a puzzle that would make the others all make sense. Like the lingering identifier in the subject line of the report Lyons sent.

"Robert, does the name *Ani* mean anything to you? Or is it some sort of psychological term? Jargon?"

"Ani?" His head tilts to the side. "Not that I can think of. What's the context?" Robert's phone buzzes before Larson can answer, and he checks it. "It's a text from Scarlett, she could tell something was off. I feel bad about convincing her to be here." He shakes his head.

"You helped, that's the right thing. This gave me more context for all the background checks that are starting to come in now," Larson says.

"I'm sure there's a lot to sort through," Robert says.

"For something like this? No stone is left unturned."

Larson follows Robert downstairs, where her gaze flicks toward the security camera hanging from the eave. The upper and lower parking lots are empty aside from her truck and Robert's Civic. The lonesome beeping of a crosswalk signal in the distance makes the street seem even quieter, the city more desolate. They wave goodbye, and Robert's trail shoes leave curved markings in the snow accumulated on the sidewalk.

Soon, everything around them will be covered in ice, she thinks.

Larson unlocks her truck as the taillights of Robert's car disappear. Her phone buzzes in her pocket, and she answers when she sees it's King calling. "Hey, I'm just leaving Hull. Interesting meeting here. Where are things at Lyons's?" The air around her face is white from her breath in the cold.

"I'm at the station, the background checks are all in."

"*Finally*. Anything interesting?"

"Are you still with Robert Barlowe?" King interrupts.

"He just…"

"Alana, do not let him leave."

SCARLETT

Scarlett is washing Iris's cereal bowl when there's a knock on the door. She's been on even more on edge since leaving Hull, and the abrupt sound makes her jump. Iris runs to the door, ignoring the hysterical voices of the cartoon she's watching on TV.

Scarlet drops the dish towel she's holding. "No, baby, don't open…" But Iris has already undone the deadbolt.

"See, Mom, it's just Robert."

He stands in the doorway, hands knitted tightly together as he glances over her shoulder. "Sorry to show up unannounced," he says.

Scarlett swallows, regretting letting Mark leave moments earlier. They may have passed each other on the road. "Mark went back to his hotel for a while," she says. "What's going on?"

Robert steps inside and gestures in Iris's direction with his eyes. "Can we talk for a minute?"

There's something he's not saying. I've felt it for days now, she thinks. "Iris, honey, go in your room? Close the door."

Her tone prompts Iris to retreat down the hall, and a moment later, Iris's door clicks shut. "Let's sit," she suggests, her kitchen chair squeaking across the linoleum as she pulls it out.

Robert sits across from her and refolds his hands on the table. His chest heaves as he draws a deep breath. then opens his mouth to speak when Scarlett's phone chimes.

"Sorry," she says, checking. "It's Detective Larson."

Robert shifts in his chair. "That's why I'm here," he says.

She presses the phone to her ear before Robert can say more.

Driving sounds come through the line, a rumble and hum. "Scarlett, are you at home now? Has Robert Barlowe made contact with you?" She says his name as if there are air quotes around it.

Scarlett holds Robert's gaze across the table.

"Yes to both. We're at my apartment."

"Scarlett, listen to me, do not say anything out loud. Take your daughter and calmly get out of the apartment. I'm two minutes away."

Reality shifts with dizzying velocity. Scarlett's pulse begins to thump.

Larson's voice says, "Robert isn't who you think he is. That's not his real name."

The last word fades as the phone is plucked from Scarlett's hand.

CHAPTER 7

LARSON

King calls back and Larson answers on the truck's Bluetooth. "He's at Scarlett Simmons's apartment. She has that little girl, Patrick. I'm almost there." She thumps the steering wheel with the heel of her fist. She should have known, she thinks, shouldn't have let him leave.

Even if knowing the truth had been impossible.

"I'm on the way with another car behind me. Three minutes," King says.

Larson hangs up, then takes a fast turn while glancing at her GPS. She hadn't known exactly where to find Robert but, based on their interactions, contacting Scarlett was an intuitive first guess that turned out to be correct.

Fresh tire tracks line the road. Larson wonders if they were made by "Robert" as he drove off from Hull Hall. The truck skids and she grips the wheel to right her course. She's probably no more than two minutes behind him, but that seems like an eternity after seeing what a knife can do—expeditiously—twice in the past two days.

He'd told her from the start he was an expert in deception.

So, why, if he knew he was hiding such a secret, had *he approached her*? The possibilities draw goose bumps up Larson's arms. Calling the meeting for her to observe behind the one-way glass had been his idea. Either "Robert" thought he could trick her more effectively from up close, or he'd planned something even more devious than she'd anticipated.

She understands something new about Tom Campbell and the visceral gnaw of his frustration. Being lied to makes anger burn in her stomach.

Anger mixed with fear.

She takes another curve, then another.

In the distance, a siren wails. King is approaching from the other direction.

Larson tells herself that her carelessness didn't put everyone in danger, but she doesn't believe herself.

SCARLETT

Scarlett looks at the man she thought she knew well.

Robert looks at his hands. "It has nothing to do with Joe and Elizabeth. About that, I'm just as sick and in shock as you. I wanted to tell you before now; I didn't want you to find out like this. I started to say something a few times, actually."

A door opens and Iris's voice emerges from the hall. "Mom?"

Scarlett's hands are fists. *Crazy how intuitive kids are*, she thinks. "Don't you dare hurt her," she mouths.

Pain flashes in Robert's eyes. "No, no…" he says, his head turning slightly. "Iris, give your mom and I another minute?" His voice is so gentle, and Iris turns and retreats to her room without Scarlett having to say a word.

A beat of silence follows. Scarlett breaks it. "Robert isn't your real name? Why would you change it?"

"It's my middle name. Something happened almost seven years ago. I learned from it. I regret it every day. I'd never put you or Iris in danger and…" A siren howls distantly, Robert cocks his head as he hears it. "I started going by Robert after prison. I needed a clean start. I had to move forward."

"Prison?" Scarlett's heart skips as she registers the word.

"I *was* a different person before all this. I got involved in drugs, I got addicted, and addicts do desperate things. I know that's not part of your world, but it was part of mine." He pauses. "I don't mean to be vague. The truth about addiction is that you stop getting high after a while, you keep using to avoid withdrawal. It made me a monster. I stole things, I sold product, I didn't sleep for days at a time. I bought and sold some stuff. I was involved in selling some narcotics that turned out to be laced, and bad things happened. I called an ambulance as soon as I saw what happened, but the guy was gone. I didn't even know him. I was arrested and charged with manslaughter."

The siren's volume increases. Robert's speech becomes more rapid.

"I worked hard to go forward, it was all I could do. That's the thing about working around the clock—it's easy to get lost. Sometimes I forgot about all of it—what I did, my life before. But no one would have worked with me if they knew."

Recognition settles onto Scarlett's features. "Except Joe. That's why you were always so loyal."

Robert nods. "He gave me a chance and kept anyone else from finding out."

The first flicker of blue light hits the sliding glass door leading to the porch.

They both look at the glass doors. Brakes squeal outside.

Feelings fly through Scarlett's chest.

"When I heard about Joe this morning, my secret didn't matter anymore. I knew it wouldn't take long for my background to come out once the investigation started. I wanted to help before I couldn't. I'm sorry I lied, but I wanted you to hear this from me."

A second later, boots rumble on the stairs like thunder.

Scarlett's heart hammers. Robert lays his hands flat on the table, his expression oddly serene. "I'm sorry," he says.

Scarlett nods, her eyes watering as officers burst through her door.

LARSON

Blue light reflects everywhere. The few neighbors still in town appear as dark silhouettes in window frames and on balconies. Robert's facing away from Larson as she enters but stands and raises his hands without being asked. In seconds, he's cuffed and in the back seat of the cruiser King arrived in.

Larson rubs her hands together on the sidewalk. "I'm going back upstairs to talk to her. She's with her daughter. They deserve some explanation."

"We've got an hour or so before the weather starts, but agreed," King says. "Want someone to stay with you?"

Larson shakes her head and begins trotting toward the stairs. "Alana?" King calls.

She stops. King leans in. "Don't take this the wrong way, but just as a reminder I'd want myself: that woman Scarlett hasn't been cleared as a suspect yet. We haven't found a motive for anyone of interest yet, including Mr. Robert over there."

Larson nods. She's heard plenty of mansplaining in her life, but King's right. Especially in this case, things are less and less what they seem.

She's thanking King when a voice calls out from the street. A man in a barn jacket approaches, a grocery bag hooked under each of his index fingers, his expression anguished. "What's going on here? What's happened?"

King faces him palms raised. "Sir, I'm afraid you can't go up there right now. We're in the…"

"I'm *telling you* my wife and daughter are in that apartment and I'm going up. Are…?" A vein appears on the man's forehead, his chest bowed out. "What happened? I was only gone for…"

Larson gets in front of him. "They're fine, they're both upstairs, safe. Take a deep breath and calm down for a second, all right? Did you say you're married to Ms. Simmons?"

"We're…divorced. But I still…" He sets the groceries on the ground and squints at the police car, the rear windows obscured by the glare and flashing lights. "Was…someone here?"

"We've detained someone, yes," King says succinctly. "Do you have ID?"

Mark produces his driver's license, which King looks over and hands back. When Scarlett's silhouette appears in the upstairs window, they all three look up.

"She's expecting you?" Larson asks.

"I brought some groceries…to make chili." Mark motions toward the bags, the dull metal edges of cans visible between the handles. "I wanted to be here, you know, with what's been going on."

"Follow me," Larson says.

LARSON

"Did he threaten you?" Mark asks, the arch of his eyebrows wrinkling his forehead.

Larson, Scarlett, and Mark face each other at the kitchen table while Iris lies supine on the carpet, pretending to draw. Outside, the sky has begun to darken from the impending storm—shades of white and gray against a thin line of pink on the horizon. Beyond the sliding glass doors, the neighborhood seems still, as if the previous twenty minutes were only a frantic dream.

Scarlett pushes up the sleeves of her ivory cable–knit sweater and rubs her forearms. "No, it was nothing like that. He seemed very calm, just sad. My adrenaline made everything a blur, but I'll try to remember the details," she says. "Robert said he'd gone to prison, and that he'd meant to tell me before now."

Larson pauses. King supplied her with the details of Robert's background check before he left, but there's been a lot of information to keep straight in the past two days. "Everything I'm about to tell you is public record that you could look up yourself. His name is Timothy Robert Bruce, but he's been going by Robert Timothy Barlowe for the last seven years, Barlowe being his mother's married name with her second husband. He moved to Colorado from California, then to here, and got a driver's license as Robert Barlowe. He was issued a new license in North Carolina and had the utilities put in that name. I'm told the registrar pulled transcripts that name him as Robert Barlowe, so it's unclear if he altered them or went by that name at UCLA. It's usually a red flag to switch name use without legally changing it, but it's not a crime."

"God," Mark says, making a *tsk* sound as he opens a bottle of beer.

Larson raises her index finger while keeping her attention on Scarlett, whose face looks pale and drained. "I...take it you had no idea?"

"None. He's been my best friend in this program for two years. I feel like I could throw up."

Larson touches her forearm sympathetically. "Can you walk me through the timeline of Thursday evening, before Elizabeth was killed? You saw him at the department?"

Scarlett nods. "There isn't much to tell. Iris and I were just there for a while after he arrived. We said hello to him and left. The next time we saw him was Friday morning when he picked me up. That's when I got the call about what happened; then we met you at the diner about an hour later."

"How did he seem when you told him?"

Scarlett's gaze drifts into the middistance of her memory. "Like he was in shock, I guess. Like I was. Upset."

"Anxious?"

"Robert's *always* anxious. He's a details person, that's why he runs point on everything in the department. I know the whole world is upside down, but he's not a murderer." Iris glances up and Scarlett lowers her voice to a near whisper. "Him doing those things makes *no sense*. He's a gentle person, thoughtful. Kids make him nervous. *Iris* makes him nervous."

Mark groans. "Now I'm going to be sick." He says the word like the syllables themselves are disgusting.

Larson shifts in her chair. Scarlett was owed this meeting after they hauled Robert away for questioning, but she's skirting the edge of what can be discussed. And in another ninety minutes maybe, snow and ice will begin to fall. "I appreciate you talking with me. I'll be back in touch soon."

Mark leans forward. "I'm sorry, but I think a little more information is needed. We just learned that the man who's been in this apartment isn't who he says he is, someone who's been around Scarlett and Iris for the past two years. I need to know any information relevant to their safety."

Larson's gaze connects with Mark's. He's overcompensating maybe, but he's obviously unsettled. Why wouldn't he be? "Mr. Simmons, the details of the case are still coming in. Even if I could legally tell you more, there isn't much to say at this point. I assure you that Mr. Bruce is detained and being questioned as we speak."

"Okay, okay, I get it," he says, backing off. "Thank you for talking with us."

As Larson walks to the door, she notices Scarlett's and Mark's fingers lace together on the tabletop.

SCARLETT

Later, Scarlett refolds the dish towel she'd literally been wringing.

"He wasn't here to threaten me, he said he just wanted to explain. I was surprised when he came to the door, but why wouldn't I let him in?"

"Can I be honest about something?" Mark asks. Scarlett knows it isn't really a question; they were married for five years. "I didn't get a good feeling about him when he came to pick you up the other day. Something was off."

Scarlett leans her elbow on the kitchen counter, resting her head in her palms. "Why didn't you say anything?"

"Because I know it would've sounded like I'm a jealous ex, sensitive to you having male friends. That's all it is, right? Just friends?" He hunches forward as if about to pray.

"I told you that," she says, half–dreamy, half–sick, a montage of her interactions with Robert playing speedily in her mind: Robert orienting her to the department the way they had for Veronica, the two of them training for and then conducting the experiment, him picking her up for school, him bantering with Iris. Robert's eyes when he smiled. Never once had her intuition issued a warning. Had she been so imperceptive? But then, maybe he'd tricked everyone just as effectively.

No one else had seemed to suspect him either.

"It's like Larson said, though: this isn't proof he murdered anyone." The word feels ugly in her mouth, foreign. "What he said was that he got involved with drugs and that led to bad choices. Years ago," she adds.

"You have to admit it's incredible coincidence: two people in the department are killed within two days; then it's revealed that a person who knew them both spent time in prison, then changed his name. You don't have to defend him, you know."

"I'm not trying to," she says softly, her thoughts too numerous to coalesce. There's no value in arguing, Mark's mind is made up. Scarlett nearly says as much, but stops herself.

Obviously, it meant *something* that Robert had concealed part of his past, but his subterfuge *not* being proof of murder was disorienting itself, in a way. The obvious suspects were all around her, and yet, in her gut, Scarlett still suspects none of them.

Nor the five students they'd pushed toward aggression.

Or Tom.

"I'm going to get something from the truck. I'll be right back," Mark says and returns a few seconds later, his expression intense. Cold clings to his jacket. "Can we talk in the bedroom?"

She leads him there and shuts the door. Their thighs touch as they sit side by side on the bed.

"What do you think about me checking out of the hotel and staying here tonight again?" he asks.

The storm would begin anytime. Scarlett runs her hand through her hair. Her thoughts spin and her chest feels leaden from loss. "I want that, yes."

Mark draws a deep breath. "What if three of us leave tomorrow and don't come back? You could stay with me until you found a place, or maybe even we could find something together."

"I…"

"Do you remember how we started?" Mark asks.

"Of course, I do." They'd retold the story to each other and to friends and acquaintances many times. Revisiting it feels like a miniature psychological vacation from the hurt and dizzying turns of the last few days.

"I remember what you were wearing the first time I saw you

when you were working at that clinic," he says. "You wore your black–rimmed glasses back then."

He loved those glasses on her, quirky as they were, and always complimented them. "I was more of a secretary than an administrator and got restless behind that desk. You were the dashing pharm rep, before you went into medical devices, charming all the doctors."

He brushes the back of his hand over hers. "I hardly sold anything there. I only kept visiting so I could run into you. And then…"

"And then the holidays came. You went to a New Year's Eve party and told me the next day you'd wanted to kiss me at midnight, so you came to my family's house that afternoon. And then you charmed my parents and all my extended family too."

"I slept in a guest room with both of your brothers."

"Traditional family," Scarlett says.

"Definitely, but I always admired that about your family, even if your dad was a little standoffish."

"Not after we got married, and not after Iris."

"No, not then." Mark pauses. "Maybe you could transfer your credits to another college. Charlotte? Chapel Hill? I know it's a lot all at once, but this is crazy here, Scarlett. We both know your department won't be the same now."

"I'll think about it," she says. "But I know what you mean."

Their hands again brush against each other atop the duvet, the fabric cool on her wrist. It's then that he opens his jacket, then sets a wrapped object between them. "Until then, I want to show you how to protect yourself."

He opens the towel and reveals a black Glock pistol.

LARSON

The sky behind Larson is now iron gray as King meets her in the lobby of Dorrance's police headquarters. The interior smells like the rock salt sprinkled over the entranceway. Already, ghostly footprints have tracked it inside, Larson notices.

King taps his fingertips together. "I waited for you before asking any real questions," he says, hurriedly, leading Larson into the building. "I cuffed him as a precaution, but he's been fully cooperative. He's in the room we use for questioning."

Larson overhears an administrative assistant patiently giving directions on the phone, presumably to the parent of a student, while a uniformed cop who looks like a high schooler quietly pecks at a keyboard. Behind her, flecks of sleet tap the front glass.

Minutes matter now.

"Anything from Ms. Simmons about him visiting her?"

Larson shakes her head. "Nothing. Scarlett said nothing but positive things, which I can't tell if that's good or bad; either the two of them are either colluding or she was as shocked as we were."

Larson enters the building's interior hallway and sees Robert through a glass partition, staring straight ahead.

His expression is tense as she enters the room; Larson understands what Scarlett meant when she said he's always anxious. "Are you going to behave if we take off those cuffs?"

Robert nods.

She rests her hand on her Taser. "I wouldn't hesitate, just so you know. You're on the other side of the one-way glass now." Larson nods at the reflective space behind him.

"Not my first time, honestly."

"Do we need to read you your rights?"

"No. But I don't know what you'd be arresting me for; I had nothing to do with Joe or Elizabeth's deaths. I loved Joe. I was trying to help."

"You can have an attorney present, if you'd like," King says.

Robert's gaze swings back and forth between Larson and King. "I'll spare you guys the questions, I want this case solved as much as you do." He nods toward the entrance. "Unless one of you two did it, whoever killed Joe and Elizabeth is out there."

King shifts uneasily.

Larson understands Scarlett's reaction after he came over to her place, her affirming take on him. "Prison records don't stay secret anymore. You knew your background would come out. But you went ahead and reached out to me to run that little experiment. Help me understand?"

"It was a matter of time. I figured if I got some evidence for you that was worth following…"

"…it might distract us? Direct our attention away from your past?"

"That's the thing, Officer. My past *is* the distraction. I wanted to improve the investigation's chances, and I knew that once you guys found out about what I'd done, there'd be no way to help." He locks eyes with Larson, his voice breaking with emotion. "My record was going to make me a suspect, not to mention get me kicked out of the university. I thought I might as well help before either thing happened. How much of it have you seen?"

"Enough to know you were charged with manslaughter,

then pled to reckless endangerment, not to mention a half dozen drugs offenses, then served three years," King says. "And that you started going by a different name after you left California."

Robert's head sinks for the first time. "I have to say, I hoped to finish the PhD before it all got out. That's one thing about education, no one can ever take it away from you. But considering the last two days, I'm reconsidering what even matters. I don't know what's happening here. Or why it is."

Larson had heard the phrase about education before but had never considered its meaning literally. It was something her mother used to say while hemming the skirt of one of her stage outfits. She flashes to her mother's joyful tears when she got her acceptance to NC State. "Nobody can take it away from you if you went, Alana. You don't want to end up a washed–up singer like your mamma." Neither of them knew then that Larson would spend the better part of her spring semester in hospital suites. Less than a year later, her mother would be gone.

Larson draws a quick breath. "Maybe you thought the credentials would give you some credibility in explaining what you did."

"I anticipated how people would think about me if they knew." He motions toward the marks on his wrists. "Correctly."

Larson looks in Robert's eyes and realizes something for the first time: *he's relieved*. Whatever else happens from here, he no longer has to carry around the secret of his past. "So Thursday night? And last night? Where were you?"

"Exactly where I told you I was. There's no change to my story for the last three days, or for the last three years." He levels his eyes at Larson. "I was an addict, bad enough that I had to steal to keep functioning. My judgment back then was gone. I'd bought the stuff an hour before, I had a lighter under it to smoke it too. I was on probation, so three years was the minimum." He rubs his hands over his face.

"This started at UCLA?"

Robert nods. "I actually earned a master's degree online while I was inside. Plenty of time on my hands, and it's amazing what you can get done when you're clean." He pauses. "I didn't know that guy's name until my sentencing, but I still think about him every day. I was responsible. You know what they say about people getting into psychology to understand their own demons? I read about what Joe was doing here and wanted to be part of it."

Larson catches King's frown out of the corner of her eye. "Give us a minute," she says to Robert; then she and King reconvene outside the room, where King leans against the wall. His chin, she notices, has added a shadow of gray stubble.

"What he's saying tracks. We're missing something, and it isn't Robert's background."

King looks out the window. Pellets of sleet have begun accumulating across the walkway. "If we're going to send him home, now's the time. And he's right, what would we be charging him with?"

"It's the right call." Larson nods. "I'll go talk to him."

ROBERT

Robert rests his head on the table. What troubled him, now that he was confronted with what he'd done, was how easily he'd slid out of one life and into another. Not to mention his obliterating

Scarlett's perception of him. Psychologists encouraged change as a matter of course—but shouldn't adopting a new identity have been marginally harder?

The best explanation he comes up for how fluidly he compartmentalized his past goes back to toggling back and forth between his parents' houses following their divorce when he was a kid. Neither one wanted to discuss the other, and so he'd learned to simply never bring the other parent or home life up. Being an only child made this simpler, obviously, making his passage between households ghostlike. Day to day, it was as if the other home didn't exist. Jail, he thinks, was just a larger house to never mention.

Some things, a person wants to forget.

The door opens. Sounds from the front offices appear.

Robert looks up as Larson reenters the room.

LARSON

She pulls a chair away from the table and sits on the edge. "We're going to release you," she says. "I do wish you'd said something earlier."

"Understood. But to be fair, Detective? It wasn't some story I made up to complicate the investigation. I'm living a very different life now. A better one."

"I think you had Scarlett Simmons fooled," Larson says. "And me too."

"I wasn't forthcoming, true, but it wasn't a game, Detective."

They stand.

"But even if I had been engaged in some kind of malignant deception, dishonesty is pretty hard to spot."

Larson lingers as they near the door. "Meaning what?"

"Meaning liars get better over time," he says. "Not to throw myself under the bus here, but I forced myself to forget the past. Deceiving is a skill like any other. Anyone who's good at lying has read the room, picked up feedback, and incorporated it into their story. If they lie and *don't* get caught, they've just practiced for another repetition, learned another nuance about what works for them."

"That's comforting," Larson says. She glances over to where King takes a call, presumably from someone on the crime scene team. Maybe it's the suspects' cell phone location data.

"That's the liar's side though; the listener—the psychologist or the cop—we *don't* get feedback. Nobody circles back and debriefs us on how honest they were in an earlier conversation."

"This thing with you surprised me, I admit, but I usually know right away when someone's lying," Larson says. "My gut tells me."

Robert faces her. They look at each other for a second. "What would tell you if someone was lying to your face?"

"Body language, for one. People have a hard time looking you in the eyes when they're lying."

Robert's eyebrow arches.

"It's conventional wisdom," she presses. "You think that's *wrong*?"

"I know it is."

Larson already has too much to do for academic theories on dishonesty, plus the weather is deteriorating. And Robert's a bit of a know–it–all, not to mention a smartass, but then, so were her favorite professors. "Okay," she says. "I'll bite on this. How do you know it's wrong?"

Robert shoves his hands in his pockets as he leans on to the wall. "Not one single study has ever demonstrated lying decreases eye contact."

"None? You've read them all?"

"I have."

His confidence is impressive, she'll give him that, but apparently he knows what he's talking about, which is even more so. He'd tricked everyone around him for three years.

"I can name three studies that show sociopaths' eye contact actually *increases* when they lie," he says.

Larson's memory circles back to interviews she conducted in the past. It might have been good to talk to Robert just as she left the academy. "Okay, so what's your method? You said you studied all this before starting the experiment."

"You really want to hear about this?"

Larson shrugs. "If you can talk fast."

"Okay, there's a few things. Number one, you have to be nice."

"That simple, huh?"

"Well…that part is. An approach doesn't have to be complicated to be effective. Maybe it sounds a little sociopathic to say it helps to be charming, but being nice works a lot better than putting someone on the defensive."

Larson remembers what a veteran told her at the academy about how the "good cop" always got more information than the "bad cop." "Everyone wants to be treated with respect," she says, agreeably.

"And people open up when they are. Two, you can't challenge too early. If you do, the person will shut down, or if they're smart, they'll think fast and alter their story. It's better to make them feel safe while you keep slowly drawing out information."

"Make them *want* to volunteer things."

"Precisely. You get them talking, then lead them into giving up information that contradicts something you know is true. Like, 'Sorry, I'm confused, you said Officer King was part of the questioning, but he's been on vacation all week.' Then, they have to backpedal."

"Noted."

"But if you really want to trap them?"

"Go on."

"You ask a question they can't anticipate. That's what customs officials and bouncers at bars do. Like if a bouncer asks, 'Are you twenty–one?' the kid will say yes, but if they ask, 'What's your star sign?' they'll have to pause to do some math. If the person is actually of age, it's an easy question, but if not, they'll have to think, and those pauses tell you what's happened."

Larson smirks at the pleasurable memories of catching people flat footed in their lies.

"You're saying I should be nice, build trust, and don't challenge someone too fast. Ask some basic questions, then ask one they cannot anticipate and watch the lag time?"

"Pretty much, yeah."

Larson squints a little. "So you were home last night through this morning, correct?"

"I was, yes."

"By yourself the whole time?"

"Yes."

"No trip to the grocery or out to eat? Nothing like that?"

He shakes his head. "No."

"What did you make for dinner last night?"

Robert doesn't blink. "Nicely done. I made chicken soup."

"Okay, go home. But don't leave Shepard."

He nods toward the door. "You've seen the forecast. I'd be suspicious of anyone trying to leave town right now."

LARSON

Larson checks messages and waits while King drives Robert back to his car. She's sure he's instructed Robert to make no contact with Scarlett Simmons for the time being. When King returns, he carries a brown bag with a handle. He hands a container to one of the remaining deputies as he walks out. "You have to eat something. Last takeout in Shepard before the storm hits. I hope you like pad thai?"

"Thanks," Larson says. King sounds a little steadier than he had earlier, but still not good.

They make their way to a small but tidy kitchen with pale yellow walls. Food had been the last thing on her mind over the past three days, but now that it's in front of her, her stomach grumbles.

King fills two Styrofoam cups with tap water and sits beside her at the wobbly table. "I wanted to update you about the janitors who cleaned Hull Hall on Thursday night. Both have worked for the cleaning service that Dorrance contracts with for more than a decade. One has no criminal record at all, and the other failed to yield at an intersection five years ago—that's it. Neither ever met Elizabeth, and they knew who Joe Lyons was because he gave them each a Christmas card with cash every year."

"You said both, meaning two, but there were three janitors, right?" Larson twines the noodles around a plastic fork.

"Just the two. They work in pairs and only mentioned the other when I questioned them."

"I'll have to take another look at the tape, but I could have sworn I saw one more."

"Maybe one walked out and then went back in."

King's phone buzzes. He glances at it, then shoves it back into his pocket. "Damn spam calls," he says. They eat in silence for a minute, Larson grateful for a moment of relative stillness.

"You said something about having problems with psychologists that first morning in the hallway," King asks. "What was that about?"

Larson dabs her mouth with a paper napkin. The takeout is indeed delicious. "It's going to sound like I'm holding a grudge, and maybe I am, but it was an employment evaluation, my first job offer," she sighs. "Contingent on me passing a physical and psych exam. *No problem*, I thought. But I guess I was too comfortable with the psychologist and made the mistake of being open about my childhood."

"Your family was involved in something illegal?"

She shakes her head. "Nothing like that. My dad wasn't in the picture and my mom was a singer. I traveled with her all over the South. Weird way to grow up, I met my share of characters, but it was nothing shady. And we had literally no money. My mom's best advice was to go to college and get a steady job."

A faint smile forms on King's lips. "So you chose police work?"

Larson finally allows a sliver of a smile herself. "I thought I could make the world a better place, as naive as that sounds, so it seemed like a natural fit. But I guess the shrink had questions about having grown up around so much chaos and gave me a diagnosis, something like 'unspecified anxiety' during the evaluation. I feel like I…"

"Should have been less honest?" King finishes.

"Maybe. Her report made my hire probationary and got me a supervisor who picked apart everything I did for a year. It was part of the reason I moved here."

King considers this. "I get that. And Shepard *is* a nice place to live. This case is like nothing else in thirty years. When I pictured my last year on this campus, I didn't imagine a double murder."

Larson forks another bite. "People can sometimes be more evil than I ever imagined, but other times give me hope, if that makes any sense."

King folds his hands over his stomach. "I bet your mom is proud of you being a cop," he says.

"Thanks, but she's been gone a few years now. Cancer. Second year of college."

"I'm sorry."

Larson reaches into the neckline of her shirt and pulls out a long thin charm that glimmers as she twists it between her fingertips. "I keep this with me, I put it on this necklace after she died."

King squints at it, the sides of his eyes crinkling warmly.

"It's a hair clip she wore onstage. Fancy, right?"

"I'll say."

"I picture her wearing it sometimes, onstage and later as she changed clothes in our little motel rooms. She'd hold it up high over her head, and the little gemstones would twinkle in the light."

"Nice memory."

Larson smiles wistfully as she tucks it away. "She'd tell me it was really a star and that when I held it, I should make a wish."

CHAPTER 8

SCARLETT

Iris presses her nose against the sliding glass door, the sky rolling in like upside-down waves. The snowfall they'd seen over two North Carolina winters is languid by comparison; this storm feels urgent, aggressive.

Iris traces an angle across the glass with her fingertip. "The snow's falling diagonally," she says, beaming from having come up with the word.

Glass containers rattle in the kitchen as Mark opens the refrigerator door. "Plenty of milk and eggs," he calls.

He sounds dutiful again, responsible. Present.

It's like they never divorced.

Connections deepen by sharing experiences, she thinks. Especially traumatic ones.

Her gaze turns back to the snow. Robert is somewhere out there. She wonders fleetingly if she'll ever see him again.

In front of her eyes, the landscape softens gauzily.

She wonders if it's possible for a person's heart to continue trusting someone after doing so stops making logical sense.

Is that what faith is?

ROBERT

Robert reaches for his duffle bag in his bedroom closet, tucked between the stack of notebooks he worked on in jail and his camping equipment. The synthetic material coolly brushes the back of his hand as he grasps the handle and then begins loading his clothes into it. There are far better ways to pack, but he can't think of any right now. In fact, he hardly *can* think—the whiskey he picked up on the way home from the police station has calmed his nerves remarkably. It's the first drink he's had in a year, but he needed it.

Outside, a branch cracks from the weight of the snow, and his head swivels at the sharp sound. Jail made his startle response hyperactive. He takes another sip of the whiskey, then sets the glass on the floor beside him, the amber liquid bitter in his throat. He's had no time to grieve Elizabeth's murder—he's worked side by side with her for a year—then his mentor was plucked from the face of the earth. *Joe. Joe Lyons is dead.* The fact washes over him in waves, each one making his stomach sink further. His thoughts spiral like a flock of startled birds: Who could have? And why? And where are they now? And who's most in danger? Scarlett? Iris?

His mind instinctually focuses on them.

His plan to engineer some sort of observation opportunity for Larson had failed, spectacularly. As had his intent to keep his past hidden. Scarlett's expression as he told her the truth and then her guiding Iris's eyes away from him as he was handcuffed had been more than he could bear. After what happened to Elizabeth and Joe, Scarlett and Iris's sense of safety in this world had been hanging by a thread.

And his lie had incinerated it.

Deep down, he'd known the day was coming. The truth always comes out. He'd jumped at the chance to work with Joe Lyons, who'd seemed to intuit his sense of duty and responsibility. And had accepted him. And after three years in jail, he'd been fully prepared to concentrate on work, which was easy compared to surviving inside. His focus had been monastic. It earned him respect around the department. He'd found his chance and nothing was going to screw it up. He was not going to get in his own way.

And he hadn't.

Fate, or someone bearing the force of fate, had.

He grabs another stack of his clothes and shoves it into the bag. He'll stay around long enough to help find the murderer, if he doesn't go crazy with regret and worry first.

From outside comes another crackling sound and he jumps. *Another branch breaking,* he tells himself.

Until three days ago, nothing ever set him off in placid Shepard, North Carolina. Now he's edgier than he's ever been. He pictures the vacant eyes of some of the men he met behind bars.

One thing about the storm, it makes the getting around harder for everyone, the killer included.

Robert imagines the angle of his Civic in the driveway.

In this snow, he doubts he could go anywhere at all.

LARSON

The springs of King's chair squeak as he rocks in it. "You're not thinking of going out in it?" he asks. At the other side of the lobby, his assistant peers out the window, her expression awestruck.

"It's not my favorite driving weather, but at least there'll be no one on the roads."

"There's a layer of ice under that snow," he says.

Larson stops herself from wincing. He means well. She wants to tell him crime hasn't taken a break, even if they're all acting like it, and that their case is gapingly open. And she hadn't given the truck's four-wheel drive an adequate test in years. "I need to get into Lyons's office to look for the other threads of that report. That subject line especially is still gnawing at me. *Ani*," she says. "And, besides, no one in their right mind will be in the building now."

"She's right, boss," the assistant calls. "There aren't many vehicles that can get around in this."

"Including mine," King says, his eyes on Larson. "Meaning if anything goes south, there's limited backup."

She pats King's arm as she slips her satchel over her shoulder. "I got this."

LARSON

Larson is greeted with a familiar beep as she swipes her access card and enters Hull Hall through the front entrance. The building is silent except for her footsteps, and she brushes her fingertips across the hair clip hanging around her neck. Funny how telling King the story of it brought her mom to the forefront of her mind. She formed a habit of talking to herself when she was scared as a kid—a "scared of the dark" phase when a dash from a bedroom to a kitchen for a glass of water seemed eternal. Now she bites at the inside of her cheek. She's always done her best to not let anyone see her fear.

Or let anyone think of me as an amateur.

You become the person you pretend to be, she thinks to herself, faking courage before she feels it.

Maybe that's what Robert did.

The doors upstairs are all closed, and the hallway is nearly pitch black; the CS investigators must have turned out the lights as they left, not having guessed anyone would be coming in later. The emptiness reminds her of the hallways in *The Shining.* She's never believed in ghosts, but standing outside the room where Elizabeth Colton was killed prickles the skin on the backs of her arms.

The doorknob to Lyons's office frigid is against her palm. Her fingertips brush against the wall until she finds the light switch and flips it on. Fluorescence flickers in both directions.

Inside, she finds a white circle on the far wall, marking off a splatter pattern of Elizabeth Colton's blood. Her throat tightens as she examines the glossy flecks dried onto the drywall. She swallows hard, composing herself. On the floor, an area is taped off in thick white strips where other evidence—a footprint, she guesses—has been collected for analysis. The remainder of the office is a peculiar mix of tidiness and disarray, but some areas appear untouched: his bookcase, for instance, appears to be just the way he left it three days earlier. A framed photo of Lyons and his daughter hiking rests there, their expressions exhausted but joyful. But other spaces seem hastily reassembled. Books and papers are stacked helter-skelter, and a jar of paper clips rests on its side.

Beside the desk is the filing cabinet, whose drawers open with a metallic whoosh. She wonders if she can thank the CS investigators for popping the lock or if someone has already rifled through. The files inside are organized with labeled green tabs atop each folder, Lyons having been as fastidious in his office as he was in his home. Larson's fingertips walk across the tops as she scans them—a large number related to coursework and various research projects he'd concluded. Near the middle, she finds the forms used for the deception project—a few photo-copied surveys with Post–it Notes indicating studies they'd been used for in the past. Her eye catches on one of the items: Fear of the Worst Happening, on a four–point scale from "Not at all" to "All the time."

She thinks, *Who would have imagined?*

And then, *What had Tom made of this form as he filled it out? Was he underreporting his anxieties, like he'd said, to get close to Elizabeth?* Larson pictures him in his disheveled apartment, either the least calculating criminal imaginable or the most cunning deceiver of all time.

She refiles the page and continues further into the cabinet until she finds a section marked "Forensics." There, files are listed by number, like the one printed at the top of the report Lyons sent.

Her gaze flips back to the green tabs atop the files until they lock onto one.

20146470

She opens her phone, then scans for the document in her email. The number is in bold at the top: 20146470.

This is it.

She pulls the file and finds a stapled report inside. It was written by another psychologist, Simon Martin, but the file numbers match. A Post–it Note is attached to the first page that says: received: 10/09/2017.

Then it clicks: This is a document Lyons received related to the report that he wrote, the one he sent her. There had been multiple asterisks in his text noting that new information had revealed the Patient had been dishonest during the examination.

Maybe she's about to find out why.

Lyons's chair squeaks slightly as Larson sits in it, the building silent otherwise.

She begins to read.

REPORT OF FORENSIC EVALUATION

—CONFIDENTIAL—

NAME	xxxxxxx xxxxx
DOCKET NUMBER	x
DATES OF INTERVIEW	October 2013
DATE OF REPORT	
DATE OF BIRTH	91
COURT	Criminal Court for
JUDGE	Honorable x

CHARGES

    Attempted First–Degree Murder

    Especially Aggravated Robbery

    Aggravated Assault with a Deadly Weapon

    Possessing a Firearm during Commission of a Dangerous Felony

    Criminal Impersonation

EVALUATOR

> Dr. Simon Martin
>
> Licensed Psychologist
>
> Certified Forensic Examiner

REFERRAL

> Xxxxxxx Xxxxxx has been charged with first–degree murder, especially aggravated robbery, aggravated assault with a deadly weapon, and possession of a firearm during the commission of a dangerous felony. All of these are alleged to have occurred on xx/xx/xx. They are also charged with criminal impersonation, which is alleged to have occurred at the time of their arrest on xx/xx/xx. They are currently free and awaiting parole review by the Alachua County Jail. Their attorney, Dxxny Ysssss, has requested this evaluation to help determine competency to proceed with the case and mental condition at the time of the alleged offenses.

Great, she thinks, another maddeningly redacted report to pore over. Confidentiality may have an essential purpose in clinical settings, but it certainly doesn't facilitate criminal investigations. The gender–neutral pronouns don't even let her rule out half of the population. Even the attorney's name is redacted.

She sighs as her gaze flicks up to the top of the page.

Dr. Simon Martin.

The report is ten years old, but with any luck, Dr. Martin has a clear memory of this case and records to go with it. And if he starts talking about client privacy, she can snag a court order.

She reads on.

FORENSIC NOTICE AND INFORMED CONSENT

At the outset of our first meeting, I clarified my role as an independent medical expert who would provide opinions about their case. We discussed the possibility that my evaluation could be beneficial, neutral, or detrimental. I explained that I would not be providing treatment and that, with their permission, I would send their lawyer a copy of my full report. I also told them that the report and anything they told me might be relayed to the court and the prosecution. I also told them that they were free to refuse to answer any of my questions. After my explanation, XX xxxxx was able to say that I was on "no one's side" in this case. When asked who would get a full copy of my report, they said their lawyer. They also recalled that a copy might be given to the judge. I reminded them that the prosecutor would also get a copy.

When we met the second time, XX remembered that I...

Larson skips ahead through the rest of the legalistic jargon and names of esoteric psychological assessments Simon Martin used and continues.

Educational Records from XX Ysssss

School records from ninth grade year indicate persistent,

severe behavioral problems that were diagnosed as oppositional defiant disorder at XX Catholic School.

XX is an extremely bright student... XX does well on tasks that require sustained attention. XX will get work done quickly and accurately...

Occasional horseplaying with other students, very aggressive with staff to the point of being assaultive, has shown aggression toward classmates as well... XX's aggression toward staff and continued horseplay with other students, which leads to fights and altercations, is a major concern.

Larson's eyebrows knit together. The report drifts into nonspecifics, but there is mention of a Catholic school. That's something, at least. She turns the page over. More than half of it is blank.

She's reading a draft, a report that was started but left incomplete while Dr. Martin was still compiling records.

Larson checks the time on her phone. 8:40. Late to reach someone, but not out of the question if she acts quickly.

She does a quick internet search on her phone for "Simon Martin psychologist" and finds several in the United States. The first one finished his doctorate two years earlier, so he would have been in high school at the time of this evaluation.

She scrolls to the next one, who seems like he's worked in Oregon and rural Washington state, nowhere near where Lyons practiced. She stumbles on an article he's written that's been published online: "Music Therapy in Geriatric Settings: Reflections from Group Work." Nothing about forensic work at all; this therapist has spent the bulk of his career in a different setting.

She wipes the sweat from her palm on her pants, gnawing at her lip. *Come on*, she thinks, following a link to the third Simon Martin.

She brings the screen closer to her face. Larson has a sense of lightness in her chest, like the feeling she gets the instant she solves a word puzzle, her gut seeming to recognize he's the author even before her eyes find the words to identify him. The photo of Simon Martin is fifteen years old but was taken in front of a plain–looking glass–and–brick structure that she can identify before reading the sign behind him: Central Florida Correctional Institute.

Bingo.

This Simon Martin is a prison psychologist, or at least was at one time, and the report she's holding made it into the hands of an academic with a background in forensic assessment.

Finally, a connection.

Larson finds her way to the prison's website and gives it a once–over. For obvious security reasons, staff and their home addresses aren't listed on these websites, but she checks for any personal listing, or maybe a board of directors.

Nothing.

She does a map search and Google tells her the prison is in Starke, Florida, which looks about the size of the town where she grew up. In her experience, professionals with advanced degrees tend to live in more densely populated areas, so it seems unlikely Simon Martin would be living nearby, even if he worked there. It's worth a quick search though, she decides, but that turns up nothing.

Larson expands the map's search radius.

The two closest cities are Jacksonville, which she recalls

only from its interstate traffic on a trip years ago, and Gainesville, the university town. She's never been there but remembers the father of one of her friends cheering loudly for the Gators on Saturdays in the fall, dressed head to toe in orange and blue.

She glances again at Dr. Martin's photo. He looks to be just out of med school, so is maybe in his late thirties by now—around the age that a person might have small children and consider the cost of living, and just maybe be attached to a school with such a loyal fan base. On a hunch, she searches Gainesville first.

She types "Simon Martin psychologist Gainsville" into Google and an office address immediately appears. It looks like he worked as an associate within a larger practice. The website seems up to date when she clicks on it, but when she scans the names listed, there's no Simon Martin. Maybe he went out on his own or joined a different practice, but no Simon Martin seems to be working as a psychologist in Gainesville. And late thirties is too early to retire.

Then she notices that below the associates, a *Sandra* Martin listed as the office manager. It's a common last name, but excellent odds she's related to Martin.

Certain that King is still where he was when she left the station, she calls him for the number, and a moment later, he's found it and reads it to her. "A lot easier than digging through the internet like this," she says. "Thanks."

Larson steps into the hall and paces as she calls Sandra Martin. The rows of closed doors create a sense of being inside something sealed, like a submarine. She's never been squeamish, but sitting alone in that office was a lot to take. And out here she can see if someone is coming.

The call picks up on the third ring, a woman's voice. "Hello?"

Larson stops. "Yes, hi, this is Detective Alana Larson from the Shepard Police Department in North Carolina. Sandra Martin?"

"Yes?" The voice is tentative with a detectable slur.

"Ms. Martin, I'm trying to reach a Dr. *Simon* Martin. Would you happen to know anything about his whereabouts?"

There's a pause. "I'm sorry, did you say you're a detective?" The slur is pronounced. Larson wonders if she should have waited till morning to reach out.

"Yes, ma'am, Detective Alana Larson. Are you familiar with Dr. Simon Martin of Live Oak Psychological Associates?"

Another pause, then the scrape of a chair being dragged across a floor.

"Ms. Martin, I..."

"Simon was my husband. What are you calling about?" Her voice is tinged with anger suddenly. "What does this concern?"

"You say he...was your husband. Are you in touch with him?"

The woman coughs a weak, dry laugh. Larson switches the phone from one ear to the other, the device warm against her cheek. The hallway feels airless suddenly.

"No one has heard from Simon in ten years."

"I'm sorry to hear that." Larson's stomach plummets. She begins to ask what happened when Sandra continues.

"He disappeared. He left for work one morning but never made it to the office. I assume he's not alive; there was never any sign of him here or anywhere. There was no note or sign of a struggle or anything. And Simon was a happy man, not the restless type. He wouldn't have just run off."

Larson's eyes shift back to the date on the report. "This was ten years ago? Do you happen to remember when, exactly?"

"Of course I remember. It was the twenty–second of October."

October, the month Simon was working on the report that's tucked under her arm. "Was there an investigation at the time into his disappearance?"

"Well, yes, of course, but the police were bumbling. I'm sorry but they were, and they never turned up anything. They wouldn't even start looking for him for two days, even though I begged. They just kept asking me questions like did we argue much and did he ever take spontaneous trips. I tried to tell them, but no one would listen. It was like he vanished into thin air. His car was found on the side of a rural road a week later."

Any investigation would have records, Larson thinks, potential hints about what may have happened. Unlikely she'd deduce the solution to a pored-over old cold case ten years later, but the thought flashes in her mind.

Sandra asks, "What's this about? You said you were a detective, do you know something?" Her voice is urgent, almost pleading.

Focus, stay on topic. "Ms. Martin, I'm sorry for what you've been through." Ten years with an unanswered question must have been an eternity, Larson thinks, her mind spinning, trying to think of the best way to answer. "I was trying to find information about a case he must have been working on at the time, a forensic report."

Larson hears ice rattle in a glass.

"Simon worked at the prison after graduation but had joined the practice two years later, where the money and hours were better. He mostly took cases from local attorneys, I…don't remember anyone…now."

Awaiting parole review, the report had said.

"We had a good life and so many plans," Sandra continues. The break in her voice at the word *plans* grips Larson's heart like a vise, but her mind whirs.

The last thing Joe Lyons did before he was killed was send her a report on someone Simon Martin had evaluated.

Someone whose lies *invalidated* the assessment, lies that were noted in the assessment.

Larson pictures King at his desk, then checks the time again.

She needs more time to concentrate, to work on fitting these pieces together. "I'm sorry to have bothered you, ma'am. It's part of an ongoing investigation in another case, but I'll circle back to follow up with you if I learn anything else."

"That's…it?"

Larson catches a glimpse of herself in the darkened window through Lyons's office door. Outside, the storm has stopped, and beyond her reflection is a blanket of white that seems tauntingly still. "I'm very sorry, but I will check back," she says, before adding, "I promise."

Larson closes her phone.

She starts toward the door when her phone buzzes in her hand. King.

She's slightly out of breath as she answers. "Hey, you're still at the station? I'm on the way back. Patrick, you're not going to believe what I've just…"

King interrupts. "Alana, you're still on campus? You're not going to believe this."

"Try me."

"An alarm just tripped, there's a break–in. It's a residence hall and not Hull, thank God, but it's close. The security company just shot me an image."

"Could you tell anything from it?"

"Not really, no. It looked like a guy, but that's it. They're wearing a hat in the video. I just wanted to let you know, most likely it's completely unrelated to the case."

"What are the odds of a break–in right beside our crime scene? What's the address?" she asks, trotting down the stairs as King reads it. "I'm on the way."

LARSON

The headlights of Larson's truck splash over the front of the dorm as she pulls into the nearly empty parking lot. At the far end is a vehicle so snow–covered, its make is indeterminable, obviously left behind over the break. She squints at the building's façade, rows of dark windows punctuating the red brick. Hard to believe how full of life a college campus can be one day and so desolate the next.

Larson climbs out of the truck. She verifies the address King texted her and steadies herself; this case has her questioning her own perceptions. A flash of light streaks across a window on the second floor, quick but clear—a flashlight on someone's phone, maybe.

Larson's shoes sink several inches with each step as she approaches the front entrance. White puffs of her breath disappear around her in the cold. Aside from her footsteps and breathing, the night is silent.

When she reaches the steps, she sees fresh tracks leading toward the front entrance, and then away, headed around the side of the building. Whoever is inside looks like they tried the front door first before finding another way in. *Clearly not a mastermind burglar*, she thinks, following.

At the side door, the lock lights up green when she swipes the all–access key card that King gave her. She shakes off the cold and looks down the long hallway before climbing the stairs to the second floor, where the flash came from. The upstairs hallway is just as dark as the first floor and smells vaguely like the vinegar–based natural products used on campus. Cleaning services must have given the building a once–over after everyone took off. An exit sign glows ghostly red.

"Shepard Police," she calls out.

There's no answer. Her fingertips brush over the handle of her Taser, her gun. Her pulse throbs in her temples as she takes a few more steps, snow moisture on her shoes squeaking with each step.

At the far end of the hall, a figure flies from one side to the other.

"Shepard Police, step back out into the hall." The quiet that follows sounds like a faint ringing in her ears. "I know you're there. Either you're coming out on your own, or you'll be taken out against your will; your choice."

A hand emerges from the doorway.

Followed by a face wearing a scared expression.

Tom.

Larson releases the handle of her pistol as her eyes pinch momentarily shut. It's like this kid enjoys playing with fire so much he'll risk getting burned.

Again and again.

"It's just me, just *me*," he says, his hands trembling as he raises them in a gesture of surrender. "I'm sorry. So sorry, so sorry."

Larson takes half a step forward. Tom Campbell had seemed squirrelly during their interview but harmless enough. Had she read him correctly? "Come all the way out into the hall and put your hands on the wall beside the door. Is it just you in here or did anyone come with you?"

"I'm alone, by myself, here all alone." His eyes are saucer sized, and his head leans forward penitently. His hair is oily and tucked behind his ears, and he's wearing some sort of baggy outfit Larson can't quite discern in the shadows.

"Stand in the hall with your hands on the wall," she tells him, and he does as he's told.

What it must be like to be so keyed up, Larson wonders, flicking on the room's light for a quick look around. It's an office for the residence hall: two neatly arranged desks with sleeping computer monitors, knickknacks, desk calendars.

From the window, she can see the angled roof of Hull Hall obscured by hazy white halos around the parking lot lights.

Could he have come in here to have a better look at the building? She hears a small thud and turns—Tom's knocking his head into the drywall as he mutters something to himself, his teeth audibly chattering.

Larson leads him into the office and motions toward the chair on the far side of the room, then sits in a chair closest to the door. "Come in here, Tom. Let's talk."

His eyes dart around the room. The overhead light is pale

blue. "How…did you find me in here?" he asks, lowering himself into a chair.

"You set off an alarm on the way into the building. Then I followed your footprints."

"Oh," he answers. "Am I in trouble?"

"It's called breaking and entering, but let me worry about that. What were you *thinking*? After everything that's happened, you wanted to put yourself back *here*?"

Tom's gaze drops to his shoes. "I…was cold. My heat got turned off."

Larson recalls the destitute sketchiness of Tom's apartment—the glances she felt from the boys congregating in the parking lot, the rusty rail on the stairwell—she hadn't felt so uneasy going into a residence in a long time. Then, once inside, squalor that telegraphed unease. "High functioning and low functioning at the same time," was how King had described some students. The description certainly fits here. "It was turned off just today?"

"About two…hours ago. I thought I could make it, but then the snow started, and I knew I wouldn't be able to get out all weekend if I didn't leave right then." He gestures toward the hall. "I used to live here. Before."

Before you were kicked off campus, Larson thinks. "Last year, you mean?"

Another nod.

She glances at the time, weighing her options. "Stay here, don't move." She moves into the hall, closes the door behind her, then calls King.

"I was getting worried," he says, his tone edgy.

"Tom Campbell is our cat burglar. He says his power's off and he's trying to stay warm."

"You think that's right?"

She angles her body away from the door, still able to see Tom's profile in the harsh office light, his knee bouncing frantically. "He says it's his old dorm. I believe him."

"So, what now?"

"Patrick, I'm taking him to the hospital. I can't leave him here but can't kick him out into the snow. This kid needs help, not a jail cell."

"You're in your truck?"

Larson lets her shoulder touch the wall. She can hear the slight edge of judgment in King's voice. Transporting him in her personal vehicle is hardly procedural. Still, the snow is six inches deep; no one is coming to help. "I don't know what choice I have," she says.

"The hospital is three blocks from that end of campus. Consider me on call, okay?"

Larson ends the call and reenters the office, Tom's hair flopping into his eyes as his head swivels around. "I'm going to get you some help, but our transportation options are limited, okay? I'm going to cuff you, but you're not under arrest, okay?"

He turns and puts his hands behind his back with practiced fluidity. "Okay."

He smells vaguely sour, unwashed, as she secures the cuffs on his wrists, taking care not to tighten them excessively. She folds the sleeve of the heavy shirt he's wearing to check the cuffs, then realizes there's another, identical shirt underneath. "What is this you have on?"

"Just something I put on to keep warm. Layers, you know."

"Layers," she agrees. "Hmm." The shirt's material is a smooth, synthetic material. She looks over the dark collar. "It's a uniform, Tom. Where did you get these?"

"The supply closet downstairs. There's a stack of them folded up," he says. "They're what the janitors wear."

She swivels Tom toward the door, her mind spinning. She'd seen three janitors in the security footage for Hull Hall, but King had only spoken to two. They hadn't mentioned a third.

Larson has a guess why.

"Show me where."

CHAPTER 9

LARSON

The following morning, King hands Larson a Styrofoam cup with steam rising from the surface. His office dates him: sports memorabilia from the last thirty years adorn the walls, the most recent date stopping at around five years earlier, when he presumably ran out of space. Most are from Dorrance's athletics, baseball specifically (the football team has never been terribly competitive), and she's reminded of how much a part of this college community King is. It's hard to picture him retiring and living anywhere else.

She knows she's forgetful when she's preoccupied, but today was a hell of a time to walk out without her winter coat. She accepts the cup with shivering hands, then brings King up to speed on Dr. Simon Martin, his widow, and the circumstances of his disappearance.

"Any of our suspects live in Florida?" he asks.

"Not that we've seen so far. Not one. It's a lead, but it's from twelve years ago in another state. We have to pull up that footage of the janitors again. Before I took the kid to the hospital, I realized if he could find them, anyone could. You said you talked to two on that team, but I was sure I saw someone else."

"On it." King rubs the back of his crew cut as he drops into his desk chair. His fingertips tap the keyboard as bluish light washes over his face. Larson moves behind him to see the screen. She leans so close to King's shoulder that she forces herself back a few inches when she senses him register her nearness.

It takes a minute to find the video clip, then to toggle to the time in question. The cursor lingers above the double triangle fast-forward icons, images blurring through time when nothing happens on the screen.

Then, it does.

A blurry figure in a navy-blue shirt appears with another beside him.

"Stop," Larson says, pointing. King freezes the frame and backs it up a few seconds, making the figure momentarily appear to walk in reverse before he starts the video in the usual direction. It's the same footage she watched the night before at her kitchen table, but she watches unblinkingly now.

One janitor enters the building, then a second. "These are the two you talked to?" she asks.

"Uh-huh." He glances at a note on his phone and reads their names slowly, taking care with the pronunciation. Time seems to move in slow motion, haltingly enough that a quick memory of the inaccuracy of eyewitness testimony flashes in her mind, something she'd read in—she's sure—her introductory psychology class, years ago.

When King restarts the video in slow motion, a sleeve appears at the side of the frame.

King's finger jumps, stopping the clip. "There's our friend," he says. They lean so close, the screen looks pixilated. He backs up the clip a half a second to replay as the sleeve moves forward and back until King lets it pass.

"This is what you saw?"

She nods. They watch for another minute, but nothing else appears. Larson can see why the image didn't solidify clearly in her memory; it's little more than a flash.

"It isn't much, is it?" King turns, his eyes reflecting her disappointment.

"It may not even be a third person. From that angle, we can't tell if one of them just walked past the camera again. And neither mentioned seeing another janitor?"

He shakes his head. "I didn't ask specifically about a third person, but they both said they saw no one else at Hull Hall that night."

Larson's eyes pinch shut. She hears the squeak of King's chair swiveling, and they open again as he's saying, "This investigation could take a while. I know you're eager, but…"

"And you know it's the first case like this in years. The more time that goes by…"

"The more evidence gets destroyed, I know. We'll find him, Alana."

Her eyebrow rises. "You're assuming it's a 'him,' but there are two men and three women in that department that knew both victims."

He folds his hands on his stomach. "Not nearly as many women commit these kinds of crimes. And whoever it was over-powered Joe Lyons. He's a former triathlete, and even if he's not in peak condition anymore, he was still strong and capable of defending himself."

"Unless he was completely caught off guard. But let's say for a second it was a male who attacked him, the two obvious connections are Chris Collins and Robert."

"Robert has a record and deceived everyone around him the whole time he's lived here. But I don't know how he would have set up that observation session with you after killing two people. No one calls the police after they've committed two murders. No one. Unless he's completely batshit."

"Or knows exactly how to lie."

King hesitates. "I suppose. But the one I don't really like is the other one, Chris, who assaulted Tom Campbell one day earlier and has a gun registered to him. We could charge him with carrying it on campus."

"Now?" she asks.

King nods like he gets the point. Chris may have broken the rules by taking the registered gun out of his car, but pursuing his arrest on the matter would squander their resources.

"Well, he needs the fear of God put in him about his carrying limits, at the very least. But I still don't think it means nothing. At some point he saw himself as capable of violence."

"I know it," Larson says. "But he has absolutely no motive beyond the fact that he didn't particularly like Elizabeth Colton. No one in the department seemed to."

"Except Joe Lyons."

King's computer emits a short chime, and they both look at the screen. A new email has arrived. The subject line is clear as Larson leans in. "That's the cell data," she says.

"Most of it," King says. "Scarlett and Veronica have a different carrier than the others, but theirs should be in anytime."

Larson pulls a chair toward the desk, and King angles the screen so she can see it. They scan the data points and times, matching each against the crime scenes and grad students' addresses.

One point stands out immediately: Britt Martinez was nowhere near Chris on the night Joe Lyons was killed. "He insisted she was with him."

"A few times," Larson says.

"I'm going to go over this, see what else pops up. Where are you going?"

Larson is already at the door.

LARSON

Larson calls Chris Collins from her truck.

"Detective?"

"Mr. Collins, I'm going to need you to clarify the statement you made earlier about Britt Martinez's whereabouts on Thursday evening."

"At your service," Chris says.

Larson grits her teeth at the polish of his voice. "You're at home?"

"I am."

Larson knocks on his door five minutes later as dialogue from a movie filters into the hall. She tenses with impatience. Only now does she sense how acutely she's pressuring herself to make an arrest. She's about to knock again when the door opens.

Chris wears sweatpants and a loose shirt, a glass of brown liquor balanced in his hand. He makes a sweeping gesture that reminds Larson of a matador taunting a bull. "Detective, come in." Behind him, Britt Martinez is seated on a couch in the living room. Her boots lay carelessly on the plush rug, and her feet are tucked beneath her. She squints at Larson but makes no indication she means to stand.

"Ms. Martinez," Larson says, her tone sounding forced.

Chris closes the door behind her with a dull click, then points a remote at a massive screen, freezing the movie they're watching. Christian Bale's character casts a serious-looking gaze.

Larson sits as Chris drops down beside Britt, balancing his glass in his hand. The only sound is the rhythmic lapping of flames in the fireplace. "Two visits in two days, Detective. What can we do for you?"

"You lied earlier about Ms. Martinez's whereabouts on the night Joe Lyons was killed. I need to find out why."

Chris opens his mouth, then closes it again. His eyebrow arches as a slight smile forms on his mouth. "*Lie* is a very strong word," he says.

"I'm not playing games, Mr. Collins, two people are dead. You told me something that was untrue. I'm here to clear that up."

Chris's smile fades as quickly as it arrived. "Two people I knew well. And yes, I'm glad you're not playing games, I'm not either."

He looks at Britt, who sets her jaw. "Same," she chimes in.

These two, Larson thinks. Her fists clench with frustration even as her gut sends zero fear signals. "You're aware that lying during a police investigation is a crime?"

"I am, yes. I'm trying to help."

"During our first interview, you told me that Ms. Martinez was with you all of Friday night, but your cell phone data clearly shows you parted ways just before nine thirty." Larson turns to Britt. "And you didn't refute it, even though you knew it wasn't the truth."

No response.

"Why?"

"You're wasting your time here," Britt says flatly.

Larson notices Britt's eyes for the first time—clear, sharp eyes. She feels like saying she'll decide what's a waste of time and what isn't, but instead says, "Then help me understand why your location was worth lying about."

"I didn't want you distracted chasing down false leads. Keep your suspicions on me, but you can leave Britt out of this."

"You know best what's a false lead and…"

"I know what she looks like to someone who doesn't know her," Chris interrupts, his head motioning toward Britt. "And no, I don't particularly want her front and center in a murder investigation. You can leave her alone."

"Chris," Britt says.

Chris turns to Britt. "She thinks what everyone does: that you look like the girl with the dragon tattoo, and I look like the president of a pledge class." He turns back to Larson, roughly setting down the glass he's holding on the coffee table, where the condensation makes it slide a little. "Right?"

"Look," Larson says. "Right now you can't provide an alibi for her, and she can't for you, no matter how much you think she's a good person. So, unless you have concrete knowledge of where…"

"I don't have to know where Britt was to know she couldn't have done it. She'd faint at the sight of blood."

Larson leans back, her expression an invitation for Chris to continue.

"When we were kids…" he pauses to take a breath.

"We survived a mass shooting together," Britt finishes. "In Elliston, Colorado. They happen every week now, but it was less common at the time. Chris saved my life."

Larson's eyes widen. She remembers grainy footage of a shooter being jerked away in handcuffs, distraught parents sobbing in parking lots. Then, temporary media coverage. "That was at a church camp, in the early two…"

"It was the summer of 2004," Chris says. "We were eleven years old and didn't have anything in common then either."

Britt rubs at the semicolon tattoo on her arm. "He was the popular kid that I thought wouldn't talk to me; then he ran into the hallway and grabbed me when the shots started. I froze and he…" She stands, pinching her lips tight, then exits the room.

A moment later, Larson hears the rush of water from a sink in the bathroom.

Chris's expression softens. "She hadn't uttered a word the whole camp, and kids were starting to say things. My sister is deaf, and people making fun of her made me sick, so I kept an eye on her. The whole camp was singing songs, then split into our breakout groups in classrooms when the screaming started. I smelled smoke and knew the shooter was nearby. Britt froze in the hallway, so I ran from where I was and dragged her into the room used for arts and crafts." He pauses. "The shots were deafening, but I couldn't tell where he was, so I grabbed a tube of red paint off the counter and smeared it onto her face and shirt, then laid on top of her until he passed by. That's how we made it: the guy thought we were already dead."

Larson swallows, or tries to, a lump of frustration and rage caught in her throat. She's seen the abundance of news reports over the years and has an identical question each time: nothing can be done?

"We just started praying together. She was so scared, I realized she'd peed. We stayed on the floor until we heard police radios."

Larson's eyes water while her lungs won't let her draw a full breath.

"I was a little jerk then, just like I'm a jerk now, but here we are. We look after each other."

It was a concept she'd learned, ironically enough, in her psychology class: trauma bond.

The two of them had a relationship forged in fire. Larson clears her throat. *Everyone has their own kind of armor,* she thinks.

"If you're suspicious of how she looks, think about why she needs that much armor."

Everyone has their own kind of armor, Larson thinks. She clears her throat. "One part of the evidence includes the word *Ani.* Does that mean anything to you?"

"Ani? No. The name?" Chris shakes his head.

From the bathroom, the sound of rushing water abruptly stops. Britt emerges, toweling her face. "I was at home with my cat the last two nights, which is where my cell phone was too," she announces. "Not that me and it are always in the same place."

Noted, Larson thinks, aware that she'll be cross-checking Britt's statement with the cell data King is getting in. She thanks Britt and Chris for their time and then leaves.

Outside the door, she shivers as she searches her jacket pocket for her truck key. None of the facts of her investigation have shifted significantly, she knows. Understandable as them covering for each other is, it's also clear that Britt and Chris have a history of scheming.

A second later, King calls.

"Alana, we need to search Scarlett Simmons's apartment."

"...*what*?"

"Today."

Larson stops in her tracks, the squeak of her shoes echoing in the empty hall. How can this be true? All she can say is, "Scarlett?" It feels like she's carefully assembling a puzzle only to have the table she's working on knocked over, scattering the pieces. She pictures the nurturing way Scarlett comforted her daughter, her forthrightness in answering questions. Of everyone who'd had contact with Elizabeth and Joe, Scarlett was the last person on her radar.

"Alana, the other part of cell data is in. All the other grad students were home when they said they were. Scarlett was in Hull Hall at the approximate time Elizabeth was killed, then was at Joe Lyons's residence between 11:40 and 12:00 a.m. the night he was killed. Veronica was at Lyons's exactly when she said she was, then evidently went directly home. No one else but Scarlett went near his house."

Disbelief rises in Larson's gut. What she wants to tell King is: *Scarlett is smarter than that.* But is that the way crimes are committed? Crimes of passion, like murder? No, her training taught her murder is almost always an impulsive act. One committed with little planning or forethought. The covering up comes later, which sets people up to get caught. New evidence can be created while old evidence is being destroyed.

But Scarlett?

Just maybe this is an instance where Larson will have to check her biases, then think critically and with an open mind. Earlier, King had said himself that he assumed the killer was a male, but the tone of his voice is resolute.

"The data doesn't lie," King says. The variation in his voice tells her he's walking, maybe already digging a path for one of the cruisers in the snow, or has had his friend with the snowplow cut out a path for him. Except the roads are unnavigable in anything other than a four–wheel drive, and even that is a stretch of good judgment.

No, he'll have to wait for her.

"I'm on the way. I'll drive us."

It's a short drive to the station. King's words echo in her mind. *The data doesn't lie.* He's right, of course; the data tells a story, and it's her job to listen. It reminds her of what Robert had told her about social science research the day before. Was the work they did studying deception so different from police work?

What if there's information in the apartment that would make the entire case click in her mind? Like the sharpening of an image through a lens, just before a photo is taken?

She rounds the last curve before the Dorrance Police Department. The windows look nearly golden against the snow–covered woods behind the building. King is silhouetted in the light, a grim expression on his face.

SCARLETT

Scarlett kneels beside Iris's bed, a triangle of light from the hallway spread across the floor. Faint sounds of the spring training baseball game Mark watches filter in from the living room. He's been a baseball fan for as long as she's known him, and the commentators' monotone and the occasional crack of the bat are a familiar comfort.

Iris's eyes are focused on the picture she's drawing. "Mom, Dad said we're snowed in?"

Scarlett feels herself smile for the first time in days. It's impossible not to in the presence of such complete innocence. "Yes, everyone is. Everything's going to be fine, kiddo. Do you believe me?"

Iris nods. "I always believe you, Mom."

Don't ever grow up, Scarlett thinks. She closes the door softly, then makes her way into the living room, where she hears the crackle and rip of packaging tape as Mark assembles a cardboard box he'd recovered from the crawl space. It's an absurd gesture, but Scarlett is warmed by it anyway. It's one of the few that survived her original move into the apartment; she'd saved it to transport something loose like clothes for donations.

"Aren't you getting ahead of yourself, just a little?" she asks, dropping onto the carpet beside him, then tucking her knees to her chest. The edge of her foot touches Mark's. It was how they used to sort out problems, sitting on the floor together. They'd called it getting "grounded" when they first started dating.

"So maybe I'm excited." He smiles. "Besides, there isn't much to do at the moment."

"There's baseball," she says, nodding at the decade-old screen. It had been the TV in their guest room before the divorce. She hadn't wanted Iris to spend too much time in front of it and knew she wouldn't have time for it much herself.

"I think my team may be more put together this year. Maybe

a playoff run. Hey, I think the snow has finally stopped," he says, nodding toward the glass door. "Hopefully the roads will be clear enough by tomorrow afternoon that the moving companies reopen. I can get a few more boxes then. We could have you into my condo by the middle of the week."

"Mark, I love the sound of that, for a lot of reasons. But what about my lease?"

"There's a fee for breaking a lease, I'm sure."

She nods.

"So, I'll pay it."

"I forgot how persistent you are!" she says, her smile wide now, warmth flooding her chest.

"You forgot?"

No, not really. She shakes her head.

Maybe they *could* work. It's been done before, certainly, couples divorcing, then getting back together. And why not? Maybe it would be a twist in a love story. Most of the best fortune in her life had been unexpected, like getting into the PhD program. She'd wanted to be a professor all her life but Mark's work schedule never seemed to allow it. His being so supportive now feels like a godsend.

Two years earlier, she hadn't thought she'd had a chance in hell when she'd hit "Send" on her application, but when Joe Lyons had called and offered her the position, she'd struggled to believe the acceptance was real, then proceeded to wrestle with impostor syndrome for the first two semesters despite feedback from academic journals, other students, and Robert's consistent reassurance.

Outside, an engine revs in the street, then goes silent.

Mark stands at the slapping sound of two vehicle doors

closing. From the side profile of Mark's face, she can tell his expression is serious.

The hair on the back of Scarlett's neck stands up.

"Someone's here," he says.

SCARLETT

There's a knock on the door that's firmer than when the police came earlier. "What's going on now?" Scarlett asks Mark, as if forgetting the previous days' reminder that anything can happen. He stands beside her as she looks through the peephole, then heaves a sigh and cracks the door.

Icy air filters inside, chilling her bare arms and the tops of her feet.

It's Officers King and Larson, their expressions concerned.

No, it isn't concern in their eyes and the tightness of their mouths, she realizes.

It's suspicion.

King speaks first. "Ms. Simmons, we have a warrant to search your property. We'll need you to stay out of the way while the search commences, either under supervision in the front room or in the vehicle outside. Are you clear on that?"

Scarlett senses vertigo, teetering over someplace high and then dizzied in a whoosh of air. She looks at Mark, whose expression is unreadable. Does he suspect something about her too? "But my daughter just laid down in the bedroom," she says, as if explaining an obvious reason why a search can't happen.

Larson steps forward. "I'm sorry, she'll have to wait out here with us. Hopefully, this won't take too long."

Scarlett nods, her trust in Officer Larson a steady foothold but her mind a swirl of confusion. She's about to ask if she can be the one to go into Iris's bedroom to wake her when she hears her daughter's voice peep behind her. "Mom?"

And all their heads turn at once, both officers looking away as the girl launches into her mother's arms. "They're just here to do a job, honey," she whispers into Iris's ear before repeating Larson's assurance that hopefully the search wouldn't take too long.

Mark steps forward, his tone aggravated as he holsters his hands on his hips. "May I ask what in the world this is about? I mean, I get that it's your job, but really? You need to search *this* apartment, right now?"

King eyes him levelly. "I'm sorry, sir, but yes, we do."

Mark frowns as he glances momentarily at Scarlett and Iris, then back at King. "Do you have a warrant?"

King patiently nods. He produces a copy of the document, which Mark's eyes swing back and forth over. "I'll need you to wait out here with Officer Larson," King says to him before slipping covers over his shoes, then turning to Scarlett. "Are there any weapons or illegal items inside the apartment that I should know about?"

Her head begins to shake back and forth before it stops. Her eyes widen. "There's a gun in the drawer of my bedside table."

"Which belongs to me," Mark volunteers loudly. "It's registered in my name and is perfectly legal to have here."

King nods. He steps into the kitchen and examines items along the countertop. With a small camera, he takes three snapshots.

"May I ask what you're looking for in the *kitchen*?" Mark asks in a huff.

"No," King answers.

Scarlett pours Iris a glass of milk, and they all four sit at the kitchen table in silence, Iris in Scarlett's lap. She watches her daughter dreamily run a fingertip through the condensation on the side of the glass as Scarlett kisses the top of her head. Occasionally, they hear the creak of a closet door opening or the thump of a cabinet shutting from the back bedroom. Twice, Scarlett hears the squawk of a police radio, then King's voice muttering in a low monotone. The stillness of the emptied town lies outside the windows, and the air inside the apartment so calm, the ticking of the hallway clock is audible.

Soon King appears in the hallway carrying evidence bags, wearing white paper booties over his shoes. The image is comical enough that Scarlett nearly laughs, but as she sees the way King and Larson look at each other, her stomach registers a gut punch.

When Larson follows King into the bedroom, it plummets.

Scarlett and Mark share a look across the table. He reaches over and touches her hand. "This is nonsense. It's amateurish, and don't think I won't contact an attorney." Mark says, squeezing her hand, and as her eyes well up from the tension, he mouths, *It's okay*.

A minute passes. When King and Larson reappear, she's holding handcuffs. "Ms. Simmons, I need you to stand up and turn around for me."

The preamble is so ubiquitous that Mark bolts up from the table. "What?! What in the hell?"

But Scarlett lets Iris slide off her lap as she stands and turns, her heart thumping in her chest. A second later, her thighs are pressed against the table and Larson has latched her hands behind her back with a sickening *zip*, her mind too panicked to register the coldness of the metal.

Could the theft of the laptop…?

No, no, that has nothing to do with this.

It's King who says the words that burn into her mind, "You are under arrest for the murder of Joseph Lyons. You have the right to remain silent. Anything you say can be used against you in a court of law…"

The moment becomes surreal montage of images, Scarlett's emotions somehow both raw and numbed. Tears stream freely down her cheeks as she cooperates, telling Iris, "It's okay, stay with your father." She falls habitually into prayer that somehow the situation will end, because there's no reason for events so fickle and horrible to continue.

But other thoughts scream throatily inside of her too. That what's happening is *impossible* and that there's been a mistake or a plot against her, and that she had no need to feel the guilt or shame she somehow does because she's *completely innocent.*

Outside, the streetlights' halos make her dizzy and vaguely nauseous. Her shoes crunch through the snow as Larson explains she's being transported to a holding cell in a personal vehicle because of the emergency weather and that she can call an attorney there if she wants to.

Mark looks down at her from the window of her own apartment as she's taken away, his and Iris's silhouettes backlit by the golden interior light.

It's all enough to make Scarlett wonder: *Am I losing my mind? Have I hallucinated parts of what's happened?*

And even more crazily: *Does this have something to do with the things I took from the department?*

Or am I missing something? Taking for granted a sharp fragment of information that would fit precisely into recent events and clarify them all?

And is it possible that I've not looked clearly at a critical fact for a long, long time?

LARSON

Back at the police station, Larson closes the door to King's office and drops into a chair opposite his desk. She pictures the way Iris looked at her mother as she was led into the night, and pain tears through her heart. The act may have been dutiful, but it was the opposite of why she'd ever wanted to become a police officer. "I feel sick, like we just ripped a mother and child apart."

"We couldn't delay that search, Alana, and it turned up even more than I'd expected."

Larson runs her hands through her hair and gestures toward the table as if they're literally about to lay the evidence across it. "Take me through it again, please. Slowly this time."

King takes a deep breath. "Okay, for starters, the cell data alone was enough for a warrant. Scarlett was exactly where both crimes were committed at precisely the times they happened."

"But she *admitted* to being in the department on Thursday night, and her daughter was with her." Flashing through Larson's mind is an image of the gore in Lyons's office; it's unimaginable

Scarlett stepped away from her kid, inflicted that kind of violence, then calmly drove home—all without the daughter sensing something was off.

"Yes, and then there's the fact that she texted Lyons about twenty minutes before he was killed. One word: *Home?*" King sighs as if Larson's objections are trying his patience for the first time. "Alana, that wasn't my favorite moment as a cop either, believe me. But of all of the grad students, two went to Lyons's house: Veronica, who was there for about ten minutes before going home, and Scarlett, who arrived an hour later and stayed for about twenty minutes. Veronica admitted she was there. And if she *had* killed Lyons, Scarlett would have discovered the body, then presumably would have called the police. Instead, she denied having been there at all. And then there's what CS found in the search. They called me too, while you were questioning Chris Collins and Britt Martinez."

Larson's head shakes back and forth, her eyes asking for detail.

King levels his eyes at her. "Direct evidence was present. Items DAs need. Forensics hasn't analyzed everything yet, but some parts match her remarkably."

"Like?"

"Like the size five women's shoes in her closet. That's a very uncommon size, and size five prints were found at both scenes. Now anyone could have been in Lyons's office, and there actually *are* seven different prints in that office, but the size fives are fresh. And they match the tracks in the snow outside Lyons's house."

Larson hesitates.

"And through the blood in his kitchen." King pulls a notepad toward him and uses it as a coaster for the coffee cup. "I think she's been lying but we don't want to believe it."

Larson winces, her voice rising defiantly. "Maybe I *don't*, fine, but I'm getting a little tired of data that doesn't make sense."

"There's more. Under the sink in her bathroom was a T–shirt with flecks of dried blood on it, stuffed up in the plumbing like she didn't have time to get rid of it discreetly. Obviously, labs aren't back on it yet, but I'm willing to bet that blood belongs to one of two people. But the last part isn't what I found in the apartment, but what CS found in the creek near the base of Lyons's driveway: a knife, serrated edge, five inches long. It was tossed into the water but lodged into the rocks instead of washing away."

"The murder weapon."

King nods. "And from the description they gave me? It matches the set on Scarlett Simmons's countertop."

Larson squeezes her hands together, then releases them, her fingertips still numb from the bitter cold outside.

"One slot was empty in the block on her countertop," King says, standing.

CHAPTER 10

SCARLETT

The holding cell is actually warm, which is a small mercy, Scarlett thinks, staring up at the air vent lodged between the bars and the ceiling. A flap of white masking tape—or something like it—clings to one of the slats, undulating with the flow of air. She paced after she was first brought in but eventually took off her shoes and laid atop the bunk for hours, feet tucked into the blanket, which is army green and oddly, comfortingly soft and thick. The lights dimmed after what she guessed was 9:00 p.m., but there was never any chance of sleep.

The night passed something like a rumination within a dream, like a living nightmare.

Now, faint light at the door's edge tells her night has passed. She's been waiting.

A bolt slides through a door at the other side of the room, its click echoing over the cell's unforgiving surfaces. She slips her shoes back on as a man in a uniform appears—she'd seen him the day before—even in her delirium, she'd thought he looked too young to be a cop.

"Ma'am, if you'd like to make your phone call…"

"Okay," she agrees, then waits patiently as the officer undoes the latch. She walks briskly to the office where the officer directs her for her call, which is empty aside from a standard office desk and chair.

"I'm going to give you space for your call. I won't listen in, you have my word, but I'll be able to see you the entire time, just so you know. Turn around, please," he says, unlocking her handcuffs, then switching on the office light. "You have fifteen minutes. If you finish early, just signal me, and I'll come back for you. There are cameras all around the building, and that glass is unbreakable, so no ideas about making a break for it. Dial nine to get out."

"Sure thing," she agrees, rubbing her wrists as she hurries inside. Through the window, icicles along the gutter have begun to glisten and drip water in the bright sun. The storm came in quickly and left just as fast.

The guard repeats his uncertain warnings about the allotted time and then disappears.

Scarlett draws a deep breath as Mark answers. She pictures his hair being wet and combed back as if he's just showered, and flecks of snow clinging to the shoulders of his barn jacket. "My God, are you okay?" he asks. His tone is something like the father of a teenager who's had a minor car accident.

"I'm…okay. Where's Iris?" she asks.

Mark clears his throat. "In the hotel here with me. Do you have any idea how traumatic that must have been for her? Seeing her mother cuffed?"

She pictures Mark's frown. Her lips pinch together.

He sighs heavily. "Look, I'm sorry, it's obviously not your fault, none of this is. I'm just feeling protective at the moment. I have a call in to an attorney for a referral, I'll make bail after I talk to him. I'm figuring this out as we go along. I don't have any experience with these things."

"Thank you. It'll be okay."

"I don't know how you *can* be okay in this situation, but that's you I guess." He hesitates. "It's something I've always loved about you."

Scarlett swallows, her grip tight on the receiver.

"Look, is there anything you haven't told me about what happened over the last few days? Anything at all about your relationships with those people? I'm not questioning you, but the lawyer may ask."

"No," she says. "Nothing. Where are you and Iris going now?"

"We have to go back to your apartment to get some of her things, clothes, and favorite toys. I called the station, I talked to every cop in Shepard, I think, before they stopped answering last night. The detective, Larson, called back. She insists on being present while I go inside to make sure I don't tamper with evidence. I'm meeting her at your place in fifteen minutes." She hears him shuffle his feet. "I don't know what we'll do if this *thing* drags on for a while. School will start back in a few days, and the other kids might talk. I don't want her to have to live in the middle of this."

Scarlett looks at the ground, the tip of his shoe nudging a small pebble.

She nods to herself. *This thing.*

"I love you, Scarlett. I'm sorry any of this happened, but especially this part. Hopefully there will be good news from the lawyer soon and the bail will go smoothly. I'm going to go by your apartment, then take Iris to breakfast. I'll come there after I talk to the lawyer."

SCARLETT

Scarlett returns to her cell, and after a short time, low voices rumble in the hall, instructions delivered and acknowledged. The deputy again unlatches the door. "You have a visitor, ma'am," he says uncertainly.

Scarlett is no lawyer, but she's pretty sure her taking visitors at the moment is against the rules. But then, when was the last time anyone was arrested for murder in Shepard? Then transported to a holding cell and kept overnight at the tail end of a blizzard? Probably no one was brushed up on every protocol. The poor deputy was clearly doing his best.

Scarlett folds her hands expectantly. *He's here so soon*, she thinks.

But it isn't Mark who appears.

Britt's hair is brushed back rather than molded into spikes, and she wears a gray sweater beneath her usual black jacket. She's without makeup, which makes her look five years younger and unarmored.

She takes a small step forward as Britt strides toward the cell. Britt's glare probably withered that deputy, Scarlett considers.

"The guy said I have ten minutes."

"How did you…?"

"I'm persuasive. Look, I wanted to see you and hear what in the *fuck* happened,"

Britt's brusqueness is an odd solace. "They came to my apartment and arrested me last night. The older cop, King, told me after I was booked that there's evidence connecting me to both crimes. He said I should call a lawyer. Mark's doing that, he said. So, I'm waiting to hear more. How did *you* know I was here?"

"I'm restless; I went for a walk and saw the detective's truck in front of your apartment last night. I live two blocks away from you, remember?" Britt explains, glancing around.

Right, Scarlett remembers, Britt walks everywhere. Besides, it's probably safer than driving at the moment.

Britt eyes the bars like she means to bend them. "This is bullshit, you didn't kill anyone. Do you, I don't know, need help with your kid or anything?"

A week earlier, Scarlett may have had to stifle a laugh, but now simply shakes her head. "She's with her father. Thank you for believing *I didn't do it*." Her voice cracks but Britt waves away the emotion, then pulls a folding chair from the wall, turns it around, and sits.

"I don't see how there's more evidence connecting you to what happened than any of the rest of us."

"I don't either, but they must have something. I'm here."

Britt's brow furrows like the circumstances have given her a headache. "Look, none of us killed them. Veronica's a supposed legal expert but seems too dumb to have carried it off. It's a wonder she knew how to drive herself up from New Orleans. Robert *loved* Joe so much that he stuck up for him at every turn.

Which leaves, you, me, and Chris. I know *I* didn't do it. And you're so pure it actually makes me sick, but you can't help it so I don't hold it against you. Remember last summer when that frog was trapped in the ladies' room? You caught it and carried it outside. I would have smushed it, I *should have* smushed it, but you jumped in and saved its little ass. You're no murderer."

"And Chris?"

"Chris, I've known practically my whole life. I've talked to him every day for the last fifteen years. We grew up in the same town, I've met his family, and he's met mine. I've cleaned up after his parties; we've spent holidays together. Remember what Joe said about assessments? They're just efficient ways of finding information that you'd come to over time? When you know someone from the beginning, they teach you what they're capable of and what they're not."

Scarlett nods. She's always liked that idea about assessments too.

Britt hesitates. "But there's something I haven't told you."

LARSON

Larson pulls in to a parking space beside Mark's BMW X5, the drive to Scarlett's apartment having become all too familiar. He'd insisted on going back into the apartment. Just standing by as he gathered a few of Iris's things seemed reasonable in her guilty frame of mind. At least the roads are slightly clearer now, she thinks, occasional patches of wet asphalt peeking through the ice. She pictures King's friend running one of the few plows through the night, imagining the amount of coffee it must have taken to keep on. Another two days, and regular vehicles might be driving again in this town.

Overhead, the sky has turned bright and expansive. It would be a beautiful day to be off, she considers, maybe sitting with a book in her living room beside Oscar. Instead, she's back to work, the truck's shocks squeaking as she shifts into park. King was right, an investigation like this is a marathon.

Mark opens the SUV's rear door, then leans inside. After a second, he returns to the driver's side door and restarts the engine. "She doesn't want to come in, and I have to say I don't blame her," he explains. "She doesn't want to revisit the scene from last night."

Larson glances back once to see if she can lock eyes with the girl but sees nothing through the BMW's dark tint.

"I know better than to leave a kid in a hot car in the summer, but this will only take a minute," he says, seemingly to himself as his phone begins to chime. Mark looks at the number, then flashes his index finger as he begins backing toward the sidewalk. He leans over. "Would you mind if I take this? It's the attorney."

"Go ahead, no rush," she says, imagining the level of recalibration that must be happening in the three of their lives. She leans to the SUV's rear window, visoring her eyes, and makes out a small hand waving inside. Larson opens the door and finds Iris buckled into the seat. "Good morning," she says, rubbing her hands over her arms as a warm burst of air escapes the interior. "I might sit beside you while your dad takes that call. Would that be okay?"

Iris nods. Larson climbs in and closes the door, the interior cave–like from the deep window tint and textured with the smell of vehicle leather and shampoo. The floorboards and seats are generally tidy—certainly more well-kept than Larson's beat-up truck—but Larson moves a plastic grocery bag to the center of the back seat. Inside are a few small items and a crumbled receipt. "You guys went to the store this morning?" she asks, making conversation. Over Iris's shoulder, Larson spots Mark pacing the sidewalk, his lips moving quickly, phone pressed against his cheek.

"My dad had to get contact solution," Iris says.

"That makes sense. It's good to have."

The girl nods and gestures toward the left side of her face. "He only wears one though, on this side." Iris's tone is calm, like she's describing an imaginary friend. "Because he has Annie in his eye."

Larson's head swivels around. The hair on the back of her neck has stood up. "What did you say?"

Iris shrugs. "He gets tired of people asking about it though, so he wears a contact lens on just that side."

"Who's Annie?" Larson asks, masking her urgency.

"That's just what he calls her. She hides in his eye. One eye is different than the other."

Sweat forms on Larson's cold palms. "Hang on, okay? I have to talk to someone." She finds her phone and calls King's number. When the voicemail comes on, she sends a text. Patrick, send someone to Scarlett Simmons's apartment now.

"Did I say something wrong?" Iris asks.

"No, no, you're okay," she says. "How long have you known about Annie?"

When Larson looks up, Mark has stopped pacing.

He is looking right at them.

SCARLETT

"The night Elizabeth was killed," Britt says, "I heard her talking with someone in the hallway; then she went back in her office for a few minutes before going to Joe's office. The next morning, I saw the police cruiser outside. I heard a deputy by the front stairs was saying Elizabeth's name into a radio, so I went around the back stairs, then took the elevator to our floor. I managed to get into her office before they saw me, and opened her computer."

"You didn't tell the police this?"

"I don't *trust* the police, you Girl Scout... I trust Chris. And...mostly, you and Robert. *Mostly*. After, Detective Larson saw me in the hall and I had to play dumb like I'd just come into my own office from outside..."

"How did you...?"

"*Listen*, because Elizabeth had never logged out. I looked at her sent email folder and there were just messages to our group. Then I checked to see the last things she looked up. Her last two search terms were Joe's old firm with Jason Gates, Gates–Lyons Assessment, and a medical term. Anisocoria. Do either of those mean anything to you?"

Scarlett had never before felt her blood turn cold.

Grew up in the same town.

Met his family.

...teach you what they're capable of and what they're not...

Scarlett's head begins to shake back and forth, "That *can't* be right."

The door at the far end of the room clatters again, and King steps through. Behind him is the deputy who'd let Britt in, his shoulders slumped. "Ma'am, you're not supposed to be in here. I'm going to need you to leave immediately."

"I need to make a phone call right now," Scarlett calls out.

"We can discuss that after your visitor leaves. You've taken your call this morning."

Scarlett's eyes shift back to Britt. "How fast can you get to my apartment?"

"I walked here, and the roads are shit. It's on the other side of Shepard. Why?"

"Ma'am," King says again, his tone sterner than before.

Scarlett's cheeks press against the bars like she means to push through. "*Listen*," she tells Britt. "Call Robert. Tell him to go to my place as fast as he can, tell him to not let Iris out of his sight."

BRITT

Britt nods as King approaches, reaching for her arm. She ducks his grasp and turns toward the hall, her phone already lit up in her hand.

King pulls the door open so Britt can pass, then closes it firmly, following her toward the lobby. Their footsteps echo in the enclosed space. "Young lady, I could place you under arrest right this second," he says.

The hallway is narrow, and the glass doors at the entrance are rectangles of white light.

"Shut up and listen," Britt tells him. "Find Doctor Jason Gates in Charlotte. Joe Lyons's old partner. *Now*. Ask him what he knows about a patient with anisocoria."

King's eyes widen from the urgency in Britt's voice. "What's…?"

"The medical condition anisocoria. *Go now, run!*"

Britt bolts from the station lobby into the snow while King repeats the name and diagnosis to himself and scrambles down the hall.

KING

Britt Martinez gives King the willies. But she's obviously an accomplished researcher, and the urgency in her voice sent a chill up his spine. Any other day, he wouldn't take directions from a recent suspect, but Jason Gates had shown up in Lyons's background check and nothing about the case has fully added up so far.

Scarlett Simmons doesn't fit the profile of a killer, and her eyes had flashed genuine surprise when she understood she was a suspect.

He's long considered his ability to read people a strength. Maybe all cops do.

But first impressions can lie.

His chair creaks as he logs on to his computer and navigates to the listing for a consulting firm Britt had called out. He finds the number easily, glances at the time, and calls.

One ring, then an answer. "Hello?"

"This is Officer King from the Dorrance University Police Department calling as part of an investigation. I'm trying to reach Doctor Jason Gates."

"This is Gates." It sounds like the man is around King's age. King hears him mutter to someone nearby, then a click. "I used to work in Winston–Salem with Dr. Joe Lyons in a practice that specialized in forensic assessment, and at times, his consultant. I saw the news this morning, it comes as a shock. What can I do for you?"

King rocks forward in his chair. "The investigation is ongoing and we may have some questions for you in the coming days, but for right now, I was hoping you could tell me about a patient who might have suffered from a condition called, and I hope I'm pronouncing this right, anisocoria."

"Just a second, let me get to my computer."

King hears a door close and shuffling sounds in the background. "Unlike Joe, I computerized our old records. The law says you have to keep them seven years post contact. Detective, there are confidentiality concerns about disclosing information on patients, I…"

"With all due respect, Doctor, Lyons was murdered. Whoever killed him may be at large, and I'm trying to keep this community safe. Take me to court later."

"Understood." Keystrokes are audible in the background. "Searching using that keyword through all our files."

A pause.

"Here. Oh, I see. It was a divorce case about four years ago, a young couple, one child. Joe was called in to do an evaluation. There aren't many reasons psychologists get sued, but one is evaluations involving child custody. Parents don't like their rights being taken away. They look for someone to blame, so Joe dotted his i's and crossed his t's. He…interviewed the father and gave him a number of tests. When the results came back inconsistent, he apparently got concerned; it can happen if a patient is misleading. There are a number of notes. Yes, there's a note about a patient's eye condition called anisocoria, where the pupils are different sizes. Quite uncommon, often the result of trauma to the eye. Joe dug into the patient's past, very deep, for any records related to his history. Initially, he couldn't find much."

King looks at the time. He's been on the call for three minutes.

"It looks like Joe eventually traced the husband's records back to a boarding school where he went years earlier, then connected those records to a forensic report from a…"

King hears keys tapping.

"…a Simon Martin in Gainesville, Florida. It was a murder case. It turned out the husband had dropped part of his name and the wife didn't know his full history. Joe was legally obligated to keep the material confidential, except for the patient and his attorney, who he obviously disclosed it to. After that, the husband dropped the case and settled, knowing he'd been found and that his past would come out if he pushed it and he would lose the case."

"And the patient's name?"

"Things don't always seem dangerous at the time, you know. You work with a lot of people, start forgetting there are real monsters in the world.."

"I need a name, Doctor."

Another pause.

"The patient's name is Mark Simmons. The wife was a Scarlett Simmons."

King drops the receiver and runs.

LARSON

Mark pockets his phone as he circles the back of the SUV and lingers at the base of the stairs. "Ready, detective."

Larson turns to Iris. "I want you to do me a favor, okay? Just stay here in the car. If more officers like me arrive, let them know I'm upstairs?"

Iris nods.

The stairs creak as Larson follows Mark up to the apartment, dialing and redialing King's number. What are the chances "Annie" means something more than a figment of a kid's imagination?

Mark opens the door and pushes inside. All the lights are off, and the apartment is eerily still—abandoned, like a place in some zombie film where humans haven't lived in weeks.

"I'll go in Iris's room now, okay?"

Larson nods, staying beside the door. She hears the shush sound of a wooden drawer opening, then Mark's voice. "We didn't have any wherewithal to pack anything last night; Iris was beside herself, wearing the same clothes since yesterday. And I'm always so silly about winter clothes. They seem so cumbersome, still."

Larson examines a photo of Iris hung in the hallway. She's beside a lighthouse on a beach, smiling toothlessly as she shields her eyes from the sun. "Still?"

There's a slight pause. "I grew up in Florida."

In the bedroom, a drawer slams closed.

Larson jumps as it does, her conversation with Robert from the day before reentering her mind. What were those steps that he'd told her?

Don't rely on body language or eye contact.

Check. She can hardly see Mark directly from the angle she's observing him.

Be nice, Robert had said. *Nice works. Don't challenge or push too fast.*

Larson hears the rolling sound of the closet opening, then the slipping sound of plastic on metal as Mark sorts through the hung clothes.

She tries King's number again, but it goes to voicemail like before. "I'm jealous," she says. "You must've gone to the beach all the time."

"People say that but not as much as you'd expect. Just daily life like anywhere else, going to school, playing sports. My dad worked in a downtown office. The beach was mostly tourists."

"I get that," Larson says. "People just idealize where they vacation."

"Maybe, yeah."

Be strategic with evidence.

"You met Ms. Simmons in Florida?"

"No, I met her up here. I had a job in medical sales, and she was doing intakes at a psych clinic. I guess she always knew she wanted to be in the field." The closet door closes with a click. His voice is so calm, so casual, almost as though he forgot he was irritable a moment earlier. A second later, Mark emerges from the bedroom and passes Larson in the hall. "I'm going to grab a few of her bathroom things, a toothbrush."

Larson nods. "Sure."

"I haven't lived with her for a few years, and you didn't ask for my two cents, but I really don't think she did anything like what you guys suspect." His voice echoes off the tile and glass. "She's always been a little competitive but not...vindictive."

A drawer slides open.

"How often do you get to visit up here?"

"About once a month." The drawer closes.

The same amount of time the security camera on the side of Hull Hall has been disabled. Mark knew neither one of the victims, but he's had access to this apartment the whole time. She rests her hand on her gun as Mark appears in the hallway, more quickly than she'd counted on, grinning at her. Can he see the change in her eyes? She can't tell. She's never been much of a deceiver, always straight–up. What people see is what they get.

"Ready?" he asks.

Her pulse pounds in her throat. What she wants is to be behind him now, so she steps into the living room.

Mark senses she hasn't moved. He's almost to the door when he stops.

Ask the unanticipated question, then watch them think.

They lock eyes.

Sociopaths actually show more eye contact.

Larson clears her throat. "How many janitor uniforms did you have to try on before you found one that fit?"

He springs at her fast, like he'd anticipated the challenge, wrapping his arms around her legs and driving her backward into the sliding door. When her head slams into the glass, the crack so loud, it sounds it feels like it originates inside her skull. Larson's hand is on her gun, but Mark grips her wrist, knocking it free. Two quick punches to her temple stun her, her vision blurring as she tries to stand, his forearm bearing down on her throat.

Everything spins.

The little girl is in his back seat, she thinks. King's the only one who knows where they are, and he's at the station. Concepts dissolve into fragments in Larson's mind, then begin falling, falling. He's turned her over, his elbow now around her throat as he drags her down the hall into the bathroom.

Larson looks up at him as her feet kick wildly, searching for leverage. His mouth shows the strain of pulling, but the calm in his eyes deepens.

From this distance she can make out the faint line of his contact lens.

He's fooled everyone. Including Scarlett, Larson realizes.

Another punch to Larson's head makes half her vision go momentarily black. White–hot pain shoots across her forehead before his arm loops under her legs; he lifts her, and for the first time she understands how physically powerful he is. The side of her shoe catches on the wall, but he knocks her leg down. She drops for an instant, then her head slams again into something hard and ungiving. Her legs and her back hit it, too, her hand sliding across something wet and moisture rising through her clothes.

He's dropped her into the bathtub. Larson partly recognizes a subtle scent around her, something sharp and floral. She tries turning onto her side but his hand is firm on her shoulder. "I'm sorry," he says, his breathing slightly labored. "I didn't want any of this for you. It's nothing personal. You'd already arrested her. You could have let this go."

Larson opens her mouth but words don't come out. What Mark must have done flashes through her mind: killed Joe Lyons and let Scarlett take the blame.

Wanted Scarlett to take the blame.

Had Elizabeth known?

He leans so close, Larson can smell the citrus of his after-shave. After all her training and experience, she knew officers got killed on duty. She'd read the stories, overheard them discussed at the station. Once, she went to a fellow officer's funeral. But it never occurred to her that her life would end this way.

Mark pulls a knife from his pocket.

She's seen in the last four days what he can do with one.

He presses it to her throat.

Then, he stops.

Through blurry vision she watches his head jerk up.

He's heard something.

She hears it too.

A car door closing, then a little girl's voice.

Then, another car door closing.

Mark pushes away, and she can feel his footsteps through the floor.

They're here, she thinks. King is here, just in time. He's called others. He has a gun trained on Mark Simmons right now. She tries again to stand, but her right wrist screams with searing pain—something structural happened inside it when he knocked the gun away. It won't take an X-ray to show it's broken; through her left eye, she can see it's bent unnaturally. Larson draws a deep breath and raises her left arm, her hand slipping along the side of the tub as she attempts a grip to pull herself upright.

She wants to get in front of Iris, to protect her; no kid should see what's likely about to happen.

Outside, an engine revs.

Then, footsteps quickly approach. Mark is above her, breathing more heavily, his eyes wide. "Going, going, going..." He's panicked, talking to himself, she realizes. "Don't go any…" His gaze darts around the room before landing on her belt. He yanks the handcuffs off with such force that her torso jerks upward. He takes hold of her wrist and pulls it upward, adrenaline resharpening her consciousness.

She yells out from the pain, a scream that echoes around the small space. Then she hears two quick metallic *zips* and understands in a flash what he's done: handcuffed her to the rounded ceramic bar above the soap dish in the wall.

Her shoulder is on fire as she pulls against the tightness of the cuff, her hand and forearm already purple from the fracture.

"Mark, think," Larson manages to say. "This can end okay. Your daughter…"

But Mark opens the knife and runs it down Larson's forearm, wrist to elbow. Pain erupts from her arm before her sleeve turns crimson.

She's too shocked to scream.

Or move her legs.

Her right side turns warm as Mark closes the knife. "That's it. Just close your eyes, and you won't hurt. I'll have to come back here."

He means come back for my body, Larson thinks as his footfalls rattle the back of her skull. She turns her arm to better see the cut: half an inch deep and seven inches long. From the color of the blood, it's clear he's at least nicked an artery. Larson's training in acute care makes her all too aware of how much time she has before passing out: less than fifteen minutes.

That's why he wanted you in the bathtub: there's a record of him coming here, and this will be easier to clean up.

She hears the front door slam and the double whoop of his SUV unlocking as he starts after whoever just took his daughter.

ROBERT

Britt's call twenty minutes earlier had been unexpected to say the least.

Right away, a tingle of adrenaline had surged through his body. She sounded uncharacteristically frantic. "Scarlett needs your help, she's in jail."

He was still in bed but sat up and put his feet on the floor. What she was saying made no sense, the sequence seemed as realistic as a worrisome dream. "I'm sorry, slow down. She's where?"

"Listen to me very carefully," she'd said in a forceful whisper. "It's Mark, he did it. And you have to get to Scarlett's apartment, he's there with the kid."

Robert stifled his questions, the realization rushing over him while he listened as Britt walked through the sequence of events, lining up the pieces. His heart had began pounding and his apartment suddenly felt like a cage. He had walked to the living room for a look at the road. He hadn't planned on going anywhere for the next day, at least. "So, we'll tell the police. You're already there, just tell them. *Right now.*"

"That's the plan, lieutenant, but will you just go and try to help keep the kid safe until they get there? Just watch the husband's car, follow him if they leave her place."

Robert was already slipping on a sweatshirt, eyeing his Nikes by the door. "I'm on it," he'd said.

He trots down the icy stairs, his heels slipping twice, before catching himself on the frozen handrail. He'd had no time to find socks or proper clothing for the cold, and the snow chills his ankles with each step. Every window in the apartment complex is dark—emergency aside, a routine fall would be dangerous right now. There'd be no one nearby to help.

At the bottom of the stairwell, Robert pats his jeans pockets, his stomach sinking with the realization he'd left his phone upstairs. He estimates the time it might take to get back up and down, then remembers Britt urging him to hurry. If Mark left before he got to Scarlett's apartment and didn't go to his hotel like he'd told Scarlett, he could slip away.

With Iris.

His Honda Civic is so snow covered, the make and model were indiscernible. A blurry flash of yellow lights peeks through as he unlocks it. He scoops snow from the windshield with cupped bare hands, his fingers numbing. Inside, he blasts the heat, praying it will melt the ice coating covering the windshield as he speeds down the empty streets.

When he'd met Mark several days earlier, had Mark recognized a counterpart in duplicity? Robert hadn't—nothing about Mark had seemed off at all. Maybe they were like two mirrors then, reflecting the other's reflection until their images vanished from sight.

He rolls down his window and squints into the rushing wind, his grip clawlike around the steering wheel. He hits a curb so hard, he's sure his front rim and bumper are dented, but there's no time to stop and check. Fifty feet from Scarlett's place, he cuts the engine and slides to a stop. Two vehicles are visible beside Scarlett's apartment: Larson's Tacoma truck and the SUV he'd seen Mark driving in the preceding days, thin wisps of vapor rising from its tailpipe. Through the back window of the SUV, he can make out the clear shape of Iris's head.

Had Mark left her inside? It was plausible.

When Robert looks up at the apartment windows, he sees Mark's expression blacken just as he lunges toward Larson.

ROBERT

Larson's hand flashes upward, slamming against Mark's jaw. Her blue uniform smashes against the glass door so thunderously, clumps of snow drop from the porch railing.

Robert bolts toward the stairs, thrusting his hand into his pocket to call for help.

He stops.

He's left his phone.

"Fuck!" he says out loud, his head swiveling toward the SUV. His stomach is sick from being pulled in opposite directions, and he wants badly to get his hands around Mark's neck.

Even if Mark outweighs him by thirty pounds.

No, the best chance to help both Larson and Iris is to call 911 as quickly as possible. Larson is trained and armed.

And surely she's already called for backup.

He looks back at Iris's profile in the SUV; she hasn't moved. His Nikes crunch through the snow. He needs to get Iris away from this and out of harm's way. Her mouth falls open when he flings open the SUV's door. "What are *you* doing here?"

"Come on. Your…mom wanted me to give you a ride to campus."

"Really?"

He glances over his shoulder. "*Yes*, really. I'm helping her out, so let's move."

Never mind that he's essentially kidnapping Iris, he thinks, luring her like some kind of predator as she undoes the car seat straps and follows him through the snow.

"Is my dad…?"

"Your dad…may be a minute." Robert hurries her into the Honda, then starts away. The Civic's tires slip on the first turn, the car sliding like a hockey puck down a small hill before regaining traction at the bottom.

"Does this car work in the snow?"

Only then does Robert realize he should have just taken Mark's BMW. He hits the windshield wipers, which scrape at the snow that's blown off the hood. "We're about to find out. It's an experiment. Fasten your seatbelt."

He catches her rolling her eyes.

Iris has been in Robert's car countless times but has never ridden up front. "It's okay for me to sit up here?"

They turn at the first light, following their usual weekday morning route straight down University Drive. He glances in the review mirror. "You know, just for today I don't think anyone will mind."

She nods, apparently satisfied. "Where…are we going?"

"The police station on campus, where everything is going to get sorted out."

They drift down another hill, then climb until they crest another. The tires have zero grip as Robert feathers the brake the way he saw in a video once online, which works temporarily, until they round a turn more sharply than he'd expected and connect with a curb. He and Iris both jolt forward against their seat belts. "Sorry. Hold on."

Robert steps on the gas and they lurch forward before stopping again. The car sinks backward as if it's being pulled. He grits his teeth and revs the engine, shifting back and forth between neutral and drive a few times. In front of them is a brick sign marking a side entrance onto campus, but they're going no further.

Robert slams his palm against the steering wheel.

Outside, everything around them is still and winter quiet.

"I think we're stuck," Iris says.

SCARLETT

The door across from Scarlett's cell unlocks again, and King strides forward holding his phone.

"What's happening?" she asks. "Where are Mark and Iris?"

There had always been something missing, she'd realized, Mark's full past. His parents had been killed in a car accident when he was in high school—she knew that was true, she'd visited their graves—and that he'd attended boarding school afterward. She had such a big family that she hadn't asked many questions about holidays or occasions; obligations were already too numerous. And he was such a devoted father.

"I missed three calls from Officer Larson in the last ten minutes. I need you to tell me as much as you can about Mark Simmons"—the cell door clangs open—"on our way to find them. Come on."

LARSON

Concentrating is harder with each passing second.

The edge of Larson's vision blurs, the soles of her shoes slipping on the tub's base as she pushes herself back, extending her legs so she can sit upright. The handcuffs' only benefit is elevating her arm, which might buy her another few minutes of consciousness.

At best.

Her time is dissolving.

She tugs the cuff to test the sturdiness of the shower handle and grits her teeth as pain shoots into her ribs. It won't budge. Already, her wrist has swollen into the metal band. She raises her knee to support her arm, then presses her forehead against the cut. Her eyes dart around, scanning for something solid that she might knock into the handle, but there's no such object nearby. And even if there were, there's isn't enough time to start chipping her way out.

Blood pools beneath her on the porcelain. She gives her head a shake to stay alert as she raises her forehead long enough to inspect the handcuff itself. If the son of a bitch hadn't taken her keys, she'd be able to spring the lock in half a second.

Her pulse slows as she lowers her head to rest against her arm. And as it does, the chain around her neck rolls forward, her mother's hairpin charm knocking against her chest.

It's long and thin, the gemstone at the base sparkling in the bathroom light.

Larson draws a deep breath, then rips it off her neck.

ROBERT

The thought flashes in an instant: he should have bought the

Subaru when he moved to North Carolina. But no, the Honda was marginally sportier and a few thousand dollars less, and he'd needed money for clothes and groceries. At the time, he'd glanced at the weather stats and decided that he could live with a few inconvenient snowy days each year.

Who anticipates a once–in–a–decade blizzard arriving at precisely the wrong time?

Not him.

Robert steps on the Honda's gas again and the rear tires whirl once more. He shifts into reverse and the same thing happens, except in the opposite direction.

"Shit," he says.

"You can't curse," Iris tells him.

Robert glances at her. There is no doubt this is Scarlett's child. "Iris, if there's ever a time it's acceptable, it's right now." He looks over his shoulder at the wintry roads extending in all directions. What does anyone do in these situations besides wait for the snow to thaw?

"Should we get out and push?"

"I'm considering that."

"You talk funny, like I'm a grown–up."

"Because I'm nervous and trying to act like everything's okay."

"Because of what's happening with my mom and dad?"

"Sure." There's no way to form an appropriate response. "Look, I don't want you to be upset so I'm acting like I have everything figured out."

"Uh–huh," she says.

"Is that *sarcasm*?"

Iris folds her arms as Robert hits the gas once more,

digging the car in deeper. "It's not about to start working now," she says.

"I'm getting that straight now, yeah."

"We have to wedge something under one of the tires like my mom did last year; you didn't know how to do that?"

"I'm from LA." He cranes his neck to look over the steering wheel. They're a hundred feet from the main library, but directly on the other side of campus from the police station. Easily a three-quarter-mile walk.

It would have to work.

He glances down at Iris's snow boots, then at his own pale ankles. "You're about to take a very unique tour of campus. Come on."

Just as they climb out of the car, Robert hears the engine of an approaching vehicle.

BRITT

The world is white except for Britt's obsidian shape and raven hair as she strides through the snow. The soles of her boots dig into the ice as she ends her call with Robert, then dials another number.

Chris answers immediately.

"Where are you right now?" she asks.

LARSON

Larson's breath comes in shallow waves.

The last time she picked a lock, she was thirteen years old, stuck outside of her mom's motel room in Baton Rouge.

Her set had ended, but her mom had "gone for a drive" and likely wouldn't be back for a few hours. Only upon returning to the room did Alana realize she'd forgotten to take a key, and there was no way she was going to sit in a sketchy hallway until God knew when. So she got creative with a piece of bent wire for the better part of an hour before eventually opening the door.

She has a sliver of that time now.

How much time has passed since Mark left? What had happened was clear enough—Larson had heard the girl's voice clearly—but she had no clue who'd taken her. As far as she knew, Scarlett Simmons was in a holding cell. If that had changed, King would be helping her right now. But no one's here.

Her right eye has nearly swollen shut, and her left stings from sweat as she wipes her sleeve over it. Based on the soft edges around her field of vision, she estimates she has a few minutes before losing consciousness. Sometime after that, she'll likely bleed out.

She bends the charm into an L shape and works it into the tiny hole. From there, she turns it sideways until she can feel the edge of the latch and nudges it until she hears a minuscule click. She concentrates on the edge of the charm, gripping it with her nails, pushing it slightly further inside, then rotating it clockwise.

Make a wish, she thinks.

The cuff makes a pop sound as it opens, too delicate and tinny for an event so consequential. Her head slips back against the bathtub's lip for a single instant before she scrambles to get her feet under her, the adrenaline surge from getting free having stopped her head from spinning temporarily.

If she can slow the hemorrhaging from her arm, she may have a shot.

Her shoes slip along the old tile as she makes her way to the sink, then she wrenches on the sink faucet and jams her arm underneath. The tap water comes out winter cold, Larson's breath hisses through her teeth as the pressure stings the wound. She maintains the flow of water despite the pain, her left hand flinging open the medicine cabinet, where her eyes land on a needful object: medical tape. In the adjoining bedroom, she flings open Scarlett's chest of drawers, rips out a T–shirt, and winds the medical tape around and around.

Her head pounds as she makes her way to the front door, pausing to pluck her phone from the living room carpet. She calls King while tromping down the stairs to her truck.

He answers on the first ring. "Alana, listen…"

She cuts him off. "It's Mark Simmons. He's free. Somebody took the girl and he followed them." She turns the key and the engine growls. Larson looks over her shoulder as she reverses, tires digging through the lot's tire–marked snow. Her eyes begin to follow two sets of tracks down the road.

"Where are you? Are you hurt? I'm calling an ambulance."

She should not be driving—she knows this—but an ambulance from Shepard General could take fifteen minutes to arrive. And the bleeding is mostly stopped. Slowed, at least. She gives her head another wake–up shake. A corny line from one of her mom's favorite action movies from the '80s occurs to her so suddenly, she almost says it aloud to King: *I don't have time to bleed.*

"They headed toward the college," she says, popping the truck into drive.

CHAPTER 11

ROBERT

"Do you know where we're going?"

It's a fair question, Robert knows. She's trudging behind him solely on faith. He'd convinced her to trust him, only to lose control of his car and lead her on an impromptu hike. And now they're both freezing.

The first time he set foot on Dorrance's campus, he admired that the acreage doubled as an arboretum. The trees were dense and lush in a way that he'd never experienced out west, and extended in all directions. Just by going to his office, Robert was immersing himself in nature. Now, under a foot of snow on the back side of campus, everything looks the same—blindingly white, any recognizable edge obscured.

"Do you want me to tell you something to make you feel better or the truth?" he asks, Robert gripping a railing with one hand and Iris's sleeve with the other as they ascend a steep driveway. As best he can tell, the stairs are a foot beneath the surface.

"Both," she says.

His shoe slips a little, and he stops to regain his footing. "I have a pretty good sense."

Iris pulls her sleeve away from his grip.

"Hey, we have to keep going. We can't stop now."

Her teeth chatter, and the bottoms of her pants look damp. "You don't know where we're going *to*."

He lets out a short sigh, then scans the lawn behind them for movement. The engine sound is gone now. Maybe just an unrelated vehicle; there are at least a few other people in town. Robert crouches down. If ever there was a crash course in interacting with kids, this was it. "I know I'm taking you to your mom, okay? And I know we're basically going in the right direction. And to be fair…"

"To be fair?"

"Yes…to be fair, I never actually work or teach in any of these buildings, so I'm doing my best. I know you're cold, but we gotta keep going here for another little bit."

She takes a small step.

"I'm ninety percent confident there's an entrance to the quad past the hedges. Once we're there, I'll have my bearings."

"Ninety?" Her voice trembles from the cold.

"Honestly, maybe more like seventy–five."

It was more like fifty–fifty. He'd been lost on the campus numerous times in perfect weather. "But come on. I'm one hundred percent sure your mom can't wait to see you. Trust me? A little further?"

"Fine."

They ascend the incline and continue through a shadowy space between two buildings. All of the windows of all of the buildings look dark, but the reflected sunlight is so bright that

Robert has to squint to see. Now on relatively flat ground, he walks by raising his feet and stomping down with each step.

"Why are you walking like that?"

When he looks back, Iris's footfalls do seem more graceful by comparison. "I told you, I'm not used to snow." He doesn't mention it's the first time he's ever actually walked through it. And the third time he's ever seen any in real life. Not exactly a confidence–inspiring admission.

They pass along a walkway and make their way around the front of the building. "See? The quad." Robert sweeps his hand. "I knew this was the way."

The sun on Robert's neck feels nearly warm. He's following Iris down the steps to the lawn when his foot catches in the ice, sending him tumbling forward, eventually landing on his back. A sharp pain stings inside his ankle. It could have happened on any set of stairs since leaving his apartment, but it happened now. Above him, the sky is bright blue and he focuses on it for half a second and tries not to think about what he's just done.

Iris looks down at him.

"I'm okay, I'm okay." But as he tries to stand, it washes over him that he's not fully okay. Pain shoots up his leg. It's a sprain and not a break, he realizes, but enough to slow him down. "We're just headed across here, and on the other side of those buildings is Hull Hall," he says, the wind knocked slightly out of him. "From there, it's just down the hill to the police station."

He favors the ankle as they trudge through the untouched snow.

At the quad's edge, Mark's voice breaks the quiet like a gunshot. "Iris?"

Iris turns around.

Mark caught up fast. The vehicle must've been his.

"That's my dad, he's coming."

It's hard to estimate the distance from the one word, but Robert guesses he's less than a hundred yards away. "It sounds like him, you're right, but the best thing will be for us to get to your mom at the police station, okay?"

Iris looks up at him.

"Look, there's been some trouble. You know that. That's why your mom asked me to get you before, and why she had to talk to the police herself. But everything's going to get figured out, I promise."

A second earlier, she'd hesitated. Now, she nods. Maybe she sees fear in his eyes?

Or senses the truth about Mark? The part of him she wanted to ignore, but now can't? "Okay," Iris says simply.

"Okay."

They find their way around to the edge of the quad and around the back of the building on the other side, and like Robert said, Hull Hall sits catty-corner on the edge of a tree-lined courtyard. Robert ignores the pain in his ankle, which has begun to swell despite being iced by the wet snow.

Mark calls out again, but Iris continues on as if she didn't hear him.

He's closer now, Robert can tell.

A few steps more and the side of Hull is in full view. "There's our building, we just have to get down the hill on the other side," he says, slightly out of breath. He can picture the slope on the far side of Hull, leaning toward the university's main entrance. On this snow, a person could practically sled down to if it weren't for the trees—two hundred yards at most.

As they make their way up the walk, they catch a look at the side of Hull Hall.

The windows are all dark, except one.

SCARLETT

"No guarantees we're going to be able to drive in this," King says.

Scarlett glares at him without breaking stride as they climb into the cruiser, this time with her sitting shotgun. Her stomach drops as King reads her address to the dispatcher over the phone. Her home had been a refuge until the last few days. Now she pictures Alana Larson there, in desperate need of medical attention based on what she can discern from King's half of the phone call.

Which means Larson learned the truth about Mark, and that now Mark and Iris are no longer there. Her mind draws a blank when it comes to Mark's reasoning for what he's done, except that by blaming her for the murders, she's out of the picture—the result Mark had originally wanted from their divorce. Fragments of their story float incongruently through Scarlett's mind but won't fit together, at least not yet. There's no time for them to.

King barrels out of the station parking lot. "We'll take Center Drive around the edge of campus to Main toward your place."

Scarlett's window is coated in ice, so she leans forward for a look through the windshield, heated air from the vents blowing against her cheeks. They're not a hundred feet from the station when Scarlett yells, "Stop!"

LARSON

Blood is everywhere inside the truck, dark red streaks and blotches strewn across the gray fabric. Larson had done her best to dress the cut with what she hastily found at Scarlett's, but the pressure is inadequate, and her clothes are soaked in places. She winces as her forearm knocks against the armrest, and then presses it against the hard surface for more pressure.

Mark got her good.

She'll need medical attention—*needed it* twenty minutes ago—but that's not an option before she sees this thing to an end. She hadn't anticipated pursuing justice playing out like this: not a desire for vengeance, not exactly, more of a need to right a wrong.

The truck fishtails as she glances at her gun belt on the passenger seat, then refocuses on the tire tracks in the snow. The blur around her field of vision has expanded. Her thoughts have fragmented. The blood loss is getting to her, it's clear. Less oxygen going where it needs to inside her body.

Larson crests a small hill and then spots both abandoned vehicles. Closer, she sees the footprints leading away from each toward the center of campus, two sets from the first vehicle—is that *Robert's* car? One trails away from Mark's SUV.

She cuts the engine and climbs out, staggering before regaining her footing. She follows the tracks up the first hill, tumbling at the top. Blood drips from her sleeve, a bright, red drizzle onto the white snow. The pattern looks like that test, she thinks, like that psychology test of inkblots. What was it called?

Wake up, she tells herself sharply. *Keep on.* Above her, the sky spins. Lightheadedness pulls on her consciousness, like she may somehow float and collapse at the same time.

Larson pushes onto her knees and then takes a few more shuffling steps through the snow, so impossibly deep. She tries to make her steps land in the footprints she's following, where the surface is at least slightly packed down, but she slips slightly with each step.

Then, she hears it—distant, but clear—Mark calling his daughter's name.

A chill runs down her spine.

She rests her hand on her gun.

ROBERT

Mark's voice comes again—from somewhere unmistakably close this time, just as Robert and Iris reach Hull Hall. "Iris, it's your dad. Come on back."

Robert can feel his presence without turning around. His voice is unobstructed, meaning he's made it into the courtyard behind them. He rests his hand on a frosty bike rack railing as the name hits his ears.

There's a choice, right then: keep running or turn.

Except at the rate Mark's caught up, they'd never make it to the police station before he reached them.

Iris looks up at Robert, lip trembling from the conflict and the cold. Fear and adrenaline surge through him, but within the feelings, heartache stabs at his chest; no kid should be in this position. "You gotta trust me here, okay?" He crouches and points toward the tree line, sloping maybe fifty yards beyond Hull's back edge. "See down there? I want you to head straight toward those trees. There's a trail that winds through the middle of those woods, and down at the bottom, you'll see a row of three buildings on the other side of the road. The middle one is the police department, go right to that door and go inside. Don't stop. Don't look back."

Robert orients Iris's shoulders directly toward the path. He can hear the footsteps sloshing behind him, the sound carried clearly on the cold air. "Now run," he tells her.

As Iris's footsteps rush through the snow, he turns to face Mark. He's closed in more quickly than Robert had guessed. Even at this distance, he can see blankness in the man's eyes—something odd about one of his pupils, one like a drilled hole showing a view into nothingness. The last time he saw anything like it was in prison.

A minute, Robert thinks, *is all she'll need to get away.*

Mark covers the distance: twenty feet, ten, charging with the determination of a bull.

Robert squares his shoulders even as he raises his hands like he means to give a hug, channeling the smart–ass sarcasm that makes everyone roll their eyes. "Mark, is that you there? Odd running into you on campus! Looks like you're in a hurry?"

Mark rears back to take a swing, but Robert lowers and springs forward off his one good ankle, wrapping up Mark's legs and driving him backward into the snow. It was his one move, a surprise, and for a second his view is of the dark fabric of Mark's jacket coated with frosty bits of snow. Robert grapples for Mark's hands but is shoved off, the immense power of Mark's arms knocking him onto his back. Mark sets a knee on Robert's neck as he looks up, scanning the horizon, and then calling, "Iris, wait just a minute, kiddo, I need you to come back. It's dangerous down there, hold up and we can walk down together."

Robert wriggles his neck, straining to breathe, his words coming out in gasps. "It's over, she's…gone already."

"She'll come back," Mark answers with eerie calm, then calls out, "*Iris*?"

Robert struggles against the ground, the pointy edges of rocks jabbing his back. Around him, the pillowy blanket of snow blocks his view as if he's fallen into a dense cloud. "*She knows*, she's not coming back. Even if she did listen, the police…know your car. Over now."

Mark brings his fist down hard into Robert's jaw. White–hot pain explodes through the side of his head, stars bursting in his field of vision. His consciousness wobbles like a monitor that's blinking out.

"Iris!" Mark yells again, his voice oddly both warm and urgent. "There we go. She's turning around now."

"No, no…" Robert opens his mouth to yell out, but Mark smashes his fist into Robert's temple, plunging him into momentary unconsciousness. His legs and fingers begin to numb as his body registers the damage of the two blows.

"You think you're so smart, don't you? You think I don't know how to start over again? She's young, she'll hardly remember in a few years. We can disappear."

"Larson…will listen."

"Larson's dead," Mark says, his mouth a tense snarl. "And now I'm in a hurry."

He flicks open his knife as Robert's eyes widen.

SCARLETT

Iris stands on top of the hill, facing the other direction. Her emerald–green coat is unmistakable amid the accumulated waves of ice on the glass. Unclear how Iris got to where she is, but surely Robert engineered it. Scarlett flings open the cruiser door and scurries to the base of the hill. "Down here," she yells, already maneuvering up the steep incline.

When Iris turns, her expression is stricken, her eyes round with terror.

"Just slide, baby. Come down." Scarlett opens her arms.

The girl begins to run down, tumbling twice onto her knees. Seconds later, she's in her mother's arms.

"Let's go inside the building, let's hurry," King says, walking them toward the police station.

Just as they reach the front door, a gunshot rings out from beyond the top of the hill.

LARSON

Larson's head jerks up as she hears the gunshot. Her shoes feel like they're made of concrete as she reaches for a railing, trying to pull herself up a set of stairs. In front of her is a narrow pass between two buildings.

The sky spins as she strains, then she feels as if she's levitating—seeming to rise from the ground and hover over herself. When the ice–covered steps rush upward to meet her chest, her lips pull into a tight, thin line. She focuses on getting up, but she can hardly gain leverage to turn over.

It wasn't supposed to be this way; she was supposed to make it to where she was needed.

But she's so tired, *so tired now*, and the snow is freezing her cheeks and neck.

She presses her left hand onto her cut before closing her eyes.

ROBERT

Pain sears the inside of Robert's eye socket, the punches to his face having blurred his vision. He needed to give Iris a head start—and he did. He presses his feet into the ground, trying to stand.

But Mark grips Robert's hair and presses his knee into Robert's sternum. Robert feels his head jerk sideways and the metal point cutting into his skin.

"Guns leave a residue on your hands," Mark says, angling the blade. "I learned that a long time ago."

Robert's body tenses. He grits his teeth as the knife ruptures his skin.

Then, a voice from somewhere behind them: "Hey, asshole."

Pressure releases off Robert's chest.

A solid thump reverberates through the air before Mark falls sideways off of him. Robert shoves himself onto his elbow, his lungs filling frantically.

Britt stands a few feet away, black jacket zipped to her chin. She bounces a shovel on her shoulder like she means to swing it again. "The grounds crew leave their stuff lying around. Comes in handy every now and then."

Mark scrambles to his knees, then his feet, shaking off the blow. He looks over his shoulder in the direction Iris ran, his whirring thoughts practically audible. *Numerous witnesses. Widening distance.* He turns the knife around in his palm, point facing down, stepping in Britt's direction. "I'll...have to make this extra quick."

"Mark, no, stop..." Robert yells.

Britt holds her ground.

She raises the shovel to swing again as Mark raises the knife.

A clicking sound cuts through the cold air.

Then approaching footsteps.

Mark freezes as Chris sweeps Britt behind him with his arm, black automatic pistol pointed at Mark's chest. "Don't fucking move, dude."

Mark flashes the knife, his jaw clenched.

"She can't stand the sight of blood, makes her queasy. But you know what? It doesn't bother me much at all."

"We called the police," Britt says, out of breath. "They're on the way."

Mark takes another step.

Chris closes one eye. "Turn around, Britt. You don't want to see this."

In the distance, a siren wails.

"Don't make me drop you, man," Chris says calmly.

But Mark lurches forward. Two steps before a shot rings out across the morning, impossibly loud. Birds scatter through the courtyard, high above the Gothic arches as Mark falls forward, clutching the back of his leg.

Still gripping the knife, he groans, angling his body toward Robert, clawing his way through the snow as Robert tries to stand.

A chaos of movement erupts, closing in from all sides. Shouting and dark uniforms seem to engulf them. "Drop the gun and step away," one of the cops yells. Three more emerge from the bottom of the hill, pistols drawn.

Chris sets the gun in the snow and raises his hands, circling back beside Britt. The police separate them, two approaching Mark, whose expression turns blank. All the energy—the pursuit and the fury—drains away.

Police radios squawk, medical and backup requests being issued.

Robert pushes himself onto his elbows and then stands. A cop stands beside him, telling him to back up. His mouth is swollen, tongue finding one of his molars loose.

"Mark?" Robert calls, "I'm sorry to tell you this, but there won't be a place for you in the next study." He spits blood into the white snow. "This is how we end things."

KING

In the police station lobby, Scarlett drops to her knees and buries her face into Iris's green coat as King unlocks an interior door for them to move further inside. "There'll be more cops here in a minute," he tells her as he strides toward the door. "I've gotta go." He rushes down the path, calculating which way to start off. His best guess is that Larson followed the others through the north side of campus. King slams the accelerator down as his heart pounds.

He brakes as he spots her truck, then flings open his door, scrambling up the incline. The cruiser's open–door ding chimes behind him as he navigates the shin–deep drifts, following the sets of footprints in the snow. The bright trail of blood makes his stomach clench as he barks directions to dispatch. "Officer in need of medical assistance. Enter campus on the north side, between Gorman and Haskins Halls."

The cruiser's blue lights flash behind him as two more sets join on the horizon. Sirens—police, fire, medical—all approach rapidly, wailing in disharmony. His breathing accelerates as he spots Larson's dark uniform in the snow. It's impossible to tell if her chest is moving, her cheek bluish and pale, torso twisted as she rests on her side.

King drops to his knees as he reaches her, mind racing through field protocols about how to apply immediate pressure and not make a bad situation worse. Behind him, doors close, voices and police radios sound. He reaches under Larson's neck and slowly rotates her head upward, tapping her cheeks. She draws a shallow breath.

King nearly laughs from relief, turns, and waves the others forward.

"Hang on, Alana. Just a little longer."

Larson's eyes blink open as she looks up.

"We got him," he tells her.

LARSON

April has brought flowers.

Spring arrived suddenly—less than a month after the grounds were blanketed by a ten–year storm, jade–colored leaves line tree branches, and flowers have budded. Around King and Larson, pastel hues are vivid and abundant, the sort of scene that prompts hurried students to occasionally pause to take photos with their phones.

They stroll Dorrance's campus, starting on the south side and winding their way toward the main quad. Administration had done magic of its own to silence new stories related to the crimes—massaging the story to sound like something that happened randomly in the city, and not inside the university's ivy–covered brick walls. Application and financial aid decisions were being finalized for the following academic year, and campus safety was on every parent's mind.

There was no place for murder, not here.

Sprinklers misting the lawns at Dorrance University have just cut off, fog hanging in the air for an instant. Like *magic*, Larson thinks. The grounds are so well tended, it's hard to believe they could harbor any evil.

"His plan was slick, I'll give him that," King says.

"Him knocking out the cameras above the rear entrance to Hull Hall a month beforehand was something I hadn't considered," Larson says. Mark had started his plan on his previous month's visit.

"Definitely had some foresight. Apparently, he stole the custodial uniform at the same time—followed a student and grabbed a dormitory door before it closed, then searched a utility closet until he found one that fit. The cleaning staff just assumed they'd misplaced one somehow. But really? I suspect he was biding his time on this for years. He hasn't admitted it, but I think he started planning this when Joe Lyons did his child custody evaluation in his and Scarlett's divorce."

"Poor Elizabeth," Larson says mournfully as they pass the campus bookstore. Already, signs are up advertising textbook buybacks. "Mark admitted through his attorney that she had nothing to do with his plan. When she saw him in Hull that night, he could tell she knew who he was. But he wasn't wearing his contact lens. His plan was already in motion, and he knew she was going to ID him."

After reviewing the facts of the case, Larson imagined the sequence happening like this: Mark was on his way to Lyons's office to destroy whatever documents might implicate him in the plan he was about to carry out. When Elizabeth ran into Mark in the hall, he saw her expression change. She looked into his eye and knew *something*, then started putting the unusual condition together with the detail in Lyons's report that only she had access to read. Mark knew enough to know he had a sudden problem on his hands.

He'd solved it by killing her.

King folds his arms over his chest as they walk, then unfolds them.

Larson recognizes the discomfort. Some wrongs can never be fixed. "If he'd found Simon Martin's report, the parts Lyons had dug up for his assessment?" Larson says, "We might never would have put those pieces together."

"Not without Ani," King agrees. "Mark did a damn good job of shifting the blame onto his ex-wife."

The details Larson learned in the days after Mark's arrest scroll through her mind: On the night he'd killed Lyons, he'd taken Scarlett's cell phone with him, texting Lyons on the way to his house. He'd even taken her car without her knowing it, in case the vehicle's GPS data was examined. Then, he'd slipped her phone and keys back into her apartment as she and Iris slept.

"He said he'd thought to bring his gun but reconsidered

having gunpowder residue on his hands, so he gave it to her. Made it look thoughtful. But you know what creeps me out the most?" King hesitates, shuffling his feet in a sort of stutter step. "He took her *shoes* the months before too."

Larson shakes her head. The detail hadn't come out for several weeks: Mark had gone through Scarlett's closet for a pair of her shoes, disassembled them, and glued the soles onto the bottoms of his own to adjust the markings of the prints. "Apparently, gunpowder and footprints connected him to the first murder he committed as a teenager, and he never forgot it."

Larson had pored over his record in the past month with the help of investigators. Mark Simmons had been adopted internationally by an extraordinarily wealthy couple outside Orlando, where he'd lived until they were killed in a car accident when he was seventeen. He was later tried for murdering the driver of the other car in the accident, although a high-powered attorney managed to have his sentence reduced to seven years after the judge considered his age and the trauma of his loss. He'd checked in regularly with his parole officer, even as he began using a different name and living in the Jacksonville area, traveling up and down the lower east coast for work.

King clears his throat. "He's only talking through his attorney, but from what I gather, he'd been planning what happened since the time Joe Lyons discovered his past and incorporated it into his assessment. Apparently even though he initiated the divorce, he held a grudge against Scarlett for going through with it. Figure that one out. His plan was that if Lyons was dead and Scarlett was in jail, he could be rid of them both at the same time. Apparently, he thought two years was long enough that he wouldn't be suspected."

"And maybe add some bits afterward that would make her sound impulsive. Violent outbursts he didn't mention during the divorce."

"Sure. For the kid's sake, obviously," King says.

"Scarlett said she thought the day she met him was her lucky day. He was a sales rep, handsome, winsome," Larson reflects.

"Do you think she ever had some idea who she was married to?"

Larson shrugs by tilting her head sideways. If Scarlett's intuition had ever hinted at Mark's dark side, she'd ignored it.

Mark was, to use her words, an ideal husband in so many ways.

"How's your arm?" King asks.

Larson pats the outside of her sleeve. "Better. The ER doctors said the timing of the storm was actually lucky, practically everyone else was stuck at home. They said the internal stitches will dissolve on their own, and I'll have the outside ones out in another week. Then physical therapy for a few months." She flexes her fingers. "See? Movement is okay, and the feeling is mostly back."

They pass beneath one of the campus's signature stone arches, King smiling as the bell tower begins to chime. It's the top of the hour, Larson realizes—but thinks again as she notices King's wistful expression. "You'll miss this place, won't you?"

"Not much, no."

Larson shoots him a puzzled glance.

"I won't be working anymore, but Helen and I aren't planning to move. We have a life here." He looks at her. "And friends. You're too young to think about it, but we've been getting retirement magazines in the mail for a decade now. Haven't you heard? College towns are the perfect place to retire."

She pictures the sports memorabilia festooning his office walls. "Which probably means more time to take in a few games in Dorrance Stadium?"

"Football season starts in a hundred and thirty days," he says. "And I might get to see some of it if I finish digging the garden, and installing the French drain, and installing the wainscoting, and manage all the projects I've put off for twenty years."

"You don't think you'll be restless, not solving crimes?"

King shrugs and glances up at a sparrow that's just then perched on a branch above them. "I'd never seen a case like the one we just worked on, and if I live the rest of my life in Shepard, I doubt I ever will again."

"But say, if any trouble were to crop up, and the lead investigator needed to access wise guidance to navigate the university…"

King chuckles. "Then she might want to call someone else. But if she was really, really in a pinch? Then, maybe, I'd pick up the phone."

LARSON

Morning sunlight streams in Larson's living room window as she opens her phone and finds the number she dialed on the night she found Simon Martin's report. A woman's answers, her tone of voice much clearer than the first time they spoke. "I promised you I'd call back when I knew more," Larson says, then proceeds to tell Sandra Martin every detail she legally can.

After she hangs up, she returns to her desk. The days are

quiet now, and Larson has time to sift through and organize fragments of the case the DA may use for prosecution. She opens a
manila envelope with a note from King.

From Joe Lyons to his advisor, written three years ago.
Sent to me after Samuel read about Mark's arrest.

She closes her door, and in the muted quiet, she drops into
her chair to read.

Sam,

*This letter is long overdue, but necessary. I hope you'll tolerate
my long–windedness, but with any situation as complex as
the one you've helped me face, there is no way to be brief. My
apologies in advance.*

*I know you'd say no explanation is needed—you've always
been gracious—but when someone seeks then disregards the
advice of a mentor, clearing the air can be helpful when a
different direction is taken.*

I hope you'll indulge me.

*I'm writing to explain myself and my decisions regarding the
matter of Scarlett S and her ex–husband Mark S, about whom I
sought your counsel.*

*Of course, the biggest question is why would I allow Scarlett
to become my student considering the dual relationship (of sorts)
and knowing what I knew about Mark.*

*As you recall, Scarlett interviewed for and was admitted
into the grad program without my having put together my*

history as a psychological evaluator in her divorce. Only after she was admitted and moved to the area did I realize the dual relationship. She had reverted to her maiden name on her application, and I, of course, had never met her during the assessment process two years earlier.

I considered asking her to leave the program but did not. Which was when I sought your advice. I went against your recommendation for several reasons.

The first is that, as I told you at the time, kicking Scarlett out of a program to which she had been admitted and was clearly qualified for would be unfair to her. She had said, on numerous occasions, that becoming a professor had always been her goal. Yes, there are other PhD programs in psychology in this country, and yes, Scarlett was qualified to enter a great many of them. But a few factors were at play.

Even though Scarlett could have sought training elsewhere, the cost may have been prohibitive. She has already qualified for scholarships because this is her home state, which negated her tuition and provided a stipend that she and her daughter will live on. The next best program is three states away and might easily sink her financially. You and I both know that being asked to leave an academic program without any explanation is a red flag that can ruin a career. Providing an explanation, in this case, would happen to break Mr. S's confidentiality.

I gave this matter great consideration, not only because of my ethical responsibilities to my clients, but because knowing the truth could put her in danger. The situation was, in some ways, a reverse duty to warn. Simply put: the more distance between the two of them, the better for her and her daughter.

The second reason is me: I'm arrogant enough to think I can make the arrangement work!

And I will.

Scarlett doesn't know I'm the psychologist who evaluated her ex-husband. And I'm bound by law not to tell her. The evaluation was done on her ex-husband, not her, after all. And if her ex puts everything together and reveals it to her, well, we can cross that bridge if we get to it.

I won't pretend to be unconcerned. I've always downplayed the risks, unfortunately—I'm a little narcissistic and think I can handle chancy pursuits—and most of the time, I'm right; I pull off whatever stunt I'm trying at the moment. I enjoy it.

This situation is an outlier, Sam. I've worked in forensic assessments for a decade and have never encountered a sociopath on the scale of Mark. All the stories you hear about hair standing up on the back of your neck, sensing the sharklike blankness in the eyes, all those things happened with him.

But here's the most frightening part: I didn't see it until the feedback session. I missed it all. I read all the reports and had the data, so I knew it was there, but I didn't sense it until I started giving him the feedback. That was when the mask fell off. The engaging, charming, dare I say warm, mask he wears around. I honestly think Scarlett had no idea who she'd married, as brilliant as she is. I wonder to what degree he'd deluded her, and perhaps deluded himself about who he is. His sociopathy had no bearing on their reasons for divorce; no, they'd simply grown apart and argued about day-to-day life and her career ambitions, like most young married couples do. No, I believe his sociopathy wasn't present during their daily life as they did usual house chores and he worked his job. It was revealed when he thought his relationship with his daughter would be severed. He'd achieved what he'd always wanted—a normal, stable family life—and then ruined it.

For now, the report is sealed, tucked safely into a file in my university office. Scarlett doesn't know who she married.

The girl doesn't know the truth about her father.

Mark wants it to stay that way.

Because of this, I feel that the greatest danger—to Scarlett and her daughter, and honestly, to me—has passed. Now, with any luck, they can go forward living their lives. It is my hope that Mark will move on.

God bless whoever he takes up with next.

The whole situation has inspired me to write grants for new research. Can you guess on what topic?

Deception.

You've always been a good friend, Sam.

Know that I've taken your advice to heart.

Kind Regards,

Joe

SCARLETT

Scarlett stands in the doorway of Robert's empty apartment, wiping her sleeve across her forehead. Iris sits cross-legged on the bare countertop.

In the parking lot, both their cars are packed up.

"I finally get to see your place just as you're moving out," she says.

Robert gazes around the open space. "I never was much of a decorator, I'll be honest. Minimalism is an improvement." Even from across the room, the dark purple under Robert's left eye is still apparent. Same with the gauzy bandage over his eyebrow where his stitches were recently removed.

Iris pushes off the counter, her shoes landing heavily on the carpet. "Mom, in our new place, is there going to be more furniture than there was here at Robert's?"

When Scarlett's gaze meets Robert's, he's smiling slyly. "It's true. Everything I own is now packed in that Civic downstairs."

"*Everything?*"

"Everything. I did manage to give a few things away. Traveling light, and *still* my car looks stuffed. Luckily it's not a long way to Chapel Hill."

"Why do they call it that? Is there a chapel? Where people get married?"

When Robert looks up again, Scarlett blushes. Iris is at an age when kids pepper adults with questions, but he's curious now too, actually. He has no idea how the city was named, but he and Scarlett are nowhere near thinking about marriage.

"Iris, wait for us downstairs while Robert and I lock up?" Scarlett asks.

Iris marches out the door and Scarlett lowers herself onto the carpet. Then Robert does as well, facing her. Dust motes float in the air between them. "We're making the right decision, here, right? A fresh start? The three of us moving to the same city?"

Robert pushes his glasses up his nose; he's not adjusted them yet. It's a new pair, the old ones having been broken by a punch. "One hundred percent. I saw this exact scenario playing out this way all along."

"Stop." Scarlett tilts her chin upward. "I'm being serious, this is overwhelming."

"It would be weird if you weren't overwhelmed, right? So, in all seriousness? Yes, there's a lot to figure out—for all three of us." He gestures in Iris's direction in the courtyard. "Iris's school, how she's handling what happened with her dad going forward, you and me fitting our research style into the work of a new team. Decorating both of our apartments. You and me...generally..."

Scarlett adjusts her ponytail with a subtle smile. Robert touches her knee. "I'm confident we're making the best next step," he says after a beat.

"Yeah? What's your confidence interval on that assessment? Ninety-five percent? Ninety percent?"

He stands and reaches for her hand. "One hundred percent certainty on the three of us moving to Chapel Hill. We'll figure everything else out from there. We can't stay here, not anymore."

"I know," Scarlett agrees, taking his hand and then standing. "Will any of the others stay, do you think?"

"Veronica left before the snow melted."

"We'll probably run into her at some conference in a few years," Scarlett says, not qualifying her obvious optimism.

"I talked to Chris this morning; he and Britt are going to stick around to work with the other professors and maybe help with the hiring process for a new faculty member."

"Is that so?"

"It is, indeed." He walks Scarlett to the door before leaving the keys on the countertop. Outside, the air smells fresh and clean. Scarlett and Robert's footsteps jostle the stairs, Robert taking each step paying mind to his ankle, on which he still wears a wrap.

"That's interesting about Chris and Britt," Scarlett says. "Maybe they're used to picking up the pieces. Maybe they know how to put violence behind them."

"Maybe."

An odd smile forms on Scarlett's lips, and Robert pauses on the last step. "What do you think they'll focus their research on?"

They step in the grassy space just before the parking lot begins, the ground moist and springy beneath their feet.

"That's anyone's guess," Robert says.

BRITT

It's a Saturday morning, and the graduate student lounge in Hull Hall is nearly empty. Chris stands at the arched windows, looking out at the students traversing the lawn. His hair is slightly longer than it was during spring break, and the way he swishes his chin to keep his bangs from resting against his eyes makes Britt roll her eyes. "I'll tell you right now, I don't think this collaboration is a good idea," she says.

"You don't think anything's a good idea, that's why you're a perfect research partner. You poke holes in everything. I'm the gas pedal," he motions toward his chest. "And you're the brake. Symmetry."

Britt checks the time. "He's late. We can't have an assistant who shows up late to things."

"Your watch is fast, weirdo. We're early."

Seconds later, there's a knock on the door.

Chris and Britt face the hallway. His hands were folded on the tabletop. "Come in," he calls.

Tom enters tentatively, peeking behind the door and then closing it behind him. He wears a plain white T–shirt and jeans and stands with a steadiness that seems new to Britt. His hair, she notices, looks clean and is neatly combed. His left eye blinks twitchily, but he has put on a few pounds of healthy weight and seems to have gotten a little sun on his face.

He glances around, weight shifting from one foot to the other.

Chris motions toward a chair. "You doing okay, Tom? Feeling well?"

"Well enough." Tom sits. "So what's up? I can't believe you guys wanted to see me. Here, especially."

"Your jaw's okay? Sorry it came to that."

Tom reflexively rubs the place where he was knocked out. The punch was cold and hard, but whatever bruising followed has healed. "It's fine," he says. "No biggie."

"Good. Well, I'll get right to it: we're running a new experiment, starting in a few weeks. We still have all the data from before but plan to run a few new conditions."

"Conditions?"

"Scenarios," Britt interjects. "Situations. We're testing a new hypothesis."

"And we need some help. The gig will average about ten hours a week and pays better than minimum wage. It would always happen here in Hull Hall, very few nights or weekends."

The attention on him makes Tom squirm in his chair, turning

his hands inward and sitting on them as if the room was cold. Britt cocks her head slightly to one side, narrowing her eyes as if assessing him, taking in his personality traits, fears, motivations.

"Interested?" Chris asks.

Tom bites at the corner of his fingernail. "Maybe. I'm open to it, I suppose. But…why me?"

Britt casts a glance at Chris, who raises an eyebrow. "You… clearly didn't like being on the participant side; we thought you might want to get in on it."

Tom shrugs but his eyes have lit up.

Which, of course they have, Britt thinks. Is anyone more drawn to psychology than people who struggle with mental health themselves?

"One other thing," Chris adds.

Tom nods expectantly, his eyes widening.

"You'd have to maintain complete confidentiality. Can you handle that? None of the details about the experiment or what happens during any of the conditions leaves this building. Understood?"

"Like, I have to keep the secret?"

"Precisely."

Tom fiddles pensively with a button on his shirt.

"I told you we should have gotten Veronica to do it," Britt mutters to Chris. "We could have convinced her to do anything."

"Hey, wait," Tom pipes up, eyes flashing worry. "I can do that. I mean, I *think* I can. I'll try."

"Well?" Chris asks. "Should I get the contract ready for you to sign?"

"I mean…"

"Clock's ticking, Tom," Britt says, tapping her wrist.

Tom's gaze shifts back and forth between the two. When he leans forward, a conspiratorial smile has formed on his lips. "What do you guys have in mind?"

READING GROUP GUIDE

1. It's clear from the start of the novel that the relationships between Scarlett, Britt, Robert, Chris, and Veronica are complicated and somewhat hostile. How did you feel about the dynamic of this research environment? Were there any times in your life when an academic environment was particularly hostile or competitive? What was that experience like?

2. When an experiment the students are running goes awry, a question of ethics comes into play. What characters, if any, cared about the morals of their research? Do you think their first experiment on deception was ethical? Why or why not?

3. How did the prologue set the tone of the novel? As you continued to read, did you have any suspicions of who the interviewee was? Why that person?

4. Despite studying the psychology of lying, each of the characters have their fair share of secrets. Discuss the irony of this. What were each of the students hiding, and were they good at hiding it? Did any of these secrets catch you off guard?

5. What role does psychological research, like evaluations and interviews, play in the story? Was the academic angle interesting to you? What did you learn about the art of deception?

6. In the story, the students discuss the idea of lying being an inherited trait, or something learned over time. Discuss this idea. Do you think we're taught to lie? Or is there something inherent that makes lying apart of our character?

7. In the end, Larson reflects that the work that she does as a detective, and the research the students are doing, might not be so different. Explain what you think she meant by this. How was her investigation a lot like an experiment? Would you agree with her statement?

8. What obstacles did the winter storm cause for all the characters? How would you feel if you were trapped on campus in a blizzard, with a murderer on the loose?

9. What was the pilot study that Joe and some of the students were revealed to be working on? Why was it kept a secret? How does the story warn readers about the implications of types of psychological research?

10. The theme of deception is the core of the novel. Discuss the many layers of lies and deception that build throughout the novel, then reflect on what deception is. Do you think it's easy for people to deceive each other?

AUTHOR Q&A

This story's focus on deception is not only twisty and makes for a gripping story, but it's also incredibly thought provoking. Why deception? What was the inspiration here?

Unreliable narrators are convention in thrillers, so I started to think about how I could get a lot of them together in one place to create a story. Some psychological experiments only work if half-truths are told, and I think a lot of us have wrestled at times with how forthcoming to be in various situations. I've certainly wondered about how to express a difficult truth kindly, and whether some things are even necessary to express at all. Research on lying is fascinating. It's common, adaptive, and seems sociopathic all at once. Even telling benevolent lies creates a kind of cognitive dissonance—or it *should*. I wanted to capture some of that tension in the story.

You have been a psychologist since 2003. How does that job help you as a thriller writer?

I'd love to have a sophisticated answer to a question like this, but I'm not sure how much it does. Broadly, it gives me a sense of how situations predict behavior more than character. But the truth is that writing is a perfect refuge from my clinical work—I love being a therapist but the process obviously involves a lot of time with people, and sometimes I look forward to working in solitude. If anything, the directionality is reversed: Being a writer makes me a better therapist. There's a psychotherapeutic technique called narrative therapy that helps patients transform difficult experiences by re-imagining them, by seeing contexts differently, and by encouraging greater sense of imagination and creativity in developing outcomes. I think writing has given me a clearer sense of how to guide a process like that.

What was it like to write from the perspective of many characters? Did it change the way you thought about putting the pieces of this thriller together? Why do you think it works for this kind of story?

This is the first novel I've written in this style. It made the story broader and it was easier to portray moments when some characters knew things that others didn't. And I think it made it easier to set up scenes that revealed who the characters actually are. But it's more complicated, for sure. Sometimes, I had to be reminded that characters didn't all have all of the same information. It was like, "Wait, she doesn't know that, yet."

What does your writing process look like? Is there a way you like to get creative inspiration?

My process has changed over the years. When I started out, I wanted to hit a certain word count every single day, no matter what, to be sure I was making progress. In the last few years, I've become more of a "plotter." I sketch out characters and create a detailed outline that I work from. Every now and then, I learn something new about a character in the middle of the story, or think of a twist that might make the plot more interesting. Those ideas come at unexpected times and I try to write them down as fast as I can.

The story features a lot of psychology and academic ideas. What research did you have to do to write the book? Did you learn anything interesting while you were writing?

Some of the research just involved reminiscing and talking with people in my grad school cohort, and those experiences were fun to recall. I work as a clinician but my Ph.D. training mostly involved experimental methods and procedures. And lots of statistics. For this book, I went back and read through a lot of classic psychology experiments on concepts like obedience and conformity—the types of studies that got me interested in psychology in the first place. As an undergrad, I helped out with a social psychology experiment for extra credit that involved a level of deception. Some of the subjects were people I recognized from other classes. It was my first experience in having to keep information confidential.

The ethical code for psychologists is designed to protect patients, the occupation, then the practitioner, in that order, to maintain the sanctity of the profession so that it can be trusted by the public. I've always loved that.

What are you working on now?

I'm working on a plot that involves a mysterious but

innovative energy start-up, a con artist, and a historic observatory. Stay tuned.

What are you reading these days?

Writing is definitely rewarding, but it takes discipline for me to stay on task. One of the best parts about taking a short break is having more time to read, and I'm omnivorous when it comes to what I choose. My last three were: Daisy Darker, by Alice Feeney, The Light Pirate, by Lily Brooks-Dalton, and Educated, by Tara Westover.

ACKNOWLEDGMENTS

First and foremost, I'd like to thank my family and friends for their encouragement and support as I worked on *This Is How We End Things*.

Much gratitude to MJ Johnston for her keen observations, suggestions, and overall help along the way. I'm deeply grateful to the team at Sourcebooks, particularly Anna Venckus and Cristina Arreola for their energy and innovative ideas.

I owe my fantastic agent, Rachel Ekstrom Courage, a debt of gratitude for her thoughtful guidance on this journey.

Special thanks to Sarah Andrews for her invaluable advice on an early draft of the book.

Thanks also to Nicole Lombardi, Amanda Stribling, and Natasha Niezgoda for their insightful feedback, as well as to Dr. Christina Jones for her guidance on the accuracy of the psychology experiment as it pertains to the plot.

And many thanks also to you, the reader, for choosing this book. I hope you enjoy it.

ABOUT THE AUTHOR

© Jason Myers

R. J. Jacobs has practiced as a psychologist since 2003. He maintains a private practice in Nashville, focusing on a wide variety of clinical concerns. After completing a post-doctoral residency at Vanderbilt, he has taught Abnormal Psychology, presented at numerous conferences, and routinely performs PTSD evaluations for veterans. He's the author of *And Then You Were Gone* and *Somewhere in the Dark*, published by Crooked Lane. Find out more at rjjacobsauthor.com.